Murder Over Gold

Penrose & Pyke Mysteries, Book 7

Rose Pascoe

Published by Flax Bay Books, 2024

Copyright

MURDER OVER GOLD

ISBN: 978-1067024314 (Softcover POD)
978-1067024307 (Epub)

Publisher: Flax Bay Books, New Zealand

Cover design: Rose Pascoe
Cover images from Adobe Stock Images

Contents

New Territory

The lady standing in the doorway of the first-class compartment examined the sole occupant's attire, starting at her fashionable hat, moving down the modest cut of her tailored gown, and finishing at her freshly polished boots.

The new arrival shifted her gaze to the occupant's face only after her inspection had been completed. "You are very young and far too delicate to be travelling alone, Miss –"

"*Mrs* Grace Penrose Pyke."

Delicate? Grace stifled the urge to add that she might be only twenty-three and of slim build, but her acquaintances in the seamier parts of Dunedin had taught her a thing or two about defending herself. However, she wanted to begin the journey on good terms, especially as the lady's luggage tag indicated she would be travelling with them all the way to the terminus of the railway at Lawrence.

Instead, Grace nodded politely. "Do come in, as long as you require only two seats. My husband and parents-in-law will join me once our luggage is stowed."

Grace straightened her back and resisted the temptation to adjust the crooked seam of her sleeve, hoping she wouldn't have to endure such scrutiny for the entire journey. Perhaps she ought to have warned the lady that her husband and father-in-law were far from delicate. Six feet of solid muscle, combined with the air of authority common to all policemen, meant they rarely had to share a train compartment.

The lady stepped inside with a satisfied nod, leaving Grace to wonder how the woman would have reacted if she had been dressed in her usual practical grey skirt and much washed shirtwaist. Grace's current outfit did not derive from a desire to be fashionable, but rather from her mother's kindness in gifting her new clothes to celebrate her change in status from wayward single woman to respectable wife. Even so, she would have worn her old clothes if she hadn't wanted to look her best to reflect well on her parents-in-law, who had paid for the trip as a wedding gift.

A gentleman entered behind the lady. His ink-stained right index finger and stiff white collar suggested a clerical occupation, while the immaculate suit and self-satisfied smirk shifted him up the ranks, perhaps to attorney or bank manager.

"How do you do, sir?" Grace said.

"Tolerably, considering my aversion to long-distance travel. Mr Fanshawe, of Fanshawe Greerton Attorneys." The man flicked a belated hand at the lady. "My wife."

Mrs Fanshawe directed a pointed glance at the forward-facing seat by the window, which Grace was guarding with her hand luggage.

Grace didn't move, but felt obliged to offer an explanation. "I'm on my honeymoon, and eager to see the sights, having never travelled south of Dunedin before."

Mrs Fanshawe still didn't take the seat by the door, as good manners would dictate, but Grace was not about to give in. "I'm from Wellington, you see, and I have had little chance to see the countryside, because I am studying at Otago Medical School." Grace could have added that she also performed autopsies as the assistant to the police surgeon, but she feared that would not be considered an acceptable conversation starter.

Mrs Fanshawe pursed her lips and sat, making a minor drama out of arranging her fur stole and other belongings. "How ... interesting. I expect you will have more time to travel now you have given up medical school to marry. Is your husband a doctor?"

Grace restrained her impulse to contradict the lady's assumption. A circle of gold around her ring finger, next to a gorgeous emerald and diamond ring, was no reason to give up her lifelong goal of practising medicine, especially for a life of idle pleasure. Thus, Grace merely smiled, albeit with gritted teeth, and answered the question. "My husband is a private detective."

The arrival of Grace's mother-in-law saved Mrs Fanshawe from commenting on this unexpected occupation. Mr Fanshawe rose and barred her entry. "This is a first-class carriage, Madam."

Grace interrupted, fearful Mr Fanshawe would add an insulting comment about "her type" being better off in second class, or indeed, in another country entirely. Jasmine Pyke's father was Chinese, and she took after him in appearance. "No need to concern yourself with the lack of seats in this compartment, Mr Fanshawe. Allow me to introduce my mother-in-law, Mrs Jasmine Pyke. Her husband, Sergeant Thomas Pyke, is in charge of the Clyde police district."

By the time Jasmine Pyke had taken the seat opposite Grace, Mr and Mrs Fanshawe had gathered their belongings.

"I'm sure you'd rather be alone with your family on your honeymoon, Mrs Penrose Pyke," Mrs Fanshawe said, before making a hasty exit, to the mutual relief of both parties.

Grace covered her disgust with a light-hearted comment. "I'd lay good odds that the respectable Mr Fanshawe is swindling his clients, since he was so quick to depart at the mention of the police. I've a mind to set Charlie onto him to find out."

Jasmine's gold-flecked green eyes, which were disconcertingly like her son's, flicked from the door to Grace. "Thank you for your thoughtfulness, Grace, but we both know the reason they left. I hope we haven't made a mistake in inviting you to stay in Clyde. I wouldn't want you to be subjected to the prejudice Thomas and I have endured throughout our marriage. Only from a minority of folks, of course."

"I expect the locals will be far more shocked by my desire to become a doctor than by my marriage, and I don't care what anyone says as long as I can spend time with your family."

Her mother-in-law's frown faded to a smile. "Ignore my foolish comment, Grace. The townsfolk of Clyde are going to love you, just as we do."

The arrival of the tall, broad-shouldered Sergeant Pyke and his son, who was a younger, black-haired version of his father, prevented Grace from replying.

"What are you two ladies smiling about? Are you up to mischief?" Charlie made a show of looking under the seats. "No dead bodies? No medical emergencies?"

Grace pulled him onto the seat next to her, breathing in his scent and hoping this newlywed glow would never end. "Really, Charlie, how could there be dead bodies when you've only been gone for ten minutes? Anyway, why would I wish to get up to any mischief on my honeymoon?"

Charlie shot her a look of such delectable intensity that Grace felt herself blushing. "Any mischief of a criminal or medical kind, I meant," she added.

"What other kind of mischief is there?" Charlie took her hand, running the tips of his fingers across her gloved palm.

While Grace struggled to maintain her composure, Jasmine and Thomas Pyke exchanged knowing glances and changed the subject. The rest of the train journey passed in pleasant conversation, covering everything from the delights of having the family together for Grace and Charlie's wedding to the latest advances in forensic techniques.

At Lawrence, they switched to the Cobb & Co coach for the onward journey to Charlie's hometown of Clyde, which was about as far from the fertile coastline as it was possible to be in New Zealand. This trip was unfamiliar territory for Grace in more ways than one, having spent her entire life in the hectic bustle of cities, never more than a few miles from the sea and civilisation.

The sight of the overloaded stagecoach awaiting its final passengers put a momentary dent in Grace's cheerful mood. The team of horses appeared fresh and strong, but the same could not be said of the coach they pulled. Grace decided to regard it as an adventure. What was a day and a half of bone-rattling discomfort, after all, compared to the two weeks of blissful honeymoon awaiting her at the journey's end?

By the end of the first day's journey, Grace's smile was at half-mast and her internal organs felt as if they'd been through a butter churner. After a night at a coach inn – an experience she wished to purge from her memory, if one could ever forget such a lumpy, stained mattress and prolonged bawdy singing through flypaper-thin walls – she was ready for a new day and a fresh start. On the second day of their journey, they would reach Clyde at last, with luck and several changes of horses.

Grace settled into her seat, fully expecting to be captivated by the promised beauty of the scenery. The other passengers intrigued her too, with their quaint views on the world spoken in a slow drawl. They filled the coach with broad-brimmed hats and dresses with bustles, like an illustration from an 1880s magazine about the American wild west. To be fair, they seemed equally fascinated by Grace's city style from the current year of 1893 and her baffling lack of knowledge about wool prices and recipes for hearty country fare.

Fortunately, Grace's conversational deficiencies were soon forgotten, as talk turned to the early days of the gold rush. As the hours passed, the tales became increasingly improbable. For every story of gold strikes beyond imagining, there were a dozen epic tales of bitter storms and shattered dreams. Grace drifted into a doze, awakening only when Charlie tensed beside her, crushing her hand. Across from her, Jasmine Pyke turned her head as if to admire the view, but her lips formed a thin, angry line. Thomas Pyke's jaws were tight enough to crack a tooth.

An elderly gentleman, who had more whiskers than face, quailed under the intensity of Sergeant Pyke's glare. "My apologies if I caused offence, sir. I had assumed you were too young to have been a policeman at the time of the infamous gold robbery. I'm sure the police did all they could."

"It's ancient history, best forgotten," Thomas said, with a thin smile, before launching into a rollicking story about a devilish highwayman who robbed his victims on the very road they were travelling.

Grace turned to Charlie, intending to ask about the infamous gold robbery, but his uncharacteristic scowl dissuaded her. She changed the subject. "The scenery is very dramatic in these parts."

Charlie's scowl faded into an expression bordering on rapture. "Isn't it glorious? Have you ever seen a sky as wide and blue, or a river as mighty as the Clutha? The gold of the tussock and the drama of the tors brings joy to the soul."

"Tors?" Grace looked out again, wondering if she had missed something, but the landscape was still arid, rock-strewn and bleak. What vegetation there was tended towards low, spiky and tenacious. The sky, whilst undoubtedly wide and blue, was a dazzling, fierce blue, devoid of clouds. They were passing through a wide valley, filled with clumps of fibrous pale-gold tussock grass, which swept upwards to rugged hills, as if God had banned the colour green from this inhospitable land.

The coach rounded a bend and descended into a gorge cut by the fast-flowing water of the Clutha River. Towering stacks of jagged rocks loomed over them like dark sentinels. Grace shivered, despite the heat.

"Tors are those tall stacks of schist rock," Charlie said. "Magnificent, aren't they? Such stark beauty is enough to make a poet swoon."

Grace murmured a noncommittal "mmm" and examined her husband's face for signs he was teasing, but he was in earnest. As a former policeman and now private detective, Charlie Pyke was not a man prone to waxing lyrical. Although well-read and intelligent, he did not care for the type of poetry written by men who had time to wander lonely as a cloud in fields of daffodils. Not that there was any flora remotely resembling daffodils here.

As the day wore on, the hills rose higher and darker, with more of the menacing tors. The company sank into numb silence, as the coach jolted along increasingly rough roads through increasingly desolate countryside until the hours blurred into an endless, dusty, hot, bruising sameness. Grace settled her head against her husband's shoulder and slipped into pleasurable memories of their first nights together as man and wife. Regardless of their different backgrounds, she had known Charlie was the man for her from the moment he helped her to sneak into the mortuary to see her first murder victim.

Finally, up ahead, Grace glimpsed a few green trees and almost cried out from sheer relief.

Jasmine Pyke leaned towards her. "Not long now, Grace. That orchard supplies fruit to Clyde, a little further upriver. If you look to your right, you'll see the top of one of the gold dredges and the pile of the tailings left behind."

Grace dredged a smile from her dwindling reserve of good cheer. She longed to stretch her legs and breathe air that wasn't one part sweat and two parts dust to three parts raw heat.

Charlie stirred beside her, looking more apprehensive than excited at their arrival in his hometown. With Chinese ancestry and a policeman father, Charlie's school years had featured inevitable bullies and bigots. Thus, a return to his hometown always came with mixed emotions. Grace was determined to show her husband in the best possible light – another reason she was on her best behaviour, no matter what.

Finally, the coach rattled over the bridge and up the cutting on the other side to the town, which was on a high terrace above the flood level of the river. Within a few minutes, the coach had turned onto the main street. The township of Clyde was smaller than Grace had imagined, having heard of the tens of thousands of men who had flocked here during the gold rush of the early 1860s. Sunderland Street stretched out before them but petered out after not much more than a hundred yards. Hotels seemed to outnumber shops.

A small cluster of old-timers looked up from their mid-afternoon slumber against the wall of the Molyneux Hotel, a little

11

further along the street. Every one of them had deep lines in their sun-darkened faces, despite the wide-brimmed slouch hats shading their eyes from the sun. Grace would have been hard-pressed to tell them apart in their near-identical blue or grey flannel shirts, dusty moleskin trousers, and high boots.

Charlie followed the direction of her gaze. "There aren't many of the old-time miners left. A few still trust to luck with nothing more than a tin dish and simple wooden cradle, but most miners are now employed by companies extracting gold by dredging the river or by large-scale sluicing. Steady money for a working man, but no chance of sudden life-changing wealth, unlike the old days."

The coach rattled to a halt outside the Dunstan Hotel. The team of horses sagged in their traces, knowing their moment of rest had come at last. One of the old-timers rose and grabbed a handcart. It was a close call whether the man or the cart was closer to falling apart. Worn-through boots and dust-caked arms pushed the rickety contraption on wobbling wheels, heading in their direction.

Sergeant Pyke jumped down from the coach and surveyed the scene with a policeman's eye, as if concerned the town might have descended into rack and ruin in his absence, leaving Charlie to put down the steps and help his mother down. Grace followed, to a murmur of "milady" from her husband. Grace stepped back to allow Charlie to assist an older woman, who was visiting her son, and the lady's maid accompanying her.

"Carry your luggage, Sergeant Pyke?" the old-timer with the handcart called.

"That'd be grand, thanks, Sylvester," Thomas said. "We have extras today."

"The more the merrier, Sarge." Sylvester's words whistled through a gap-toothed mouth, black with decay.

Grace, who was no stranger to the diseases of poverty through her medical work at a women's refuge in Dunedin, noted signs of an arduous life in Sylvester's gaunt frame. The harsh winter conditions had left him with frostbite scars and a rattling wheeze in his chest, and a scar trailed out from under the hairline of his misshapen skull. Clyde may have the reputation of a town built on gold, but it was clear that not all prospectors had found their fortune here.

All eyes were turned in their direction. Grace guessed the arrival of the thrice-weekly Cobb & Co coach was one of the highlights of the week, especially when strangers arrived. For the most part, the stares seemed innocuous, if verging on unfriendly in some cases. One man raised his hand in a wave, but he was only swatting a fly away. Perhaps it was simply that the loafers were unenthusiastic at the return of their diligent local police sergeant. Thomas Pyke must have been used to their mistrust because he showed no signs of unease, but the scrutiny left Grace with a sinking feeling in the pit of her stomach.

One particularly burly fellow rose to his feet, a simple act that nevertheless conveyed menace. Perhaps it was the slouch hat, pulled low, or his bunched fists, or the scowl on his face cold enough to freeze the Clutha River.

Thomas Pyke ignored the man and focused on unloading the trunks. The top of Sylvester's head was barely level with Thomas's shoulders, and he looked as if he'd struggle to lift a shovel, but Sylvester set to work stacking the trunks onto his handcart with surprising strength and dexterity.

Charlie gazed around, frowning, as if he couldn't quite work out how he had arrived in this strange but familiar place.

"Charlie Pyke," Sylvester said, extending a gnarled hand. "You've been away a long time. I wouldn't have recognised you if you weren't the spitting image of your pa."

Charlie shook his hand. "I was back for a short time last year, but only to see my folks." He shot a dubious glance at the piled cart. "We can do it in two loads if it's too much, Sylvester."

"Ain't knocking on the devil's door yet, young Pyke." Sylvester proved it by pushing the cart into a slow roll down the dusty street. "How've you been, lad?"

Charlie walked beside Sylvester, exchanging news and lending his weight to the cart, while Thomas and Jasmine checked that all their possessions had been removed from the coach.

Grace was still standing back, dazed with relief at being on solid ground again and lost in thought. Charlie had been in low spirits when he was in town last year and he had kept a low profile. It had not been a happy time, because he had been forced to resign his position in the police force, and he had left Grace after telling her he wasn't good enough for her. A short glitch in their rocky road to happiness, best forgotten. She hoped coming here wouldn't bring back those unpleasant memories.

A stench of tobacco and sweat closing in on her from behind brought her back to the present. Grace turned to see the scowling man breathing down her neck. She struggled to make out his features against the backdrop of brilliant sunshine. Sun-browned skin, dark brown hat pulled low, dusty brown clothes, and sludge-brown eyes. Even his teeth were stained a vile shade of yellowish brown from tobacco.

He leaned towards her ear. "You want to watch yourself around that one, girl, despite his pretty city manners. The day that mongrel Pyke boy was born, the town was cursed with ill fortune. He should've stayed away."

Dark Places

Charlie had walked twenty yards down Sunderland Street with Sylvester before he noticed Grace wasn't with them. He looked back to see her taking a rapid step away from a disreputable-looking man. Jake Blackthorn, by the look of it, and he sure wasn't welcoming her to town.

Grace was already hurrying towards him as Charlie ran back to her. He took her hand, sensing her agitation. "Grace, what was that about?"

She glanced back to Jake Blackthorn, who was still watching them with disconcerting intensity. "I'll tell you later, when we're alone."

Charlie had noted Grace's uncharacteristic silence on the latter part of the journey, which had only grown deeper as they got closer to Clyde. To him, the town was filled with memories of a happy home and a childhood spent roaming wide-open spaces with the freedom of a country upbringing. Not all of his memories were pleasant, of course. His school years hadn't always been easy. Now, he saw the town through his wife's city eyes. A small, dusty collection of buildings in the middle of nowhere, where their welcome had been less than friendly. Perhaps they shouldn't have come.

But it was too late for doubts now. Charlie hooked his arm through hers. "It's been a long journey, my love. It'll be good to get settled in."

They walked in silence to the Pyke's stone cottage, where Thomas Pyke was handing the carter a generous payment for his services. He probably felt sorry for Sylvester, who had received a short ration of both brains and luck. Or perhaps, as the local police sergeant, it was worth his father's while to be generous in the hope of cultivating cordial relations with a group who could be troublemakers.

Charlie helped his father to unload the trunks from the handcart, while his mother took Grace into the cottage to rinse the layers of dust from her face.

The front door was open, letting the breeze freshen up the house after the Pyke's absence at their son's wedding. A local woman, who helped when needed, had been busy preparing for their arrival. A jug of deep crimson roses sat on the table next to a loaf of fresh bread, a bowl piled with apricots and peaches, a cake tin, and a copy of the local paper, the *Dunstan Times*. They were welcomed by the sound of a kettle coming to the boil on the top of the coal range and a delicious aroma wafting from the oven. His mother already had her mixing bowl out, whipping up some new treat. Charlie's favourite meatloaf, judging by the ingredients.

These simple pleasures were enough to revive Charlie's spirits. He looked around the familiar room. The cottage still felt as homely as ever, but, for the first time in his life, it no longer felt like *his* home. The last time he had been here, Charlie had had nothing. Now he had a life he could scarcely have dreamed of back then: an extraordinary wife, a private investigation business, and a home in Dunedin.

When he returned from having a wash, his mother was taking a casserole out of the oven and putting the meatloaf in, while Grace cut thick slices of fresh bread and made tea. Charlie's stomach grumbled. After two days on the road, eating at roadside inns, he was looking forward to a home-cooked meal and time alone with his family.

When the casserole had been devoured to the last lick, Jasmine pushed her chair back and gathered the plates, stopping Grace when she rose to help. "You must be looking forward to being alone after a long journey. I suggest you and Charlie take a stroll through town to stretch your legs while we deliver your trunks and provisions to the cottage in the buggy. I need half an hour or so to make sure the cottage is ready for your arrival. And don't feel you have to be visiting us all the time. It is your honeymoon, after all. Enjoy the rare opportunity to sleep in and do whatever you wish."

Knowing his mother would want to make the cottage perfect, Charlie took Grace's arm and set off on a slow stroll around his hometown, starting with the bridge. The Clutha River was the most powerful river in the country, and always an impressive sight. At sunset on a perfect evening, with his new wife on his arm, the rush of deep green-blue water seemed impossibly romantic.

But it seemed romance was not the only thing on Grace's mind as she stared at the water below, rather than into the eyes of her adoring husband. "Who was that foul man who accosted me the minute I stepped from the coach?"

Charlie leaned on the bridge railing beside her. "His name is Jake Blackthorn. Black Jake, some people call him, which fits with his reputation. Jake encourages the name, but Pa refuses to use it, because it makes him sound like a folk hero."

"He's no hero." Grace shuddered. "One whiff of him was enough for me."

"Stay away from Jake, Grace." The words came out sharper than he intended.

Grace put her delicate hand over his and linked their fingers. "There's only one man I want to be near for the next two weeks. But I need to know why Jake sought me out. Is he as bad as he looks?"

"The unfairness of lady luck can turn some men rotten on the inside. Jake was one of those men. Jake never struck it rich as a goldminer, so he took to prowling the diggings, looking for successful men to rob. But those days are over. Now he rides around on a big bay horse as if he has money to burn. Pa has tried to pin him for sheep rustling, but Jake is a slippery devil. I hope he wasn't offensive to you, my darling. Jake Blackthorn is not an admirer of the Pyke family."

"I gathered as much. He said something about you bringing ill fortune to the town the day you were born."

"Was that all Jake said?"

"He warned me to stay away from you and said you should not have come back. What did he mean about your birth bringing ill fortune, Charlie?"

It seemed to Charlie as if he would never escape the unfortunate coincidence of the past. However, it would be better that his wife heard about it from him rather than the town gossips. "The largest and most infamous robbery in Central Otago history occurred while I was being born. A vast sum of gold and cash went missing."

Grace turned to face him, her expression incredulous. "You can't be blamed for being born during a robbery, for heaven's sake."

"My birth was a bad omen according to a foolish minority. 'Evil comes to town when the child of a mixed-race marriage is born', or some such nonsense like that. Victims seek someone to blame in any crisis."

"Poppycock. The robber or robbers were to blame. Surely even a one-eyed imbecile could see that."

"Can we forget about it, please, Grace? Jake Blackthorn had more reason to be angry than most. A small portion of the stolen gold was his – the only decent find he ever made. Worse still, Jake's brother was the trooper guarding the gold lock-up that night. The following morning, he was found dead outside."

"The robbers killed him?"

"No one is certain whether they drugged him to get the key or whether the guard passed out from drinking too much and the robbers took advantage of his incapacitation to steal his key. Whichever it was, the robbers left the guard outside on one of the coldest nights of the year. He froze to death."

"Were the robbers arrested?" Grace asked.

"Only one was caught, but the robbery was ambitious for one man to attempt on his own, not least because of the sheer weight of gold stolen. The arrested man admitted he had an accomplice and implicated the guard. The general feeling was that the guard was either innocent or only complicit in handing over the key under duress, but of course that could not be proved for certain. Jake was furious that his brother's reputation was tarnished after the tragedy of his death. Jake Blackthorn has been an angry man ever since."

"I feel a tiny bit sorry for him now," Grace said. "If one of the robbers was caught, I take it the police recovered the gold?"

"Ah, that's the nub of it. Only about a third of the gold was recovered, a devastating blow for a small town like Clyde. Somewhere out there is a colossal fortune. As you can imagine, many people have been obsessed with finding the missing gold over the years. If you ask me, there was a second robber, who is now hundreds of miles away, living a life of wealth and ease. After almost a quarter of a century, there is no chance of recovering it. But people here have never forgotten the robbery, and never will until the missing gold is found."

"I still cannot believe anyone could view the birth of an innocent child as a bad omen. Perhaps it is time for the townsfolk to build new memories of you." Grace reached up and kissed him. "Charlie Pyke, successful detective and happily married man, the new favourite son of Clyde."

Happily married indeed, Charlie thought as they lingered on the bridge, their bodies and lips fitting together as if they were made for each other. He was about to suggest they retire to the cottage with all haste, when Grace got in first.

"I'm longing to see our honeymoon cottage," she said, "but I think a short stroll down the main street is in order to show off my new husband."

Knowing how short the main street was, Charlie agreed. In truth, he welcomed the opportunity. Pride might be a sin, but he couldn't deny he had been looking forward to his hometown seeing him with Grace Penrose on his arm. They had known each other for three years, been engaged for three months, and married for almost a week, but Charlie still woke up at night fearful it had all been an impossibly wonderful dream.

After Grace's unpleasant initial introduction to the town, their stroll provided a delightful reminder of normality. All the passers-by nodded politely. If their eyes followed the newcomers, it seemed to be out of interest rather than any other motive, which was reassuring. Several people recognised Charlie and welcomed him back, while a few friends stopped to catch up on old times. Grace charmed them and dropped unsubtle hints about how proud she was of her husband and his successful private detective business.

By the time they reached the far end of the shops and hotels, the approaching twilight had drawn deep shadows on the rapidly emptying street. The only people still out were those in search of a drink after a long day – and a few who had already imbibed far too much. Charlie farewelled a last acquaintance and turned for home. He lengthened his stride, not wanting to be travelling to the cottage in darkness, or for his wife to be the focus of the stares of the men propping up the walls of the seedier hotels.

A plaintive cry drew their attention to an alley beside the most disreputable hotel of all, the Molyneux. Charlie felt Grace's fingers tense on his arm, but he dragged her onwards. The cry trailed off into a high-pitched sobbing.

"A woman is in trouble, Charlie," Grace said.

"I don't think that's a woman." Every nerve in his body warned Charlie to steer clear of trouble, but what if Grace was right? The voice cried out again. "Stay in the street, Grace. I'll be back in a moment."

Grace glanced around at the men watching them from the front of the Molyneux Hotel. "I'm coming with you."

Charlie went first, with Grace close behind. The alley went around to the back of the hotel, where horses shuffled in their stalls and piles of rubbish and old casks lined the rear wall. There was no sign of a damsel in distress. Charlie turned back towards the

20

main street, but a raucous laugh close behind him forced him to turn back, with every muscle tensing for trouble.

A man in a beer-stained barman's apron sneered down his nose at them. "Well, well. If it ain't Charlie Chink, turned up again like a bad penny. Never could resist a whimpering woman crying for help, could you, Pyke? You want to watch this one, girl."

Charlie cursed himself for a fool for being lured into a dark alley by his old foe's trickery. He sized up the school bully from head to toe with as much casual disdain as he could muster. Nathaniel Summerfield had always been fair of face when he chose to smile, which ought to have made him popular with girls, especially with his blue eyes and blond hair. But his heavy brow had a way of making him appear belligerent when he was sneering, which was far too often, and thus respectable girls, and boys for that matter, had avoided him. Of course, there were always plenty of others of similar ilk who hovered around him like flies on a dung heap.

How ironic that Nathaniel was now the barman at the Molyneux Hotel. His mother had been a barmaid here before sudden wealth had elevated the family fortunes. Nathaniel had been teased at school about his mother's reputation as a woman of loose morals, and he had taken out his rage on easy targets, like Charlie.

"Nathaniel Summerfield," Charlie said. "Thought I smelled something off in this alley. I guess nothing much has changed. Ten years on and you're still a bully and a loser. Charming as it was to see you again, we will leave you to lugging crates and pulling pints for your Mama."

Charlie backed away, keeping Grace behind him. He had no intention of turning his back on the man. Lugging crates had added muscles, while throwing drunks out at closing time had no doubt honed his bullying skills.

Nathaniel came after him. "Running away again, Pyke? It's you who's the loser. I'll own this hotel soon, while you left town with your tail between your legs years ago. Word has it you came

21

crawling back last year when the police force chucked you out and your slag left you, but you didn't stick around long enough for me to settle our old scores. I hope you will not disappoint me again."

Charlie gestured for Grace to go back to the street. She didn't budge. He loved her beyond measure, but sometimes he wished she would put her reckless courage aside and retreat when he told her to retreat. There was no arguing with her loyalty, but he prayed she wouldn't escalate the situation.

Grace stepped out from behind him and faced Nathaniel. "You heard wrong, Mr Summerfield. Charlie left the police force of his own accord to start a business in Dunedin. A business that has brought him fame, fortune and respect. I suggest you return to the miserable fleapit you call a hotel and leave your betters to their evening stroll."

Nathaniel's ruddy cheeks flushed crimson. He grabbed a bottle from the top of a pile of empties. One crack against the stone wall and he had a lethal weapon. "I don't take kindly to insults from a half-bred Mongol with a criminal grandfather, and I certainly won't tolerate insults from a woman who debases herself by associating with him."

Charlie pushed down the anger seething inside him at this quarter-century old nugget of baseless gossip. His priority right now was to get Grace out of here before Nathaniel worked himself into a fury. He took Grace's arm and hauled on it. She shook it off.

"Charlie's grandfather was a respected man," Grace retorted. "It is you who is the intolerant numpty for not seeing the good in men, regardless of their origin."

There was no way out now, Charlie realised. Time to fight fire with fire. "My grandfather was cleared of any involvement. Your father, however, remains high on the suspect list, Nathaniel. Quite the coincidence that his wealth appeared from nowhere within weeks of the robbery, don't you think? A lucky gold strike, I believe he said. Quite the rags to riches story. Now, if you will kindly excuse us, we have somewhere else we would prefer to be."

22

"You ain't going nowhere until you tell me why you're back in town. Word has it you're here to recover the gold your grandfather stole. Take my advice, Pyke. Tell me where your grandfather hid the gold, or I'll cut your ugly face until even your Mama won't love you."

Charlie let out an overly dramatic sigh. "How many times do I have to say it, Nathaniel? My grandfather had nothing to do with the gold robbery, and none of the Pyke family knows anything about it."

"In that case, I suggest you turn tail now before I run you and your doxy out of town." Nathaniel turned to Grace with a leer, holding the broken bottle within stabbing distance of her lower abdomen. "On second thoughts, the doxy can stay. The brothel could do with a bit more class, even if she hasn't much in the way of flesh to grab hold of."

Years of practice had trained Charlie to keep his composure in the face of loathsome bullies, but the situation was getting out of hand. Tempted as he was to punch this idiot, he tried one last time to calm the aggression. Not for Nathaniel, or Grace, but because two men were coming down the alley behind them with lengths of stout wood in their hands. The focus of their malice told Charlie they were on Nathaniel's side.

"I'll ignore your despicable insult, Nathaniel, because you know no better. Allow me to introduce my lovely and talented wife, Mrs Grace Penrose Pyke."

"Knock her up, did you, Pyke? Can't see any woman marrying you otherwise."

"Let's go, Grace. He's not worth it." Charlie tipped his head to indicate the men approaching from behind.

Grace's eyes flicked to the side, then back to him. Her hand slipped to the buttons on the front of her skirt. For once, Charlie was relieved to think she might have a concealed weapon. Being a medical student, a knife was his wife's weapon of choice, but he had long since ceased to be surprised by her inventiveness. If she brought out a blunderbuss from under the folds of her skirt, he wouldn't bat an eyelash.

When Charlie glanced back to see what the two accomplices were up to, Grace proved she could take him by surprise after all. She lunged forward and slapped Nathaniel Summerfield. Grace might look slim and delicate, but she had years of practice handling unruly patients at the hospital and drunk husbands at the women's refuge. When she slapped, the alley ringed with the sound of flesh on flesh. Nathaniel reeled backwards.

Grace glared at the bully with the full force of her best don't-mess-with-me glare. "How dare you insult my husband, you disgusting little creep? Charlie Pyke is worth a thousand of you."

Nathaniel had his hand to his cheek and seemed to have lost the use of his tongue. He snapped back to life when he heard laughter from the gathering crowd of onlookers at the end of the alley. He crouched into a fighting stance with the broken bottle in front of him. "Can't handle your woman, eh, Pyke? Perhaps I should punish her ill manners for you."

"Watch your tongue, Summerfield. Grace could trounce you with one hand tied behind her back." Charlie would never have risked her safety under ordinary circumstances, but the stumbling footsteps of Nathaniel's drunken friends were now too close behind him to ignore. Besides, for all their difference in size, he would back Grace against Nathaniel any day. "I'll leave it to my wife to teach you some manners. Personally, I wouldn't bother bloodying my knuckles on the likes of you."

Nathaniel gaped at Charlie, obviously taken aback by the confidence behind the insult. Charlie gave him a superior smile and didn't move an inch. Nor did Grace, who was looking at Nathaniel as if he was an annoying mosquito she would be forced to swat. Nathaniel hesitated, but then his eyes flicked behind them. The sight of his friends brought a twitch of glee to his lips.

He jabbed the bottle in Grace's direction. "That wench is so scrawny, I could push her to the ground with one finger. A wife is only good for one thing, Pyke, and I would be happy to show you how a real man does it."

"Brutes and drunkards aren't good for anything, Mr Summerfield," Grace replied. "Look at you. You can scarcely hold that bottle straight. I fear if you don't put it down, the jagged edge will cause a nasty cut, and not to me."

With a roar, Nathaniel lunged at Grace, who stepped aside at the last minute. Her leg went out, tripping her attacker, and a sharp elbow between his shoulder blades finished the job. Nathaniel hit the ground with a wail, catching his arm on the sharp edge of the broken glass as he fell on it.

"Oh, dear," Grace said. "Didn't I tell you to be careful with that bottle?"

The crowd of onlookers laughed louder and longer this time. They had moved closer to the fight, egging on both sides and taking bets on the outcome. It seemed nothing ever changed. The men around here would bet on a flea fight given half a chance.

Charlie only had time to flick his wife a smile before the other two attackers were on him. He ducked under the wildly swinging slab of wood wielded by the first man and plunged a fist into his stomach. The man staggered backwards, retching a tankard or two of cheap ale against the wall. The second man was less drunk and more cautious. He approached Charlie slowly, judging his moment. Charlie glanced back at Grace, who had pulled out a clean handkerchief from the stash she kept on hand for medical and emotional emergencies.

Charlie stared in disbelief at his wife as she knelt beside Nathaniel. Grace ought to be running away, but she was examining the slash wound. In his moment of distraction, the second man swung the wood at his head. He ducked on pure instinct and felt the whip of wind on his face as the weapon missed him by a whisker. The miss put the assailant off balance, allowing Charlie to step in and sweep his legs from under him. His head hit the brick wall with a thump and he went down in a heap.

"You'd better check that one's injuries, Charlie, as I have my hands full with this idiot." Grace was busy wrapping Nathaniel's bleeding arm in the handkerchief as her patient watched on, speechless. "I suggest you give this a thorough wash in clean water, Mr Summerfield, and see the local doctor for a couple of stitches. Fortunately, you haven't severed a blood vessel or tendon, but I suggest you refrain from assaulting innocent people for a day or two."

Nathaniel finally found his voice. "Get off me, you witch."

Grace obliged. "You're lucky my husband left you to me, Mr Summerfield. As this country's foremost private detective, Charlie Pyke has captured dozens of hardened criminals. He'd have had you in handcuffs before you could cry out for your Mama."

Nathaniel spewed a string of profanities, which only made the crowd of onlookers laugh louder. He rose and came at Grace again, with more deliberation this time. Charlie couldn't come to her aid, because the first man had stopped gawking at the unfolding fracas and was advancing on him again.

By the time Charlie had both his attackers moaning on the filthy cobbles of the alley, Grace was brushing dirt off her boots, while Nathaniel writhed in agony, clutching his private parts.

"Come, husband," Grace said, holding out her arm. "I think I have met more than enough of the fine citizens of Clyde for one evening. Shall we finish our stroll before the night turns chilly?"

"By all means, my dear." Charlie straightened his cuffs and picked up his hat.

"I'll have you up before the magistrate for attacking me, Pyke," Nathaniel groaned.

"Are you sure you want to do that, Nate?" Charlie asked. "The *Dunstan Times* will take great pleasure in publishing the account of you being beaten by a lady you insulted. In fact, I have an acquaintance who writes for a rather notorious Dunedin newspaper. I do believe you could become a laughingstock across the entire colony if you played your cards right. Or you could grow up and leave decent folk alone. Your choice."

Nathaniel slunk away. Charlie was tempted to stop and ask what odds the bookie had given on Grace, but there was no need. Charlie's bet would always have been on his wife.

Night Mare

Grace linked her arm through her husband's and strolled out of the alley past the crowd of grinning onlookers. Her heartbeat refused to return to normal and her face felt flushed, but she held her head high as if she hadn't a care in the world. The most discomforting aspect of the last few minutes was not the fight, but the unladylike elation she had felt during the encounter. What did it say about her that she hadn't felt so alive since they had put a double murderer behind bars two days ago?

How ironic that she had feared small town life might be a trifle dull compared to her usual busy schedule, especially as she had no experience of idleness. Grace was not about to admit it to Charlie, but she had tucked a textbook on surgical procedures into her trunk, just in case she needed a distraction. Not that she had expected to read it, given the newfound pleasures of time spent in her husband's intimate embrace.

When they were out of earshot of the crowd, Charlie whispered, "Nice work, Mrs Penrose Pyke. Having you by my side is a constant delight."

She loosened her grip on his arm. "I do hope the rest of the local populace is more civilised, my dear."

"I expect they will be now. I am sorry that our first night in town has been spoiled."

"Not your fault, Charlie. And it hasn't been spoiled. The best is yet to come. However, if we wish to enjoy a peaceful honeymoon, we may need to put a stop to these rumours that you are here to find the missing gold."

"Herding a score of feral cats would be easier than stopping a rumour in this town, Grace. Our best option is to ignore it and escape to the delights of our secluded cottage. I'll have to have a quick talk to my father before we leave, though. I wouldn't want him to hear about our altercation with Nathaniel Summerfield from anyone else."

"Isn't it a little late in the evening to be leaving town?" Grace asked. Especially with danger lurking around every corner, or so it had seemed thus far.

"It's a fine evening. Even if we leave after twilight, there will be plenty of starlight until the moon rises. Besides, Rose Cottage is not far from the edge of town."

Charlie's parents were already back at their own cottage. Grace noted that the buggy had been stowed away in the shed, so she assumed they would be staying at the Pyke's cottage after all. Jasmine Pyke took Grace inside, while Charlie and Sergeant Pyke went next door to the police station to talk.

Jasmine watched them through the sitting-room window, her face tight with a mother's worry. "I hope Charlie hasn't landed himself in trouble on his first night back in Clyde. For such a sweet-natured boy, he did get into an awful lot of scrapes."

"It wasn't Charlie's fault," Grace replied. "We met a trio of his former school bullies by the Molyneux Hotel. A pathetic specimen called Nathaniel Summerfield had the gall to call him a …" Grace bit the words back, not wanting to insult her dear mother-in-law.

"Let me guess," Jasmine said. "Mongol half-breed teacher's pet? Or words to that effect."

"Close enough. Suffice to say, Nathaniel appears to harbour a deep antipathy towards Charlie, even after all these years have passed."

"It ought to be the other way around," Jasmine said. "Nathaniel bullied Charlie at school until he was big enough to fight back. I hope there were no injuries during tonight's altercation."

Grace hesitated, but the fight had been observed and wild rumours would soon fly. "Nathaniel cut his arm on the broken

29

bottle he threatened me with, and he will also be sore in the nether regions for a day or two. His own fault entirely, as many witnesses will attest."

Jasmine shook her head. "I can understand Charlie getting angry when you were put at risk, but he ought not to have hurt Nathaniel."

"Actually, it wasn't Charlie." Grace cringed at the thought of how Charlie's parents would react when they heard their new daughter-in-law was seen brawling in an alley within hours of arrival. "I'm sorry if my actions bring shame on the Pyke family, but I could hardly stand back and do nothing when razor-sharp glass was thrust towards my face. If my boot came down a little harder than I intended on Nathaniel's groin, it was only because he was so rude to my beloved husband. I hope Sergeant Pyke won't have to arrest me."

Grace risked a glance at her mother-in-law.

A delicate hand covered Jasmine's lower face, but it was clear her eyes were smiling and she was struggling to hold back laughter. "Oh, Grace, it's so wonderful to have you here, so we can share in your adventures. I have no doubt who started it. Thomas will arrest Nathaniel, if necessary, but I expect Charlie will tell him to let it lie. The townsfolk are more likely to want to award you a medal than have you arrested. Young Summerfield and his friends are trouble."

"Didn't Nathaniel's parents discipline him when he was younger?"

"They protected him with their wealth. Over the years, Thomas has failed in several attempts to arrest Nathaniel on various charges of abusive behaviour, after the victims were recompensed generously for dropping their complaints. The Summerfield family feels they are above the law, especially when the law is administered by a man who sank so low as to marry a woman of mixed race. It's not as though they were born with a silver spoon in their mouths. Nathaniel's father was scraping a living as a prospector until he stuck gold, and his mother was a barmaid at the Molyneux Hotel. Now Mr Summerfield owns shares in one of the biggest dredging companies in the region and his wife fancies herself as the pinnacle of local society."

Grace thought the Summerfield family must be fools if they looked down on the Pykes, especially if they hadn't been born to elevated status themselves. "It must have been difficult for you, Mrs Pyke, coping with irrational prejudice all these years."

"I turn the other cheek and try to prove my worth by my actions, not my words." Jasmine's eyes twinkled as she added, "no one could have stopped me marrying Thomas Pyke, least of all the likes of Vern and Constance Summerfield."

A smile snuck onto Grace's lips. "I understand perfectly. The Pyke men are utterly irresistible."

Jasmine clasped Grace's hand as they shared a moment of unity. "Please don't feel that the townsfolk are all so prejudiced, Grace. We have many good friends here. For the most part, the Chinese and European communities rub along. The Chinese miners mostly searched for gold in the tailings left behind by other men, and caused no trouble, so they were accepted by most people, albeit not as equals."

"Nathaniel Summerfield seemed to have a specific issue with Charlie's grandfather, calling him a criminal and asking where the gold was buried. I hate to bring it up with you, Mrs Pyke, but I am even more reluctant to talk to Charlie about it and risk ruining our honeymoon. I wouldn't ask at all, but I don't want any repeats of tonight."

Jasmine walked to the window and stared out into the growing darkness. Just when Grace thought her mother-in-law would not reply, Jasmine returned to the table and placed her dainty hand over Grace's again.

"The men will be back soon and it's getting late. I suggest you and Charlie head to the cottage and get a good night's sleep after our long journey. Come over around noon tomorrow for a meal and we'll talk then. It would be better if Thomas gave you the facts of the case."

Grace took the hint. "I'm looking forward to seeing the cottage. How long will it take us to walk there?"

"It's about forty minutes on foot, but it'll be quicker with the horses. Thomas is lending you his own mount, Erebus, and Charlie's favourite horse, Nyx. Charlie adored Nyx. He must miss her dreadfully."

Grace didn't know how to respond. Charlie had told her that his father bred horses for police duty, but he had never mentioned having a horse of his own. "He doesn't talk much about his life here, other than how much he misses you. Tell me about Nyx."

"She was the first horse Charlie trained. Thomas guided him, naturally, but Charlie has a way with animals. Sometimes, I worried about my son spending so much time roaming around the wilderness on Nyx, instead of being with other young folk. Leaving Nyx behind when he went to Dunedin was a wrench."

After only a few hours in Charlie's hometown, Grace was realising how little she knew of her husband's former life. "Do you think Charlie regrets leaving his hometown?"

"I suspect he was homesick for a while in the early days," Jasmine said. "But we all knew that leaving was the right decision for him. Charlie was clever at school and determined to become a policeman. In Clyde, he was just a part-Chinese boy too big for his boots, following in his father's footsteps. Look at him now. He has never been happier, and we couldn't be prouder of what he has achieved with you by his side."

The two women sat in companionable silence, contemplating the men they loved. When the silence drew on, Grace said, "Erebus and Nyx are unusual names for horses."

"They are the Greek god and goddess of darkness. You'll understand when you see them. In fact, since it is getting dark, you may not see them at all. A truly black horse is a rare thing, and they are absolute beauties. Nyx is seventeen hands high, with the muscle and intelligence of her Percheron ancestors. Erebus is even bigger. Thomas and Erebus terrify the bejabbers out of most of the criminals they encounter on police duties."

Grace could well imagine it. A tall, muscular policeman on a powerful black horse would be a fearsome sight if one was running from the law. "Does Sergeant Pyke still ride Nyx?"

"Nyx is mostly used as a broodmare now, as her mother was before her. She'll probably be retired soon. She's had a full life and deserves a rest, although she's still lively at thirteen. If you could see her running wild on spring grass, you'd think she was still a filly, not a mature lady. She and Erebus will enjoy their time with you, not least because Rose Cottage is next to a field of green grass and has plenty of shade trees. Thomas will use his spare horse."

A clatter of boots interrupted their cozy chat. Charlie said goodnight on the doorstep and led Grace around to the rear of the police cottage. "Wait here, Grace, while I get the saddles."

"Saddles? Aren't we taking the buggy?"

"Where's the fun in that? I can't wait to get back into the saddle again. Nothing like a ride in the countryside to bring joy to the day. Or night, in this case."

Charlie left Grace standing in the dark under a tree, next to a gloomy expanse of paddock. She wanted to call out after his retreating back, but it was too late to admit her lack of riding experience. How hard could it be to ride a short distance on a road? Perhaps Charlie could arrange a quiet pony for her, while he rode the lively Nyx. His footsteps padded back towards her before she could decide.

"Nyx," Charlie called into the darkness.

Across the other side of the field, Grace heard a whinny, followed by the thunder of hooves on hard ground. She saw nothing but a blur of black on black, until an enormous head loomed up over the wall, pushing her equine nose against Charlie. He rubbed her between the ears, as a second, even larger, black head appeared beside them.

"Grace, meet Nyx, the other lady love of my life. And this fellow is Erebus. Pa has lent them both to us for our honeymoon."

33

"How kind." Even from her position out of biting range, Grace found the giant horses intimidating. Now was the moment for her to admit the truth. "Perhaps we should take the buggy, Charlie. I realise it will seem unfathomable to you, but I grew up in the city. The only time I have been on a horse was when my country cousin led me on an ancient pony around their orchard. I'm sure Nyx and Erebus are excellent police horses, but perhaps somewhat beyond my riding ability."

Charlie appeared startled, as if it had truly never crossed his mind that she couldn't ride. It was not as if he had ever seen her on a horse, although he knew she could drive a buggy. After a moment's hesitation, he slipped halters on the looming heads. "Nyx has the sweetest nature of any horse I know. She'll look after you, Grace. I promise, she is as quiet as a lamb."

He had to be joking. No way was Grace getting up on that massive beast. "Charlie dearest, I've seen lambs in the fields, and they are usually frisky little demons. Your sweet Nyx looks about as safe as a thoroughbred racehorse with her tail on fire."

He laughed, as if she was the one joking, and led the horses to a hitching post by the shed, where he saddled them with practiced efficiency. Grace, never one to admit defeat, said no more, although she considered going to say farewell to her parents-in-law in case she never saw them again.

Charlie flipped the reins over Nyx's head. "I promise you'll love riding once you get the feel for it. It's an essential skill out here." He waved towards the rugged hills looming on the horizon, picked out by the pale starlight.

If her husband thought she was going anywhere near that terrifying wilderness on a horse the size of Goliath, he was insane. Charlie cupped his hand and waited for her to put her foot up. With a sense of impending doom, Grace allowed him to boost her high off the ground into the saddle, before she could have second, third or fourth doubts about riding.

Her riding skirt separated into wide trouser legs as she thumped onto the stiff leather of the saddle. When her parents had given her the skirt, saying she would need it for riding, Grace had foolishly imagined it as being suitable for a bicycle, as well as comfortable walking attire. She had been here only a few hours and already had discovered the split skirt was also suitable for riding gigantic battle horses and fighting vicious bullies. Had she really thought she might be bored on their honeymoon?

Charlie stroked Nyx's nose and told her to be on her best behaviour, because she was carrying precious cargo. The mare turned her massive head and eyed Grace up with apparent interest, or possibly scorn for her riding prowess. In truth, the mare did have sweet eyes under long lashes, but Grace was not altogether convinced that her nature was as placid as the eyes promised. Her husband put the reins in her hands and deserted her to mount his own horse.

Erebus shook his mighty head and crabbed sideways, but Charlie brought the beast under control with a squeeze of his legs. "Relax your muscles, Grace, and move with the horse, not against her. Unless you want me to put Nyx on a lead rein?"

Grace tapped Nyx with her heels. If she was going to do this at all, it would not be on a lead rein like a child. The mass of muscle beneath her surged as Nyx walked forward. Grace grabbed the pommel of the saddle and tried not to look at the ground, now six feet below her.

"We'll do a loop past the cemetery so I can show you where my grandparents are buried," Charlie said.

Terrific, Grace thought. Nothing like a spooky graveyard at nighttime to add an extra layer of terror to her ordeal.

Charlie headed off into the night in the opposite direction to the main street of Clyde, keeping up a steady stream of chatter about the sights, which comprised a scatter of houses and a dark recreation ground where he had played games as a child. Grace had to admit that it was very pleasant to be swaying gently on Nyx's broad back, walking through the darkness with little effort on her own part.

By the time they reached the cemetery, Grace had drifted into a state of sleepy acceptance. The horses' hooves crunched on the finely crushed gravel of the path to the gate. Beyond the gate, rows of headstones cast long shadows under the rising moon, but the fresh scent of the pine trees and the tranquillity of the night gave the place a feeling of serenity.

Charlie pointed out the headstones of his grandparents. "My parents had to insist they were buried together. Usually, Chinese people are buried in the mixed section, not the Anglican section, despite my grandfather being a practising Anglican. In some graveyards, Chinese people are buried outside the walls, as heathens. Most of those born in China prefer their remains to be returned to their homeland, but that is not always possible."

Grace nodded her understanding. "We'll come back another time with flowers."

As they continued down the road, Grace struggled to keep her eyes open with the gentle sway of movement and the hypnotic clip-clop of hooves on the road. The night was dense with the smell of green grass and ripe fruit, as if she was dreaming of somewhere other than this arid place. When she opened her eyes, Grace realised it wasn't a dream.

"Lovely, isn't it?" Charlie said. "Rose Cottage is in the biggest orchard in the area. The original owners planted thousands of fruit trees and grapevines over the last thirty years. They won awards for their wine. There's grazing land for dairy cows as well, and pigs, chooks, a market garden, and fields of oats. A Garden of Eden and a blessing to the town. In the early days of the gold rush, miners had to survive on what little food they could bring with them, supplemented with meat from the sheep stations which already existed in the region. Scurvy and similar diseases were rife back then."

"How did they grow such a lush garden when the land around is bare of trees?"

"The land is fertile enough. All that was needed was a supply of water. Half the enduring family feuds in town are disputes over water rights."

"Your grandparents had a market garden too, didn't they, Charlie?"

"Further along this road. Small by comparison, but they eked out a living from it by long hours of hard work."

They turned off onto a side road, passing a farm gate with a splendid line of poplars forming an avenue to a house and several other stone buildings.

"I'd love to hear more about your grandparents, Charlie, not least because I want to know why Nathaniel implied your grandfather had a connection to the gold robbery. But not tonight."

"Definitely not. I think we have had enough talk of the past for one day, and certainly enough unpleasantness."

"Indeed. If this first day is a foretaste of what we can expect from the inhabitants of Clyde, I am inclined to stay in the cottage for the rest of our honeymoon. Perhaps we should get a fierce dog to guard our privacy." Grace yawned. "How much further?"

"We're here."

They turned onto an overgrown path. The horses' hooves swished through wildflowers dancing in the long grass, turned silver by the moonlight. A dry-stone wall of stacked schist rock ran beside them. The natural plane on the top and bottom surfaces of the rock made it ideal for stacking. In contrast, the jagged side edges reminded the onlooker that this countryside had been wrenched from a rugged wilderness by blood, sweat, and tears.

Mature trees hung heavy with peaches and apricots on the other side of the path, wafting the heavenly scent of ripe fruit. Grace plucked an apricot as she passed. When its juice filled her mouth like pure heaven on earth, it was all she could do to suppress a groan. Beneath Nyx's hooves, the aroma of crushed thyme drifted up. Grace leaned low over the mare's withers to inhale the scent, but lost her balance. Only Charlie's steadying hand stopped her from slipping from the saddle.

The track ahead widened into a clearing in the trees with a little wooden cottage on the far side.

"Oh, Charlie, it's perfect."

And it was. From the climbing roses around the veranda posts to the trickle of smoke coming from the chimney and the welcoming lure of the open door, Rose Cottage was absolutely perfect.

Grace slid from the saddle, dropping the reins in her haste to enter this sanctuary from the world.

"Wait," Charlie said. He gathered her into his arms and carried her over the threshold.

Inside, the marks of Jasmine Pyke's thoughtfulness were evident. In the main room, a vase of roses stood on the table next to a lit candle and a covered platter of food. A large pot of water simmered on top of the coal range. Another candle glowed through the open door of the second room, revealing a wide bed, its patchwork quilt scattered with rose petals. Their trunks were arranged side by side in one corner.

Charlie put her down and wiped a tear from her eye. "Ma made the quilt years ago for my marriage bed. As you can see, she is delighted that the time has come to use it." He dropped a kiss on her cheek. "Why don't you make yourself comfortable while I see to the horses."

Words still wouldn't come, so Grace nodded. She shed her dusty clothes, washed in glorious hot water from the stove, and went into the bedroom to search her trunk for her new silk dressing gown. She was brushing out her hair when Charlie returned. He shed his clothes in the sitting room and sighed at the touch of hot water, as she had done.

"Grace, are you still awake?" Charlie said in a low voice.

"Just getting ready."

"I hope you are not cross that an old bully ruined the start of our honeymoon. Or rather, our trip away, since the honeymoon started the instant I slipped a ring on your finger." He sighed. "Best few days of my life, give or take a murder or two."

Grace came out of the bedroom with her long hair brushed to a shine and hanging loose over the front of the dressing gown. "Our encounter with your schoolmate only served to remind me how fortunate I have been in my choice of husband."

"You look beautiful," Charlie whispered.

"From now on, this honeymoon is about us enjoying our new life together." Grace undid the tie of the gown and shrugged the silk to the floor.

The moon had risen above the trees by the time they emerged from the bedroom again. They shared a late supper on the veranda under a sky awash with stars.

Charlie leaned back on the bench seat with a contented sigh and plucked a rose petal out of Grace's tousled hair. "What a wonderful way to start our time away, my love."

Grace had to agree, apart from the unwelcome encounters with Jake Blackthorn and Nathaniel Summerfield. However, there was one tricky subject she had to raise, if she could find a way to do so without upsetting her husband. The time of the month was fast approaching for them to be restrained in their lovemaking, or Jasmine Pyke might be switching her sewing talents to baby quilts.

Before their marriage, they had both agreed that children would have to wait until Grace had graduated from medical school. Unfortunately, that longed-for date was almost two years away. Meanwhile, Grace wasn't sure that her husband understood the sacrifices this would entail. Indeed, she doubted her own resolve now that she had experienced the joys of the marriage bed. She had wanted to talk with him before, but finding the time in between

39

work and wedding preparations had been difficult. It hadn't been urgent then, so she hadn't pursued the matter.

"Charlie …," Grace began.

Charlie tensed beside her as if he knew what she was about to say. "Shh. What's that noise?"

"What noise?"

"A scratching sound, coming from under the veranda."

"Rats, probably. Charlie, we need to talk."

"Can it wait? It sounds like whining as well as scratching." Charlie rose to investigate.

He had to lever up a loose slat from beside the steps to get underneath the veranda. When he emerged after a few minutes of wriggling and cursing in the pitch blackness, he had an armful of black and white fluff. A dog. Grace went into the cottage ahead of them to light candles near the warmth of the stove.

"This is no stray," Charlie said. "She's a young border collie. One of Duncan MacEwen's probably. He breeds them as heading dogs."

"Heading? Do you mean herding?" Grace was already busy prodding the stove into life. Fortunately, she had brought a medical kit with her from force of habit. It made a change not to be tending to her husband's wounds.

"Heading dogs are the artists of sheep handling. A well-trained dog can move a flock of sheep precisely where the shepherd wants them. Border collies are masters of the art." Charlie ran careful hands down the collie's sides and limbs. "Poor lass must have crawled under the cottage and become stuck. She's dehydrated, but not injured apart from a ripped ear, which looks like it has been clipped by a shotgun pellet. Luckily, border collies are exceptionally quick on their feet."

Grace brought over a bowl of water, which the collie lapped to the last drop. Her tongue switched its attention to Grace's hand, with a slobbery lick she took as thanks. "I must have conjured her up when I suggested getting a fierce guard dog. Although fate is

40

playing a trick on us. I've never seen a dog who looks less fierce that her. The only way she'd stop an attacker is by licking them into submission. Perhaps we could call her Fluffy?"

"Over my dead body. She's a working dog, Grace, not a pampered lapdog, and deserves a noble name." The collie laid her head on Charlie's feet, gazing at him with adoration and pushing her nose into his hand until he patted her grubby coat. "She'll be hungry. Can you slice up a little of the meatloaf Ma made for us, please? I'll clean her up properly tomorrow."

Judging from the smitten expression on her husband's face when Grace came back with a plate of chopped meatloaf and more water, a love affair between dog and man was already blossoming. Grace resigned herself to sharing her honeymoon with two other females: Nyx and the collie. She rubbed the dog's head, being careful to avoid the ripped ear. "With that jagged strip of white down her nose, we could call her Blaze."

"Best not to name her at all," Charlie said. "Her owner will be looking for her. A top border collie is worth a fortune in sheep country." He eased his feet from under the ball of bedraggled fluff. "Let's leave Blaze to rest. After two days' travelling, I'm looking forward to a soft bed with only my wife for company. In fact, I agree with you about not leaving this cottage at all for the next two weeks."

Strays and Scones

Charlie woke up with a weight pinning his legs. The sun angled through the curtains, telling him he had slept late. He turned to ease Grace's body off him so he could get up, but her side of the bed was empty. Blaze's lolling tongue and bright eyes welcomed him instead. The rescued collie was taking her guard duties a mite too seriously.

After a quick wash, Charlie donned a pair of old trousers. He added a cotton shirt, but only because they might have unexpected visitors. His tie and waistcoat didn't get a second glance. This was the life. Yawning, he ambled into the main room of the cottage, which was empty. The meatloaf platter was also empty. Charlie made do with a hunk of bread and cheese, and a couple of boiled eggs he found cooling in a pot.

He found Grace sitting on the veranda with a pot of tea and a bowl of peaches. Blaze padded over and laid her head on Grace's lap.

Grace ruffled the fur around the collie's neck. "Enough of the soulful eyes, Miss Blaze. You've already had the rest of the meatloaf. What will my mother-in-law say when she finds out her fine cooking has been feeding a stray dog?" Grace pushed an empty cup in Charlie's direction. "I gave her a brush too. Blaze is looking much recovered from her ordeal, don't you think?"

"All of us are." Charlie poured tea and sat on the step in the sun, devouring his breakfast. When it was gone, with peaches for dessert, he leaned back on the veranda post and closed his eyes. "Bliss. After I've taken Blaze home and visited my parents, I don't want to see another soul for the rest of our honeymoon, except for you."

Blaze's low growl roused him from a doze a few minutes later. The collie crouched on the edge of the veranda, poised to launch herself at the broad-shouldered man moving rapidly towards them through the trees. A black slouch hat shaded the man's eyes, but his mouth was puckered with anger and the cocked shotgun gave an unambiguous message.

Charlie rose, with one eye on the collie. "Blaze, sit." The dog sat but remained alert.

The man stopped a few yards away, with his shotgun under his arm. "What are you doing here? This is private property."

"Good morning," Charlie replied. "Mr Trent, isn't it? I'm Sergeant Pyke's son, Charlie, and this is my wife, Grace. My parents have hired Rose Cottage for the two weeks of our visit to Clyde."

"Oh, aye. I thought I saw Sergeant and Mrs Pyke here yesterday evening with a buggy." The shotgun dropped to the side of his leg, but Mr Trent's mouth remained stubbornly down-turned while he inspected them. Finally, a single finger lifted the brim of his hat half an inch in acknowledgement of the presence of a lady. "Pardon my caution, but you wouldn't believe what the ne'er-do-wells of this town get up to when the grog is in them. No respect for a man's property, those youngsters. Weren't like that in my day. Every boy had a proper day's work to do as soon as he could walk, and a boot to his backside if he so much as talked back."

"I'm sure you're right, Mr Trent," Charlie said. "We won't be any bother, I promise you."

Trent glared at the collie, who was sitting on the step with her eye on Charlie, in case further commands were forthcoming. "Caught a feral dog bothering my cows a few days back. Black and white, it was, like this 'un."

"I'm sorry to hear it, Mr Trent. This is one of Mr MacEwen's purebred border collies, not a stray. You can see she's cared for and under control."

Grace moved beside the dog and held out her hand. "Blaze, shake." Blaze put her paw into Grace's hand. "Down, girl. Roll over." Blaze complied. Grace rubbed her exposed belly. "You see, Mr Trent, she's not the least bit feral."

Trent grunted. "Reckon I winged the mongrel with my shotgun a few days ago, so happen it's long gone."

"I expect so, Mr Trent." Charlie stepped forward to shake their neighbour's hand. "You can be sure we will keep a lookout for dangerous strays."

"Right, I'll be off then. Haven't got time to loll around all day." With that, Trent stomped off the way he'd come.

When their neighbour was out of hearing distance, Charlie resumed his spot in the sun. "How did you know Blaze could do tricks, Grace?"

Grace gave the collie a final rub. "I taught her while you were still dead to the world. She's highly intelligent and a quick learner."

"I didn't know you had experience of training dogs."

"I don't. But chunks of meatloaf are an excellent motivator. Dogs and husbands have a lot in common." Grace smiled and poured another cup of tea for him. "I must have tired poor Blaze out, because she went back to bed after our training session. It'll take her a day or two to get her strength back, I suppose."

"I'm surprised how well she has recovered already."

"Dehydration must have made her weak, but it's also quickly remedied," Grace said. "I take it you know the man with the shotgun."

"Bob Trent. I don't know him well, although he and his family have lived in Clyde forever. He's not the most sociable of men. You'll be pleased to hear that Trent is our neighbour rather than our landlord. Rose Cottage belongs to the farm and orchard on the other side. Bob and his wife, Matilda, have a smallholding running dairy cows. He's not a bad fellow, just a little surly. Matilda Trent is a ray of sunshine compared to her husband. She is renowned for her jolly laugh, her delicious cheeses, and her capacity for hard work."

"They do say opposites attract."

"Do you think we're opposites?" Charlie asked.

Grace lounged back on the bench seat. "In some ways, I suppose, but that only makes us perfectly compatible. I am very much looking forward to having a peaceful honeymoon to prove all aspects of our compatibility, once I have a nice little loll around in this glorious sunshine. I cannot recall the last time I sat down with nothing better to do than nap in the sun."

Charlie felt the same, but there was one task he couldn't put off. "I'd better take the collie back to Mr MacEwen straight away. Harassing livestock is a capital offence around here. Regardless of how many adorable tricks Blaze learns, Bob Trent will shoot her if she goes onto his property again."

In the end, they both took Blaze home, because they wanted to spend as much time together as possible. Besides, it was a splendid day for a stroll through the countryside.

While Grace was changing into visiting clothes, Charlie taught Blaze the names of various items and the "find" command. Within ten minutes, the collie had taken to the game with boundless enthusiasm until Charlie had sticks, boots, water bowls, and sundry other items piled in front of him. When he heard his wife coming through the bedroom door, he tested Blaze on a new item. "Find Grace." Blaze was off in a flash, cutting Grace off as she attempted to return a glass to the sink, and herding her to the door.

"Why is Blaze treating me like a sheep, Charlie?"

"I'm teaching her to track and recover. You're right, she's a quick learner."

"What's the point when you're taking her back to Duncan MacEwen?"

Charlie had no answer for that, except that it was a pure joy to have a dog around again.

They set off at a comfortable pace, enjoying the tranquillity of the countryside. He kept Blaze close to his side, which she accepted only after several reprimands for chasing down alluring scents and incautious wildlife. Their route took them on the road to Springvale, past the plot of land Charlie's grandparents had turned into a market garden during the gold rush.

"I wonder why Blaze ran away," Grace said. "I'd have thought Mr MacEwen would have had her working hard for her supper. What's he like?"

"A fine country gentleman," Charlie replied. "His family was one of the first to lease land for sheep in Central Otago. The original landed gentry of New Zealand. The land might have been cheap back then, but help was scarce during the gold rush and getting the wool clip back to Dunedin was a nightmare when the roads were little more than rough tracks. Even so, the land suited sheep and vast fortunes were made in the early days for those willing to risk capital and put in the hard yards."

"They are a wealthy family, then?"

"They've had their ups and downs. When old Mr MacEwen squandered most of the wealth, the family had to sell off some prime land. Duncan inherited a run that was too small to be efficient, but he has built it up again over the years. Hamish, their oldest son, and his brother now run the high-country station. Duncan and his wife live in the original homestead a mile or two beyond town with their two youngest children these days, where they breed and train border collies and raise sheep for local consumption."

"Do you know them well?"

Charlie could almost smell Mrs MacEwen's famous scones. How many hours had he and Hamish MacEwen spent in that welcoming kitchen over the years? Oh, the adventures the two of them had had away in the wilderness, when Duncan could spare his son from the farm. Happy days.

"Charlie?"

"Sorry, Grace. I was wool-gathering. Apart from my friend Amelia, Hamish MacEwen was my best friend at school. I spent almost as much time at the MacEwen's home as my own. Hamish even lived with us for a short while after his mother died. I don't remember it, because we were both babies."

"You never told me." Grace slapped a hand over her mouth. "Oh, heavens, if you two were so close, I expect the MacEwen family will be upset we didn't invite them to the wedding."

"I wrote to invite them," Charlie admitted. "Apologies, Grace, but there was so much to organise, I forgot all about it. It was merely a politeness. At this time of the year, there was no chance that they could come to Dunedin."

"I take it Duncan MacEwen remarried."

"He was lost without his wife. Eventually, his family rallied around to run the sheep station, and baby Hamish came to live with us while Duncan went down-country to recover. He met the second Mrs MacEwen at a country dance and lived happily ever after. Hamish never knew his own mother, of course, and he has always been treated exactly the same as the other children they went on to have."

"How lovely. I'm looking forward to meeting some friendly locals, especially as they will have no interest in an old gold robbery."

Charlie wasn't so sure. *Everybody* was interested in the missing gold. Over the years, Charlie had witnessed more than one prominent citizen, and a great many ordinary citizens, poking under rock piles along the trail to Arrowtown, where the gold was reputed to be hidden. Or rather, such had been the case when he was a lad, and it was too much to hope that anything had changed. The town seemed to churn on the same path year after year, like a water wheel endlessly circling in place even as fresh water flowed though.

Even the social gatherings had followed the same pattern on every occasion. The farming men would cluster in one corner, grumbling about wool prices, the state of the roads, the unfair share

47

of water rights assigned to gold ventures, and the difficulty of getting shearing gangs. The gold syndicate men would cluster in another corner, grumbling about gold prices, the state of the roads, the excessive use of water by farmers, and the difficulty of getting competent engineers and spare parts for the dredges. The women split along similar lines, although with slightly more mingling because of their shared charitable concerns. Other notables – the magistrate and law enforcement, attorneys, land agents, bankers, shopkeepers, and so forth – mingled as they chose or talked amongst themselves.

Once the mandatory grumbling session was over, each group would then discuss the latest social events: who was stepping out with whom, whether a second cousin twice removed might be a suitable wife for a lonely bachelor, and other matters of social import. Finally, inevitably, there would be a lull in the conversation, and somebody would fill the gap with speculation about the gold robbery. Charlie was glad to be out of it, although he missed the sense of close community and the wildness of the countryside. Not for the first time, he worried Grace would not be comfortable here.

Grace broke the silence a few minutes later, as they approached the MacEwen's driveway. "You didn't answer my question, Charlie. Please tell me Duncan MacEwen wasn't another robbery suspect."

Blaze charged ahead up the driveway, confirming to Charlie that she was one of Duncan's dogs. A shame, but for the best.

"Duncan? No more of a suspect than any other law-abiding citizen. The police kept an eye on any man whose fortunes improved after the robbery, but Duncan's improved situation had a solid explanation. Mrs Julia MacEwen was one of the well-to-do Matheson family, who are landed gentry from down south. Her dowry allowed Duncan to expand the sheep station and prosper."

"He married her for her money?"

"By no means. Duncan and Julia fell in love at first sight, or so the story goes. Once you see them together, you will believe it.

Nevertheless, her dowry was welcome. Julia MacEwen has been a blessing to both Duncan and the local community. Intelligent, kind, loving, and a supporter of worthy causes. A wife like that is better than any amount of gold, as I well know."

Charlie looked around for Blaze. In the adjacent field, a small flock of ewes were running in circles, bleating. Up ahead, a cat shot under the gate and across the drive with the collie in hot pursuit. If Duncan MacEwen was watching, he would be furious.

"Tarnation mongrel," an angry voiced bellowed from the house end of the field. "Heel, ya mangy beast!"

Blaze raced back down the drive to Charlie. She darted behind him, holding her head and tail low and avoiding his glare. Too late to slink away now. Boots stomped across the yard towards the drive. A lean man strode around the corner and came to a dead halt, shotgun raised in their direction.

The horrified look on Grace's face showed she understood. She gripped Charlie's arm. "Don't let Mr MacEwen shoot Blaze, Charlie."

A blue-flannel clad arm came up to shield the sun from his face – unnecessarily, since he was wearing a wide-brim hat. Then his sunburned face cracked into a broad smile and he broke open the shotgun. "Charlie Pyke, as I live and breathe. Good to see you, lad."

The gap between the two men closed as if Charlie had never been away. Duncan MacEwen pulled him into a bear hug, accompanied by much good-natured backslapping. "Darned shame we couldn't get to your wedding. Julia will insist you and your wife come for a meal. We'll get Hamish and the others down."

Charlie stepped aside to reveal Grace, who had been shielded by his broad back. "Mr MacEwen, I would like you to meet my wife, Grace Penrose Pyke."

Duncan MacEwen strode forward and enveloped Grace in a hearty embrace. "A pleasure to meet you, Mrs Pyke. You're part of our family now, and most welcome."

Grace seemed stunned but pleased by the unexpected show of affection. "You must call me Grace."

"Grace it is. How good of you to call on us so soon after your arrival."

Charlie gestured at the shotgun. "Is this the way you greet all your visitors these days, Mr MacEwen, or are we special?"

A flush rose to their host's already ruddy cheeks. "Sorry about that. Some no-good spawn of Satan has been stealing my stock. Four lambs last night and two prime breeding ewes a few nights ago. I've been keeping watch, but the thief is slipperier than a greased pig." He bent to scratch Blaze's ears. "The dog disappeared the same night as the ewes, so I assumed the rustler had dog-napped her. More fool him, stealing the worst sheepdog I ever raised."

"We found your dog trapped under Rose Cottage," Charlie said. "Maybe she got away from the thief and hid there. If we hadn't arrived, she'd have been a goner."

"Stupid beggar. She probably took off to go chasing rabbits again. Sniffing out trouble is all she is good for. I've used every darn trick in the book to train her, but she doesn't have the heading instinct. A disgrace to the noble breed of border collie. She's not worth a brass farthing to me if she runs off every time a rabbit pops its head up when she is supposed to be working the mob. Especially not when there are more rabbits on our run than specks of gold in the Clutha."

Blaze had sunk so low in shame that her body was splayed out on the ground.

"Don't give me that look, dog," Duncan said. "You know I'm too soft to get rid of you. Maybe I'll try training her to fetch rabbits to feed the rest of my dogs. Anyway, come on in for a brew. If we're lucky, Julia will have made a batch of scones, especially as she knows you're in town."

Charlie brightened at the prospect. "You're a lucky man, Mr MacEwen, to be married to the best scone maker in the county."

"Don't I know it, lad. And she manages all the accounts. All those columns of numbers dance in front of my eyes like so much gibberish, but Julia knows it all down to the nearest penny." Duncan paused at the open front door to kick off his boots and bellow that they had company.

"No need to shout, dear. I saw you in the yard." Julia MacEwen already had a huge pot of tea and a plate piled with fresh scones and jam waiting on the kitchen table, along with silver teaspoons and starched white linen napkins, which should have seemed out of place, but somehow didn't.

Julia MacEwen exuded the same odd mix of elegance and comfort, with her carefully coiffed hair and sparkling eyes setting off a dab of flour on heat-reddened cheeks. She stripped off her apron, revealing a simple, well-cut gown, and pulled Charlie into a tight embrace. "Wonderful to see you, Charlie, my dear, simply wonderful. And all grown up and married too." She pulled away and turned her rosy cheeks on Grace. "Come here, Grace dear, and give Charlie's second mother a hug. I cannot tell you how delighted I am to meet the woman who has made our Charlie so very happy."

"Thank you, Mrs MacEwen," Grace mumbled from within the embrace. "I'm overwhelmed by the warmth of your welcome."

Mrs MacEwen released Grace and gestured for them to sit. Mr MacEwen reached for a solid enamel mug, which appeared to have seen duty over a campfire, while Mrs MacEwen set fine porcelain cups and saucers in front of the other place settings. "You've had an eventful time since you arrived, I hear." She made the words sound matter of fact, but her eyes danced with laughter.

Grace looked mortified, so Charlie stepped in. "News still travels faster than lightning in these parts."

51

"Duncan took the last of the season's lambs down to the butcher's shop this morning. The butcher said his lad had heard from the stable hand at the Molyneux Hotel that a young lady had given young Summerfield a right walloping. About time somebody taught young Summerfield a lesson. Help yourself to sugar, Grace, dear. We don't stand on ceremony around here."

"We assumed it was you and Charlie," Mr MacEwen mumbled through a mouthful of scone.

"Really, Duncan," his wife said, "must you speak with a full mouth like a peasant? Thomas and Jasmine have told us tales of your exploits, Grace. We're as proud of you both as they are. It's not easy becoming such a success in challenging professions."

"Have another scone, Charlie." Mr MacEwen passed the plate and took one for himself. "Must keep up your energy on your honeymoon, especially if you are here to solve the mystery of the gold robbery as well."

"We have no intention of doing any such thing, Mr MacEwen. All we want is a few days of peace to enjoy a much-needed rest." Charlie had said it so often, he was beginning to sound desperate. "Please feel free to tell anyone who asks that I am not here to solve any old mysteries. The Pyke family has no knowledge about the robbery and never did." He bit down into layers of sweet strawberries, rich cream, and soft-as-a-cloud scone, letting out a groan of bliss. "You haven't lost your magic, Mrs MacEwen. Biting into one of your scones is like a trip to heaven."

"Glad to hear it, Charlie," Mrs MacEwen said. "I'm sick of hearing about ancient crimes too. No point stirring up that old nonsense again."

Mr MacEwen tapped his nose with his index finger. "Enough said, lad. All we ask is for a heads-up if you get a sniff of the gold. Price of wool these days is criminal. There'll be more than one sheep station around here up against the wall if this damnable socialist mob in government doesn't get off their lardy arses and focus on the people making the country's wealth, instead of breaking up productive farmland into smallholdings."

"Ladies present, Duncan." But Mrs MacEwen's admonishment was said without rancour and was met with an apologetic pat on the hand from her adoring husband.

"Don't mind me," Grace said. "I volunteer in a women's refuge. There isn't much left to shock me, especially not when it comes to colourful language."

Duncan MacEwen ignored the linen napkin his wife had put in front of him and wiped a blob of jam off his chin with his fist. "I still think Vern Summerfield had something to do with it. The robbery, I mean."

"Why do you say that, Mr MacEwen?" Charlie couldn't conceal the shock from his voice. Vern Summerfield had produced a witness who swore he was at his diggings up Cromwell way on the night of the robbery, several hours away, even on horseback in good conditions. The witness statement had eliminated Vern from the inquiry. "Mr Summerfield was at his Bannockburn diggings."

"That's what he said, but one of my shepherds was sure he saw Vern in town that night, sneaking down the main street in the middle of the night. I told Quinney he had to return to town immediately and tell the police. I asked your father about it when I next saw him, weeks later, but the police had ruled Vern out by then."

"I don't recall any such evidence," Charlie said. "But then I only heard the story much later, when I was old enough to ask questions. I suppose my father only gave me enough of the facts to satisfy my curiosity. What was the shepherd's full name and what exactly did he see?" Charlie pulled a notebook out of his pocket and flicked to a fresh page.

"Jethro Quinney." Mr MacEwen's lower lip pushed out as he struggled to recall long-ago events. "Quinney had to have a finger amputated due to frostbite, and he reckoned the whisky at the Molyneux Hotel would be a better painkiller than anything they had at the hospital. Anyhow, Quinney woke up in the early hours with a throbbing hand. He saw Vern Summerfield outside the Molyneux Hotel, heading toward the bridge. Or the gold lock-up.

Vern was a dirt-poor miner at the time, but struck it lucky soon after the gold robbery, or so he said. The old rogue thinks he owns the town now, the way he lords his wealth around like he was a born aristocrat."

"Connie is even worse," Mrs MacEwen said. "You'd think Mrs Constance Summerfield was the Queen the way she demands her way at every social event and on every charitable committee. I overheard her say once that Vern Summerfield would be nothing without her. I must say, it crossed my mind to wonder if it was Connie who had some role in the robbery, rather than Vern. She was very close to that Yarwood man for a time."

Connie had been "very close" to several men before she settled on Vern, if the rumours Charlie had heard were to be believed. Connie had also been seen on the night of the robbery and had been questioned as a witness. She had denied seeing anything.

But this sighting of Vern was news to Charlie. "Was Quinney positive it was Vern Summerfield, Mr MacEwen? After all, it was at night and Quinney was in pain." He had probably been drunk too. Shepherds lived a lonely life and made the most of any chance to go into town.

"My shepherd knew Vern by sight, after a disagreement over a gambling debt. As I recall, Quinney said he was certain of the man's identity because he struck a light for his pipe. He reckoned Vern looked mighty pleased with himself. Quinney's long gone, of course, so I suppose we will never know the truth."

"Charlie and Grace are here on their honeymoon, Duncan," his wife reminded him. "I never want to hear another word about that robbery, and I'm sure they don't either."

There was a firmness in her tone, which Grace must have noted too, because she dabbed her lips with a napkin and let out a satisfied sigh. "Charlie is right, Mrs MacEwen. These are absolutely the best scones I have ever tasted. I do hope I have the chance to meet your son Hamish while we are here. I'm longing to hearing what Charlie was like as a boy."

And thus, the topic of conversation veered onto more acceptable subjects: Charlie's boyhood antics, the difficulty of finding suitable wives for high-country farmers like Hamish and whether Grace might perchance have any sisters or cousins, the dire state of the roads, an ongoing dispute over water rights, and the difficulty of getting shepherds.

After another half hour, Charlie mentioned another engagement, and they exchanged warm farewells, but only after Mrs MacEwen had extracted a promise from Grace to accompany her to a charitable morning tea the next day. Grace queried whether Jasmine could come too, but Mrs MacEwen assured her that dear, kind Jasmine preferred actual charitable work, rather than fundraising morning teas with the gossiping classes.

As soon as Charlie and Grace stepped out into the yard, Blaze jumped up from her patch of shade and raced to their sides.

"Stay, Blaze," Charlie ordered.

Blaze stayed, but her head stretched forward, nose quivering. They waved to Mr and Mrs MacEwen, who were standing arm-in-arm on the doorstep, and hurried to the gate. Charlie willed himself not to turn back, no matter what. As soon as they opened the gate, Blaze could restrain herself no longer. She raced for the gate, slipping through before Charlie could close it. He opened the gate again and tried to get the reluctant collie to go back through.

Duncan MacEwen strode towards them but made no attempt to grab the dog. "Looks like you've made a conquest, Charlie. Perhaps you could do with a dog for company? I'd let you have her for a knock-down price."

Charlie hesitated. He imagined the collie shedding hair over Mrs MacMillan's furniture back in Dunedin and pining while he and Grace were out all day. Border collies needed the constant stimulation of their work and had a habit of herding anything they could find if that stimulation was lacking, even if it meant herding small children by nipping at their reluctant heels. Worse, she might try to herd Grace's elderly great-aunt and knock her over.

Blaze shoved her wet nose into his hand, but Charlie was determined not to be swayed by an intelligent pair of dark eyes and a pleading expression. "I'd love to have her, Mr MacEwen, but we can't afford to buy her, or even to feed her."

Mrs MacEwen arrived and took her husband's arm. "What my dear husband means to say is that she's no use to him and he'd be happy to see her go to a good home, especially as we owe you a wedding present. He'll even throw in a sack of the dried meat that's been stinking out our barn since last summer. Won't you, dearest?"

Duncan looked at her fondly. "Of course, Julia."

"Wouldn't she hate life in the city?" Charlie's willpower was slipping. He looked to Grace for support, but Grace was busy scratching Blaze under the chin and making cooing noises.

By the time Duncan returned with the sack of dog food, Charlie accepted they were now the proud owners of a purebred border collie with no herding instinct. He told himself they could sell her for good money if they had to, but he knew in his heart it wouldn't happen.

After all, Duncan MacEwen had said that sniffing out trouble was all Blaze was good for – and sniffing out trouble was Charlie's business.

Echoes from the Past

Grace was melting in the dry heat by the time they turned onto the track to Rose Cottage. She had enjoyed their visit and had been especially impressed with Julia MacEwen, who was a good friend to Jasmine Pyke, despite their very different backgrounds. But they had lingered too long and a glance at her pocket watch told her they would be late for their midday meal at the Pyke's house.

Fortunately, they found Thomas Pyke waiting for them with the buggy. He had his back against a tree and peach juice running down his chin. The look of total satisfaction on his face was pure Charlie. Grace could never quite get over how similar father and son were, as if she was looking at her husband in the future. Fortunately, Thomas Pyke was a fine figure of a man, even in his fifties, although he lacked Charlie's gorgeous almond-shaped green eyes and silky black hair.

"Morning, Pa," Charlie said. "Has Nathaniel laid a complaint? Are you here to arrest me or because you are escaping Connie Summerfield's wrath?"

"All's quiet at the police station this morning, thank heavens," Thomas said. "Your mother sent me to pick you up. Who's your canine companion?"

"Meet our new dog, Blaze," Charlie said. "A wedding present from Mr and Mrs MacEwen."

Thomas half-heartedly fended off the collie's licked greeting as he ruffled the fur around her neck. "What a beauty she is. That was mighty generous of Duncan and Julia. A top border collie is worth a small fortune."

"Blaze doesn't have the herding instinct, but I'm thinking she might make a fine tracking dog. She's a quick learner." Charlie picked up the enamel bowl they had been using for water. "Blaze, find water."

Blaze cocked her head to one side, so he tapped the bowl and repeated the command. She trotted around to the rain barrel beside the house. Charlie made a fuss over her as he filled her bowl.

Her husband may have put up a show of turning down the MacEwen's offer, but Grace could see he was smitten with the collie. Grace had never had a dog before, having grown up in a house bursting at the seams with children, but Blaze had already captured her heart too. She went inside to freshen up, then Charlie helped her into the buggy, before lifting Blaze onto the jump seat.

Grace sat beside her father-in-law. After they'd exchanged pleasantries, Grace had to restrain herself from asking about the gold robbery. For all that she had told Charlie to forget everything but the honeymoon, she couldn't escape the fact that even Mr and Mrs MacEwen, welcoming as they were, seemed to think Charlie was in town to investigate the old case.

"Jasmine said you wanted to know about the robbery of the gold lock-up," Sergeant Pyke said.

"Only because everyone in Clyde keeps mentioning it," Grace replied. "I don't understand why everyone thinks Charlie is here to investigate an old robbery, or indeed why he would have any interest in it, simply because he was born the same night."

Thomas Pyke exchanged a look with his son. "It's not the coincidence of Charlie's birth, Grace. It's that a fair proportion of the town is convinced Charlie's grandfather was the second robber or knew where the gold was hidden. My guess is someone has started a rumour that Charlie has deciphered a clue left by his grandfather, pointing to the location of the gold. It's nonsense, of course, but I sometimes think we'll never put it behind us."

"Duncan MacEwen said something interesting," Charlie said. "His shepherd, Jethro Quinney, saw Vern Summerfield in the main street of Clyde late that night. Duncan said he told Quinney to inform the police."

"I wasn't on duty at the time," his father replied, "but I know the police file off by heart. Jethro Quinney never made a statement. Vern Summerfield produced a witness who swore Vern was in the miner's camp near Cromwell on the night of the robbery. We had no reason to suspect Vern, aside from his sudden wealth. He had a gold mining licence for Bannockburn, and other gold diggings in that area had yielded fair amounts of gold, so his lucky gold strike could have been legitimate. Was Quinney sure he saw Vern?"

"Quinney knew him well enough to be positive it was Vern Summerfield he saw that night."

Thomas Pyke was thinking so hard he missed the turn onto Blyth Street. Fortunately, the horse made the turn out of long habit. "Duncan MacEwen did ask me about Vern a few weeks after the robbery, but he didn't mention Quinney's evidence. Of course, Duncan had other matters on his mind at the time."

"Other matters?" Grace prompted.

"His first wife had died in childbirth and wee Hamish was only a few months old at the time of the robbery. I'm not sure how Duncan coped with no wife and a baby to care for. He'd hit a rough patch, because wool prices had slumped shortly after he took on debt to buy a flock of pedigree merino sheep. Beautiful fine wool, but an expensive capital outlay. His family and neighbours did what they could, and he had household staff, but Duncan wasn't one to admit he was struggling. He really only became his old self again when he met Julia Matheson a few months later."

Which meant Julia MacEwen was not in town at the time of the robbery, Grace thought. No wonder she was tired of hearing about it. "Mrs MacEwen has doubts about Connie Summerfield too. Apparently, Connie has said that Vern would be nothing without her. Mrs MacEwen wondered if Connie was the one who made the fortune from the robbery, because she was close to a man I presume was a suspect."

"Ezra Yarwood," Charlie said. "Mrs MacEwen was only speculating. She doesn't have any proof, as far as I know."

Thomas Pyke pulled the buggy to a halt by the front door of the Pyke's cottage and handed Grace down. "Charlie, do you have a moment to come over to the police station?"

Grace saw Jasmine Pyke waving from the window and detected the rich aromas of soup and fresh bread wafting across the garden, so she opted to leave father and son to whatever they were up to. Besides, she wanted to give her mother-in-law a warm hug after the gift of the beautiful marriage quilt and all Jasmine had done to make their honeymoon cottage a blissful retreat.

Jasmine brushed off her thanks but looked pleased at the compliments. She set Grace the pleasant task of stirring a vast pot of thick soup, which was simmering on the coal range. Grace inhaled the mouth-watering aroma of meat and vegetables in a rich broth, with a spicy edge she didn't recognise. Despite the earlier scones, Grace's stomach rumbled.

Clyde may not have given them a wholehearted welcome, but Grace already felt right at home in the Pyke's cottage. Everything about it was cozy, from the smell of cooking, to the rugs and cushions jumbled on the worn chairs, to the shelves filled with books lining every available wall. Grace recalled Charlie saying his maternal grandmother instilled a love of reading in both her daughters and her grandson.

Jasmine set to work slicing a loaf still warm from the oven. "Thomas has been up since five o'clock this morning, going through the cases his constable dealt with while he was away. He was worried that an apocalypse of crime would hit Clyde while we were at your wedding, but it has been as quiet as a tomb. A few men the worse for drink and a minor altercation over unlicensed siphoning of water from a water race."

"I'm glad to hear it," Grace said. "Peace and quiet sound perfect to us." She had just decided to make no more mention of the gold robbery when Charlie and his father returned.

Charlie had a police file in his hand and was in mid-discussion with his father. "…had diggings near Arrowtown and a mother in Clyde, didn't he?"

"Ezra Yarwood started prospecting for gold near Arrowtown," Thomas Pyke said. "But he was never a patient man. He tried his luck near Cromwell for a while, before moving down to the Conroys Gully area after his father died, presumably to be closer to his mother."

Charlie kissed his mother's cheek. "Soups smell delicious, Ma. Is there a soup bone I could give to Blaze to keep her busy? Mrs and Mrs MacEwen gave us a border collie as a wedding present."

His mother handed him the bone. "As long as you don't feed the dog my good meatloaf."

"Mr MacEwen gave us some dried meat," Charlie said, carefully skirting the truth. "I'll take Nyx out tomorrow morning and shoot some fresh meat for Blaze. I'm looking forward to getting out into the hills again."

"You're not abandoning your new bride, I hope, Charlie Pyke."

"No, Ma. Mrs MacEwen is taking Grace to a morning tea to introduce her to the young ladies of the town."

Thomas Pyke threw up his hands in mock horror. "No wonder you're escaping into the hills, Charlie. That lot terrifies me. I have nightmares that Constance Summerfield will resort to violence to get her way, and I'll have to arrest her."

"Connie is not as domineering as you make out, dear. She does a lot of charitable work about town." Jasmine tasted the soup and added some fresh herbs. "You'd better make it crystal clear that you are married, Grace. Any new single woman in town is set upon by a pack of she-wolf mothers trying to find a bride for their sons. Even as a married woman, you can expect to undergo a rigorous interrogation on everything from the latest fashions in Dunedin to your favourite pastimes. New blood is a rare treat in a small town."

Grace tried to stifle her nerves. She knew little about fashion, and she doubted her favourite pastimes, which included dissecting bodies and catching criminals, would be well received. She steeled herself with the thought that a ladies' charitable morning tea could hardly be worse than facing the examination board at the medical school or the various murderers she had come face to face with over the last few years.

"I'd rather face a gang of cut-throats than that mob," Charlie murmured unhelpfully. He had returned from giving Blaze her bone and was sitting in an armchair with his nose in the police file.

"Tell me about the robbery," Grace said, seeking distraction from the perils of polite society. "But please start at the beginning this time."

"It happened in mid-winter," Thomas began, "when the amount of gold and cash in the lock-up was at its peak. Winter is the best time to get gold from the rivers, because the water level is low."

Grace didn't understand, but she didn't want to interrupt. Charlie put down the file long enough to explain that water was held in the snow on the mountains and the ice of the glaciers in winter. In spring and summer, water was released again, frequently as devastating floods. Many a miner's carefully hidden hoard of gold had been washed away in a flash flood, and many a miner with it.

"The roads had been impassable that winter too," Thomas continued. "The usual fortnightly transfer of gold to Dunedin was changed to monthly. Thus, there was an exceptionally large quantity of gold and cash in the lock-up. Four boxes full. It cannot have been a coincidence that the lock-up was targeted that night, right before the Gold Escort was due to take it to Dunedin. Local knowledge, it seemed, and yet the only man apprehended was from Arrowtown, which is fifty miles away across rugged terrain. They arrested him two weeks later. He had been considered an upstanding citizen before the robbery."

"And then there was the fact that the robbers had a key to the outside door," Charlie said. "There was a bolted and padlocked inner door too, but they got through that by removing the screws in the bolt plate. You can see why there were grounds to suspect

62

the man guarding the lock-up, who was Jake Blackthorn's brother. Jake swore his brother didn't know the man who was arrested, but he wouldn't have hesitated to lie to protect his brother's reputation."

Thomas took over the story again. "The arrested man's name was Zachary Dawson. The only reason the police caught him was because the weight of the stolen gold was too much for his horse. Dawson stashed gold along the route to lighten the load, but the horse eventually foundered in the icy conditions and Dawson was forced to make camp. Unluckily for him, his fire was seen and the evidence he left at the campsite was enough to track him down eventually. He was caught red-handed with all that he could carry of the gold stashed in pickle jars in a tanning tub. Dawson knew his only hope of clemency was to tell the police inspector where he had stashed the rest of the gold and claim that the robbery had been planned by the dead guard. The government had offered any accomplice a free pardon, and Dawson tried to use that to get himself off. He swore he left the guard in his guardhouse, drinking a bottle of rum so he could pretend he was drunk when the robbery took place."

"What happened to Zachary Dawson?" Grace asked.

"The consensus was that Dawson lied about the guard being involved, because the guard had an excellent reputation. Dawson was convicted of the robbery but acquitted of the guard's death, as there was room for doubt about whether it was murder. Dawson's lawyer contended the guard was so drunk he wandered outside and collapsed, freezing to death. Dawson got twelve years' hard labour, which meant back-breaking work hacking a road through the mountains. He died in a landslide only two months after he was sentenced. If he buried the missing gold, his secret died with him."

"He must have had friends and relations," Grace said. "Did they have any connection to Clyde, which might have explained his local knowledge?"

"They found an old letter at Dawson's lodgings from a sister. Her last known address was the country estate of a wealthy family who lived near Cromwell, where she worked as a parlourmaid. Cromwell sent a constable out to see her, but Dawson's sister had already left her position to get married. It was unlikely she knew anyone from Clyde, which is close to twenty miles downriver from Cromwell."

"Friends?"

"Nobody was admitting anything beyond a passing acquaintance with Zachary Dawson. It may be true. Gold prospectors can be a solitary breed, although it's likely he shared many an evening at taverns with other miners. The only connection the police could find between Zachary Dawson and Clyde was Ezra Yarwood, who had partnered with him at diggings near Arrowtown a while back. Yarwood was considered a strong suspect from the start, and even more so after Dawson's arrest. He was interviewed within hours of the discovery that the gold was missing. Naturally, he claimed he knew nothing about it. His mother gave him an alibi, and no evidence was found to link him with the robbery."

"Ezra Yarwood's mother still lives on the outskirts of Clyde," Jasmine added. "Next door but one to Rose Cottage, in fact, with the Trent's dairy farm in between. You won't get much out of the old lady, though. She sees most visitors off with a shotgun."

"What is it with folks around here and shotguns?" Grace said. "We've been threatened with two of them already, and now you're warning me another of our neighbours is a gun-toting maniac."

"Welcome to country life, Grace," Thomas Pyke said.

Grace raised her hands in surrender and laughed. "I was promised peace and tranquillity."

"Not if you visit Mrs Yarwood," Jasmine said. "Even if you do get past the gate, Mrs Yarwood is an old woman now, who struggles to remember what day of the week it is. She gets by well enough, though. She has essentials like coal and flour delivered, and her neighbour, Matilda Trent, keeps an eye on her."

"I can't blame old Mrs Yarwood for being fed up with talk of the robbery," Thomas said. "The police sergeant at the time assigned the men from the Gold Escort to dig up every inch of her garden, and search the house from top to bottom, but they didn't find any gold or other evidence her son was involved in the robbery. Ezra disappeared after he was interviewed and never returned to Clyde. A fair proportion of the local townsfolk believe Ezra is living a life of ease and plenty far away."

Grace studied her father-in-law's expression. "But you don't believe that, do you, Sergeant Pyke?"

"Can't say I do. Ezra Yarwood was no saint, but he loved his mother. I can't see him leaving the old lady to fend for herself all these years if he was alive and wealthy. He did give her some gold before he disappeared, but we couldn't prove it came from the robbery. Ezra was a goldminer, after all."

"Who else was a suspect?" Despite Grace's protestations that she wanted a quiet honeymoon, she felt herself being sucked into the whirlpool of intrigue around the robbery.

"Anyone with a yearning for riches, which doesn't exclude many people, except men who were too old and infirm, or too young. Jake Blackthorn always springs to mind when it comes to easy money and lack of morals." Thomas shrugged. "But you've seen the man. He's far from living a life of silk cravats and mansions. Besides, Jake's brother was the guard and there was no chance Jake would have left his brother to die. I think it is possible that Jake was the source of the information on the amount of gold in the lock-up, though, as he had inside knowledge via his brother."

"Maybe that is why Jake is still so angry about the robbery," Charlie said. "Not only losing his brother, but possibly left with no payment for his role in the robbery."

"You could be right, Charlie," his father said, "but there was never any evidence to suggest Jake was involved. He was only ever a suspect because of his reputation. Shame it was his brother who died. Jake Blackthorn's been bad to the bone since he took his first breath, whereas his brother was a solid citizen and a reliable member of the Gold Escort. Personally, I thought the brother must have been drugged rather than drunk the night of the robbery. Either way, I still believe the robber or robbers callously left him outside in the depths of winter. Dawson ought to have been convicted over his death."

If Zachary Dawson was killed in a landslide while doing hard labour, he had certainly suffered a worse punishment than a quick death at the end of a noose, in Grace's opinion. "Charlie said the gold was worth a fortune and not much more than a third was recovered."

"That's right. Almost £14,000 in gold and cash was stolen, of which around £9,000 is still missing."

"£14,000! One could purchase an entire street of desirable houses in Dunedin for that amount." Grace could hardly get her head around the concept that such a colossal fortune was sitting in a small-town lock-up. No wonder the robbery had remained so fresh in the minds of the people of Clyde, especially with so much gold and cash still unaccounted for.

Thomas winced at the memory. "It was a disaster for the town and for local law enforcement. I was glad to have been a lowly constable and not on duty that night. But the fact the robbery took place within shouting distance of where our baby was being born still rankles. I might have looked out the window and seen them pass. The robbery took place between twelve-thirty at night and four-thirty in the morning, when Jasmine was in the final stages of a difficult labour."

"Poor Thomas, I must have cracked every bone in your hand, I was squeezing so hard." Jasmine gave the pot one last stir. "Time to eat."

Thomas took the soup bowls from his wife as she filled them and placed them on the table. "The birth of our son was worth all the gold in the Clutha to me." Thomas shook his head, slopping soup to the brim of the bowl. "I don't believe the truth will ever come to light after all this time, but I hate the thought that I can't retire in peace with it still hanging over the reputation of the local police. There was a £500 reward offered for the return of the gold. I imagine it still stands."

A reward of that size represented several years' wages for a working man. Enough to encourage anyone with information to come forward. Grace had to agree with her father-in-law's assessment that the truth would lie buried forever. Still, there was always a chance that fresh eyes could spot a new lead, especially when the eyes belonged to a private detective. Not that she could see her husband's lovely green eyes, as his head was over his bowl, focusing on getting spoon to mouth as if he'd been starved for a month.

Grace followed suit. The soup was certainly worthy of her full attention. When the last of the fresh bread had scooped the remnants of soup from the bowls, she hazarded a final question. "What do you think happened to the missing gold, Sergeant Pyke?"

"In my opinion, the gold is long gone," Thomas said. "A robbery that audacious most likely required at least two men. In which case, the second robber probably got away with his half, by lying low until it was safe to cash the gold in. He is probably sitting back on the veranda of an ostentatious mansion far away, with no one the wiser to his dark past. Even now, I keep an eye on the possible suspects, to no avail. There have been no new leads in almost a quarter of a century, so I think it is safe enough to let you and Charlie look at the file. I wouldn't hold out much hope, though."

"Charlie and Grace have better things to do, Thomas," Jasmine said. "If it wasn't for the damage to your reputation and my father's, I'd have thrown that file into the fire years ago."

Thomas Pyke saw the anguish in his wife's face and covered her hand with his. "Everyone worth knowing believes in your father's innocence, my love."

Grace wished she had never asked about the robbery now that she understood the pain it still caused Charlie's parents. Now was definitely not the time to discuss it further. Instead, she flicked a napkin at her husband, who was uncharacteristically silent. "Come on, lazybones. After that fine meal, we have dishes to do. You're on washing, since you're cruelly abandoning me to the ladies tomorrow morning."

"While I go out hunting to feed my growing family." Charlie looked positively smug as he gathered up the dishes and took them to the sink.

After their duties were done, Charlie declared they would walk back to the cottage.

Grace's fears were confirmed when he picked up the police file on the way out. Jasmine noticed it too. Despite Grace's profuse thanks for a lovely meal, Jasmine Pyke's cheerful wave farewell did not hide the worry lines around her eyes.

Lingering Suspicion

The police file on the gold robbery, flimsy though it was, was a lead weight in Charlie's hand as he waved farewell to his parents. He hadn't missed the worried glance his mother had exchanged with Grace. He'd taken the file on impulse after finally understanding how much the robbery had affected his parents. Out of guilt too, that he'd spent his childhood fretting about the effect of his grandfather's reputation on himself, without paying enough attention to the pain his parents felt. On the other hand, this was supposed to be a honeymoon and a chance for Grace to leave the cares of the world behind.

"Grace, we don't –"

Grace put a finger on his lips. "We are going to clear your grandfather's name, Charlie, no matter what it takes. We owe it to your parents." She raised her hand to silence his thanks. "You need to know too, after all these years of baseless suspicion. Why don't we start at the scene of the crime."

Charlie wanted to wrap his wife in his arms and kiss her, but they were in public, so he made do with taking her arm and pointing out the location of the gold lock-up and the trooper's camp. The proximity between the Pyke's residence and the scene of the crime had always been a thorn in his father's side. How many times had his father berated himself for not looking out the window in the early hours of that fateful morning? Not that he would have seen the robbers, who would certainly have approached by a more circumspect route.

They walked in silence for a while. Charlie reflected on how different it was to come back to Clyde with a growing reputation as a detective and the love of his life by his side as his wife. And yet so little had changed, including the dark cloud over his grandfather's reputation.

Grace stopped him as soon as they were out of sight of the last house. "I hope you don't mind me reopening old wounds, Charlie. You don't have to investigate if you don't want to, but please know that I'll support you in any way I can, whatever you decide."

Blaze bumped her nose into Charlie's palm, as if agreeing with the sentiment.

"It's not you who is reopening old wounds, Grace. It's all the people here who cannot let go of the past. I think you need to hear the rest of the story before we decide what to do, because I don't want any secrets between us. To be honest, it's probably a waste of our precious time anyway, as I doubt we will shed any new light on such an old mystery."

Grace took his hand and resumed walking. "It's your grandfather's rumoured involvement that is the main concern, I presume."

"The police investigation exonerated him. A regional police inspector was brought in to handle the case, because of the size of the robbery and the fact the guard who died was implicated. Even so, there are still people in town who think my grandfather, Lee Hope, was either a robber or an opportunist who took some of the gold. If I could have a shilling for all the times my grandparents had to chase intruders with shovels out of their market garden, I'd be a rich man."

"How dreadful for them. Did the craziness last long?"

"It went on for months. My grandparents took turns staying up at night with a shotgun and a dog. To be honest, I think it almost became a game for the local ruffians, because there was not an inch of their property that wasn't dug over a dozen times. My grandfather used to make light of it, saying he was grateful to them for turning the soil while searching for the gold. But my grandmother was furious at the destruction of their livelihood and feared for their lives. They went everywhere together and never without the shotgun, in case someone tried to force the supposed

70

location of the hidden gold out of them. Eventually, they sold up and moved into town. Not that it was any better, as the townsfolk refused to let go the lingering suspicions about their involvement in the robbery. Lee and Elsie Hope died a couple of years later, within hours of each other."

Grace squeezed his hand. She hesitated for a minute or two, chewing her lip. "You'd better tell me why Lee Hope was a suspect. Please don't tell me it was only because of the country of his birth or some ludicrous notion about the evils of a mixed marriage."

Charlie checked the vicinity for watching eyes, before pulling Grace into a quick embrace. When their lips separated again, he murmured. "How can there be anything evil about love? Did I ever tell you that Lee and Elsie chose the name Hope as their new surname, when people couldn't pronounce their Chinese name? They hoped it would make their marriage easier, as well as being a positive note to start their life together. Hope was all they had in the early days, before they moved to New Zealand for the gold rush."

"I'm glad they could be buried together," Grace said. "Perhaps we could honour their memory in one of our children's names, if we should be so blessed. Hope would be a lovely name for a girl. Mind you, we have a lot of other people to remember. Jasmine Louisa Anne Lily Hope Penrose Pyke is rather a mouthful. And don't even think of suggesting we have five girls simply to use up the names."

"I was thinking of calling our first daughter Nyx Blaze," Charlie teased, "in honour of my favourite animals."

"Then you'll be sleeping in a separate bed for the rest of your married life." Grace bent down and ruffled Blaze's fur. "No offence intended."

"Louisa Anne it is." Charlie pointed to a cottage on their left, almost obscured by a straggling hawthorn hedge. The cottage was a twin of Rose Cottage but had been left to the whims of nature. "That's the Yarwood's place."

"Ezra Yarwood? The robbery suspect who disappeared leaving his mother alone?" Grace squatted down to look through a gap in the hedge.

"Don't get too close, Grace. Mrs Yarwood really is handy with a shotgun and intolerant of trespassers." Charlie held Blaze tightly in case her curiosity got the better of her. He had always feared the old lady when he was a child, because the local children had told tales about her being a witch. Now he felt sorry for her. She had suffered in the same way as his grandparents had, tarred by the brush of suspicion through no fault of her own. Worse still, Mrs Yarwood had lost the son she depended on.

"How does she manage on her own?" Grace asked.

"The old folk around here know the meaning of tough times and don't ask for much. She's not as badly off as some, because her husband had done well enough at the gold diggings to purchase an acre of land. She'll have eggs from her hens and fresh fruit and vegetables from her garden. As my mother said, she has essential supplies delivered, and the neighbour keeps an eye on her."

Charlie knew many old miners, who hadn't had the luck of their peers, were in far worse circumstances. Those who hadn't moved away from Central Otago now lived however they could, sheltering in caves or mud-brick huts or kerosene-tin shacks.

Grace scrambled to her feet. "Maybe I ought to see if I can get Mrs Yarwood to talk. With judicious use of bribery in the form of food provisions. Perhaps a nice cake would stop her from shooting me."

"I don't think she's of sound mind, Grace."

"Some old people who seem to be rambling actually have good memories for events in the past. But not today, Charlie. I want to get back to our cottage and rest for a while."

They continued past green pastures surrounded by dry-stone walls. Cows with swollen udders milled by the far gate.

"The Trent farm," Charlie said. "Not far from home now."

Back at Rose Cottage, Blaze flopped to the ground in the shade. Charlie topped up her water bowl and checked the horse trough. Nyx and Erebus were snoozing under a tree with their muzzles next to each other. Charlie's eyelids sagged at the restful scene. The only active creatures were the tiny birds darting through the grass, chasing insects, and bees feasting on pollen.

Charlie returned to the cottage, where he found Grace on their bed in her undergarments, fanning her face. He put two glasses of cool water on the side table and went to lock the door.

Grace patted the bed beside her. "Tell me why your grandfather was suspected."

He stripped off and dropped onto the cool sheets. "My grandparents went to my parents' cottage in their cart when they got the message that my mother was in labour. After I was born in the early hours of the morning, my grandmother stayed with us, while my grandfather left to return to their market garden. He delivered fresh vegetables to the general store every day, and not even the birth of his first grandson was going to stand in the way of that commitment."

Charlie paused to drain his glass. "When he got home, my grandfather gathered what he needed from the garden and got back in his cart to return to Clyde. He was stopped by the troopers from the Gold Escort as he entered town. The robbery and the dead body of the guard had been discovered by then, and the troopers had been ordered to prevent anyone from leaving town. When they inspected Lee Hope's load, they found traces of gold dust on his sack-barrow. They arrested him and took him to the local police sergeant, who was in charge until the police inspector arrived. My father was a constable back then and, of course, he was with his family and unaware of what was going on until he heard of Lee's arrest."

Grace curled into his side. "Let me guess. Lee Hope's cart, with the sack-barrow in it, had been left outside your parents' cottage."

"Exactly right, Grace. The robbers realised they would need a means of transporting the boxes when they saw the colossal amount of gold in the lock-up. The man who was eventually arrested, Zachary Dawson, admitted as much to the police inspector."

"They probably didn't realise how much they would find."

"Quite so. Presumably, they used the sack-barrow to move the boxes of gold to a safer place, where they could unpack the contents without being seen. The boxes were found discarded in a nearby pond. The sack-barrow was returned to my grandfather's cart, probably to frame him for the robbery. Dawson then left on his horse, heading for Arrowtown with all the gold he thought the horse could carry. Dawson either buried the rest to retrieve later, or there was a second man or men in the gang, and the gold was split between them."

"How long was it before Lee Hope was released from police custody?".

"Several hours. The local doctor was quick to tell the police sergeant that the guard had been dead for hours, based on how frozen the body was. My father swore that Lee Hope was at their house until five o'clock in the morning, right before the robbery was discovered. My father's word, as a respected police constable, combined with the testimony of the midwife, was enough to secure the release of my grandfather, although he was required to stay at my parents' house until the police inspector arrived the next day. When Zachary Dawson was finally caught a couple of weeks later, he named the guard of the gold lock-up as his accomplice, not Lee Hope, which put the end to any lingering doubts held by the police inspector and local sergeant."

"But suspicions still lingered in the minds of some of the townsfolk," Grace said. "Presumably, they thought your father was shielding his father-in-law, while the midwife was either mistaken or paid off."

"You're always so quick to understand, Grace." Charlie gathered his wife in his arms. "News of the gold dust found on the

74

sack-barrow was enough evidence for some folk. A new rumour went around that Lee Hope had seen where the robber or robbers had hidden the rest of the gold and taken it for himself."

"Did your grandfather see anything suspicious that morning?"

"That's what I was looking for in the police file," Charlie said. "The morning was freezing, so my grandfather said he hunkered down under a blanket and let the horse follow the usual route. He recalls seeing only two people that morning. One was Ezra Yarwood, whom he saw with a spade and a lantern in his mother's garden. That was why the police were so quick to interview Ezra."

"Digging the garden in the early hours of a freezing morning? No wonder the police were suspicious."

"As Pa said, the police dug over every inch of the Yarwood garden and searched the house, but found nothing. When Ezra was interviewed, he claimed he had a long list of jobs to do for his aging mother, which meant he had to start early. Ezra visited his mother for a short time every month or two, so his excuse for being in the garden so early was plausible. He showed the police the various jobs he had already completed and told them he intended to leave town again soon, which means his disappearance was not unexpected. However, Ezra Yarwood never returned. He had denied any involvement in the robbery, of course, and nobody had seen him out the night of the robbery. His mother swore Ezra was with her all night."

"Who was the second person your grandfather saw on the morning of the robbery?"

"The Yarwood's neighbour, Matilda Trent. She waved to my grandfather as she was bringing in the cows for milking. Matilda Jacks she was then. She was only sixteen at the time and had recently started at the dairy farm as a general servant and milking hand. A sweet girl who grew up to be a sweet woman. Needless to say, the police didn't believe she had any involvement in the robbery. Matilda didn't see Ezra that morning and nor did she see anyone leaving town, which makes sense. Zachary Dawson had headed in the other direction, north-west towards Arrowtown, not south-east past the Trent farm."

"When did Matilda marry Bob Trent?" Grace asked.

"About two years later, as I recall. Bob was the oldest son of the owner and inherited the dairy farm on his father's death."

Grace was silent for a minute or two, digesting the fresh evidence. "I agree with you it sounds like a hopeless case. All we can do is read the file to see if anything was missed at the time. I suppose we could do a little discreet poking around as well when we tire of more pleasurable activities."

Charlie lay back on the pillow with a smile hovering on his lips. "I'm not sure I'll ever tire of more pleasurable activities."

Grace leaned over him, tickling his chest with her long hair. "Then think of the £500 reward, Detective Pyke. We could buy a mountain of dog food with that amount, and still have money left over for an extended honeymoon every year."

"I like that idea." Charlie pulled her into his arms and kissed her. "What did I do to deserve a wife like you?"

"You didn't run away fast enough," Grace replied, "and now you're stuck with me forever."

Social Graces

The next morning, Grace pulled every gown from her trunk and tried them on in front of the cracked looking glass in their bedroom. One by one, she discarded them onto the bed. One was too grand, another too plain, a third too hot for the sweltering weather. The fourth she threw down in disgust for no reason she could fathom.

Unfamiliar social situations were always stressful for Grace, who was more at home in a surgical apron than a gown. However, she was grateful for Mrs MacEwen's kindness in inviting her to a morning tea to meet the ladies of the town, and didn't wish to let her down.

The problem was, she simply did not understand the rules of country society. When they had visited the MacEwen's grand homestead, Mrs MacEwen had worn a simple dress, complete with an apron, and served tea and her own homemade scones at the kitchen table as if she was a common housewife, not a member of the landed gentry. Yet her pale hands and shapely fingernails were not sullied by working in the garden, laying fires, cleaning the abundant silverware, or starching the linen napkins. Grace had heard three women laughing in the scullery as they washed up and prepared the midday meal, and had seen glimpses of other staff both indoors and outdoors.

Fortunately, Charlie had left Rose Cottage early, and thus was not present to witness her nail-biting indecision. All she had seen of him in the dim pre-dawn glow was a figure clad in a checked cotton shirt leaning over the bed to kiss her. "I'm off to hunt rabbits with Blaze and Nyx," he'd said, as he tugged on high leather boots and pulled a broad-brimmed hat low over his eyes. She had scarcely recognised this rugged country cousin of her city husband.

Grace's hand hovered over the discarded fourth gown, a pale blue dress of fine cotton lawn, beautifully cut and tailored with a fitted bodice and embroidered flowers. Was it too elegant for a charitable morning tea? Or too pretty and girlish for a married woman? She didn't expect Clyde would be a centre of fashion, but nor did she wish to let Charlie down, especially as he stirred up mixed emotions in town. By the time she was finished with this group of locals, Grace hoped, Mr Charles Penrose Pyke, private detective, would be reinvented as the town's favourite son. That is, if they weren't too busy gossiping about the shocking new wife he'd brought home, who'd slashed a man outside the seediest hotel in town mere hours after arrival.

Definitely the fourth gown, she decided. No woman wearing such a pretty garment could possibly have fought in a filthy alley. Besides, it was cool enough for the hot weather, respectable enough for a married woman, and of the high quality to be expected of the wife of a successful man.

I can do this, Grace told herself, as she forced her hair into a stylish knot. Think of it as going undercover in disguise to advance an investigation, she told herself. With a huff of frustration, she pulled the knot loose again, realising it would not fit under the dainty straw hat she intended to wear. Through the bedroom window, she saw a buggy coming towards the cottage. With a last determined tug, she secured her hair in a knot behind her head. Grace dashed to the door in a fluster, only to double back for her hat and basket, which held the bundle of herbs she had gathered from the overgrown garden as her contribution to the fundraiser. She made it back to the veranda as the buggy drew to a halt.

Mrs MacEwen was driving the buggy herself. She must have been close to fifty years old, but her back was straight, and she had the rosy glow and open smile of a country woman. Grace's heart leapt when she saw her escort was wearing a gown of similar type and quality, albeit in a more mature style.

Julia MacEwen drew the horse to a halt with the gentlest of tugs on the reins with her gloved fingers. "Good morning, Grace.

Don't you look splendid in that divine gown. And how thoughtful of you to bring a beautiful bouquet of herbs for the fundraiser."

As soon as Grace was aboard, Mrs MacEwen clucked her tongue, and the horse set off down the drive. When they were safely back on the road, her eyes went sideways to Grace again. "You look perfect for the role of a sweet newlywed lass from the country. I must admit I had formed a different image of you in my mind based on Jasmine Pyke's recounting of your exploits. I expected a rather terrifying bluestocking carrying a medical kit, and possibly a weapon of some sort. I don't know why, because Charlie and Jasmine have repeatedly said how lovely you are."

Grace sagged with relief at this further evidence of a lively humour and kindness, not to mention the compliment on her dress choice. Perhaps the morning tea would be a pleasant experience after all. "Charlie speaks highly of you, too, Mrs MacEwen. He has great admiration for the way you coped with the demands of the farm and four children."

Mrs MacEwen chuckled. "Dearest Charlie was always the sweetest boy. Although I thought it was my culinary skills he admired most of all."

"That too, of course. Keeping Charlie Pyke fed is a full-time occupation."

As they travelled the short distance to the Clyde community hall, Mrs MacEwen explained the event was a fundraiser to purchase more prizes for the upcoming Vincent County Horticultural Show – the inaugural one and clearly the social highlight of the year. "They're good people, Grace, but I must warn you that a new young lady in town is bound to spark interest, especially one such as yourself."

Grace hesitated to ask what she meant by "one such as yourself". A city woman? The new bride of a local man? A woman who chose to fight convention by studying medicine? She told herself not to worry.

When they reached the community hall, Mrs MacEwen halted the horse with an expert tweak of the reins next to a trough and hitching post. After she secured the horse, she took Grace's arm and walked towards the hall with an air of natural confidence.

A group of young men lounged around outside, smoking and attempting to give the impression they had gathered there by chance. Several men gave Grace an appraising once over. She felt as if she should paint a number on her rump and do a circuit of the stock auction ring, but she ignored them instead. She hurried towards the hall, not wishing for another encounter with one of the young men in particular. Apparently, Nathaniel Summerfield felt the same. As soon as he saw her, he pushed himself off the wall he had been leaning on and disappeared around the corner.

Mrs MacEwen apologised for the men's excessive scrutiny and explained that any social event was an opportunity for the town matriarchs to parade their unmarried sons, because the ratio of suitable young ladies to unmarried sons was lamentably unequal.

Closer to the door of the community hall, a group of young women hovered under the watchful eyes of an older chaperone. Most of the girls were no more than twenty years old, in Grace's estimation. Their fresh faces and pretty dresses made Grace feel old, although she was only twenty-three.

Mrs MacEwen greeted them and entered the hall, which was filled with women aged from eighteen to eighty. The volume of conversation rang in Grace's ears, but, as Mrs MacEwen had said, everyone seemed to be cheerful, and the faces that swivelled towards the newcomers were friendly and welcoming.

Grace smiled back, but her nerves had her wishing she had skipped breakfast. She was out of place here. What on earth would she talk about when she couldn't make a scone to save her life, let alone arrange flowers or herd sheep or whatever it was these women did.

Mrs MacEwen's name was called from the far side of the room, where a statuesque lady was holding court amongst the middle-aged matrons of the town. "My apologies, Grace. I have been summoned by the Chairwoman of the Horticultural Show Committee. She probably wishes to lambast me for not yet having arranged all the prizes for the Baked Goods and Homecrafts categories of the show." She took the herbs from Grace. "I'll put these on the table as a peace offering. Sorry to desert you."

Grace wanted to cling to Mrs MacEwen as a life ring in a storm, but her escort was already gone. Mrs MacEwen stopped along the way to have a word with a woman of Grace's age.

The woman hurried over to Grace. "Hello and welcome. Mrs MacEwen says you're a friend of hers, who is new in town. My name is Lucy."

"I'm Grace."

"You arrived on the coach yesterday, I believe. You were seen talking to Charlie Pyke, who must have travelled on the same coach. I must warn you, Grace, tongues are already wagging. We are all keen to know why Charlie is back in town. I heard his parents went to Dunedin to attend his wedding, but other people are saying Charlie's girl jilted him and he is here to investigate an old robbery. He's a famous detective now, so we hear."

"The wedding rumour was the correct one, Lucy. My wedding to Charlie, in fact. I am Mrs Grace Penrose Pyke." Grace had little hope that her full name would be used here. She would be Mrs Charlie Pyke to the locals.

Lucy's eyes widened, then her gaze dropped to reassess the woman in front of her. Grace wondered what she had heard about "Charlie's girl" that left her in such a state of surprise. Perhaps, like Mrs MacEwen, she had expected a weapon-toting, terrifying bluestocking. Grace was glad she had left behind the knife she usually carried strapped to her calf.

Lucy recovered quickly. "Oh, how lovely. The townsfolk will be delighted Charlie Pyke has made such an excellent match. Does that mean you are on your honeymoon, Grace? Or would you prefer Mrs Pyke?"

"Grace is fine, and yes, we are here on our honeymoon." Lucy hadn't mentioned the altercation in the alley, which gave Grace hope that her reputation was not already ruined in the eyes of these

81

charming young ladies. Perhaps she could stop the other rumour too. "It's true that Charlie is a well-known detective now, but I can assure you that he did not come to Clyde to investigate any crime. We are taking a short break from our usual work, so I can get to know my new parents-in-law."

"I remember little Charlie Pyke sitting in the row behind me at school, quiet as a mouse most of the time. How well he has done for himself. You must be proud of him." Lucy took her arm. "Come and meet my friends, Grace. I do hope you will stay awhile in Clyde. We are a lady short on the tennis team."

"I'm afraid I don't play tennis, and we are only here for two weeks. Perhaps we can come and watch a game instead."

Grace hoisted a smile on her face as Lucy introduced her. She was terrified she wouldn't know what to say, but the young women of the town saved her by supplying all the small talk she lacked. She fended off questions from all quarters with a volley of appropriate, if censored, replies.

How did she and Charlie meet? A tricky one, since they had met after a gruesome death. Grace went with the simple version – she had reported a crime to the local police station, where Charlie was a constable.

Was it love at first sight? Absolutely. No need to mention that Grace fell for him because Charlie allowed her to help him identify the cause of death of a mislaid corpse.

Was your wedding wonderful? Another tricky one, since there had been a fatal fire during the wedding, which turned out to be a murder. Grace said it was the happiest day of her life.

The questions flowed into slightly safer territory. What were the latest fashions in Dunedin? No idea, but nothing as lovely as Grace could see in the hall today. Do you attend the theatre? Regularly, she replied, without mentioning it was an operating theatre. Is Charlie a good dancer? At last, an easy one. Most definitely, Grace replied.

"What a shame you were not here for the dance last week," Lucy said, perhaps sensing that Grace was floundering under the weight of genteel interrogation. "The dance before that caused great excitement, because a kerosene lamp blew and set the place afire. Our little town is not without its excitements, you see."

The other women added their stories of past entertainments and suggestions of local activities to try. Everyone insisted that she and Charlie must stay for the upcoming horticultural show, which was to be one of the highlights of a busy social season of cricket, tennis, horse racing, choral societies, amateur dramatics, and more.

"Come now, ladies," Lucy admonished. "Let poor Grace catch her breath."

"Not before Mrs Pyke tells us what Charlie Pyke is really in town for." The speaker leaned towards Grace with eager eyes and pink cheeks. "I have heard he has fresh information on the old gold robbery. Has Ezra Yarwood been found at last?"

"No," Grace said, holding back her exasperation. "We came to Clyde for a peaceful honeymoon and nothing else. I had never heard of this robbery before the rumours started."

"Charlie ought to talk to Bob and Matilda Trent. Their farm is next door to the Yarwood's place. Mother believes if anyone knows what Ezra was up to, it would be the neighbours, especially as Matilda was rumoured to be sweet on Ezra Yarwood."

Grace couldn't recall the speaker's name, but she didn't get a chance to reply anyway, as another woman chimed in.

"I feel sorry for Matilda, being married to Bob Trent. I'd rather be an old maid than married to that sullen oaf, especially with Matilda being such a lovely woman."

"Better Bob Trent than Ezra Yarwood," another woman said. "My mother said Ezra was flirting with half the girls in town and probably other towns too. I overheard Mother say he was bedding the barmaid at the Molyneux as well. Charming, but definitely unsavoury, she called him."

"Matilda loves Bob," another said, "and they've done a fine service to the town's bachelors by producing four bonnie daughters. Can you believe she is with child again? She must be forty years old, at least. I expect Bob is desperate for a son."

Grace felt as if she was at the tennis match already, watching the chatter being batted back and forth in front of her. She wanted to know more about Ezra and the barmaid, because she recalled that Connie Summerfield had been a barmaid at the Molyneux Hotel at the time of the robbery and was rumoured to have been close to Ezra.

She looked around, wondering if Mrs Constance Summerfield was here. If so, the speaker had better take care that the former barmaid did not overhear, as Connie didn't sound like the type of woman who would care to have gossip spread about her lowly past. After the incident last night with her son, Nathaniel Summerfield, Grace was eager to avoid a meeting. Even Mrs MacEwen seemed in awe of her rival.

Grace was so intent on listening that she jumped when somebody tapped her shoulder. For a horrifying moment, she feared she had conjured up Mrs Summerfield, but the middle-aged woman who had tapped her shoulder was wearing a maid's uniform. Grace had seen her pouring cups of tea and slicing cake with the precision of a surgeon.

The maid bobbed at the knee and addressed Grace with beautifully rounded vowels. "Excuse me, ma'am. My mistress wishes to meet you." She inclined her head towards the intimidating Chairwoman of the Horticultural Show Committee, who was watching from across the room.

Mrs MacEwen intercepted Grace when she was halfway across the room and whispered a warning in her ear. "She'll want to know if you are a single lady, come to town to find a husband. I only said you are a friend visiting from Dunedin. She didn't give me a chance to explain that you are married to Charlie. Forgive me that I did not press the matter, Grace, but I couldn't resist letting her find out for herself after she summoned me so rudely."

The cluster of smartly attired middle-aged women parted at Grace's approach. The Chairwoman evaluated her with the condescension one can only manage with a height advantage. Her battleship bosom was inadequately tucked inside an expensive gown, whose girlish ruffles did nothing to soften her appearance. Likewise, the little hat perched on top of her elaborate pile of hair only emphasised her intimidating bulk. Her saving grace was her face, which had the perfectly symmetrical bone structure for which words like "handsome" were used, because "pretty" was inadequate.

Mrs MacEwen straightened her back as they approached. "Grace, may I introduce Mrs Constance Summerfield."

Grace's heart clenched into a knot, while Mrs Summerfield examined her prey with the ice blue stare that her son Nathaniel had turned on Grace in the alley. Evidently, she decided Grace passed muster as a sufficiently ladylike prospect, because she bestowed a smile upon her. The smile softened her in a way the ruffles did not. Grace found herself smiling back, despite her misgivings.

"Charmed, I'm sure," Mrs Summerfield said in a low voice that nevertheless seemed to carry across the voices around her. "What an elegant gown you are wearing, my dear. You must come for afternoon tea while you are here. My oldest son, Nathaniel, is always delighted to meet young ladies with city refinements."

How to delicately disabuse this terrifying woman of the notion that her son would wish to meet the newcomer, after their inauspicious first encounter? "I'm rather busy with –" Grace began.

Constance was not to be interrupted. "Nathaniel is responsible for the management of our hotel enterprises as present, while he learns the finer points of his father's extensive business interests."

The prospect of tea with Constance Summerfield, the former barmaid and current committee tyrant, was about as welcome as a broken bottle to the face. Grace felt safe in the knowledge that the offer would never be repeated once Constance found out about the incident in the alley.

Meanwhile, Grace did not wish to play games. "I am only in Clyde for a short time, Mrs Summerfield, on honeymoon. My husband runs a successful business in Dunedin and does not wish to disappoint his many clients by being away for too long. I am afraid I have little time to spare while we are here, as I wish to spend time with my parents-in-law, Jasmine and Thomas Pyke."

Constance Summerfield's impressive jaw tightened as she failed to find the right reply to this unwelcome revelation. Mrs MacEwen had a positively devilish grin on her face. Grace suspected her new friend had enjoyed scoring a point against her rival for dominance in the social circles of Clyde. The grand dame of the landed gentry versus the upstart rags-to-riches barmaid. That was a battle Grace had no intention of getting caught in the middle of, but she couldn't think of a way out.

A rosy-cheeked woman came to her rescue. From the bulge pushing out under her simple muslin dress, this must be Matilda Trent. "Welcome to Clyde, Mrs Pyke. Naturally, we are delighted that young Mr Pyke has found himself such a lovely wife, and we wish you all the best for your honeymoon. Will you be staying long enough to attend the horticultural show? Mrs Summerfield is certain to win the prize for the best roses, but perhaps you have some more of those lovely herbs you can enter. The prizes are quite splendid. A pair of ducks for the herbs, so I hear."

Grace smiled gratefully at her saviour, who had not only diverted the conversation, but had smoothed the hackles of Mrs Summerfield with a compliment to her prize-winning roses. "Unfortunately, my husband and I will not be in Clyde long enough to attend the show. A shame, as I have heard such excellent reports of it."

"Oh, but you must stay, if you can," Mrs Trent said. "We are offering such lovely prizes. A silver brooch for the best scones made by an unmarried lady. You wouldn't be eligible to enter that, naturally, and Mrs MacEwen is bound to win the prize for married lady's scones. Perhaps you might enter the best bouquet of flowers, which wins a pair of lovely gloves."

"If my pickled onions do not win that pretty pair of photo frames, I shall be most put out," another woman said. "I have some lovely cheese this year, but there's no beating our Matilda in the cheese contest." She patted the arm of the rosy-cheeked woman. "Matilda Trent is our very own Dairy Queen."

Matilda blushed and denied that she was worthy of this great honour. Grace studied the former Matilda Jacks, rumoured admirer of the missing Ezra Yarwood, and now married to the unpleasant Bob Trent. Grace had to agree with the assessment of her new acquaintances. Matilda Trent seemed far too nice a woman for either of these men.

Grace would have to find an excuse for visiting Matilda to find out more. Fortunately, she loved cheese. "Mrs Trent, your reputation precedes you. We are currently neighbours. Perhaps I might call on you and buy some of your delicious cheese?"

Once the words were out, Grace realised how rude it would appear to be paying a call on Matilda Trent after refusing an invitation from Constance Summerfield. Grace kept her eyes on Matilda, who was quick to answer with gracious tactfulness.

"I would be delighted to show you my cheeses, Mrs Pyke. Drop by any time your busy schedule permits. If I am not there, my husband or one of our girls will help you. In fact, come this afternoon if you wish. I have a lovely line in French-inspired soft cheese that you and your husband might enjoy."

"Wonderful, thank you, Mrs Trent. My grandmother was born in France and instilled in me a love of soft cheeses. And now, if you ladies will excuse me, I have another social engagement arranged this morning. After I have stopped by the table of goods you have for sale, naturally. One must support local charity, especially when all that is required is the purchase of delicious cakes."

The circle of ladies stood aside, looking pleased at the compliment to their baking. Grace didn't wish to appear discourteous by leaving early, but their time in Clyde really was short and she didn't want to spend it making endless social calls when she could be spending the time getting to know her parents-in-law and stealing all too rare private moments with her new husband.

Mrs MacEwen accompanied Grace to the fundraising table. "You handled Constance superbly, Grace. My apologies if you thought I'd thrown you to the lioness. Nathaniel Summerfield always behaved abominably to Charlie, and he infected his mother with his prejudices. I wanted Constance to see what a splendid match Charlie had made."

Grace regretted her earlier thought that Mrs MacEwen was simply scoring points when her true intention was to support Charlie. "How kind of you, Mrs MacEwen, but it is me who made the splendid match. Amongst his many fine attributes, Charlie is the only man I have ever met who accepts me for who I am and encourages my ambition to become a doctor."

"Oh, Grace, how lovely it is to hear you say that. I know exactly what you mean. To have a man love you for yourself is a special gift indeed." Mrs MacEwen embraced her. "I'd better get back to committee tasks or Constance will be after me with her horsewhip – figuratively speaking, of course."

Grace purchased two cakes from the fundraising table for the purposes of entertaining and bribery. A winsome young lass persuaded her to add a buttercup-yellow square of thin cotton to her purchases. A neckerchief is vital in these parts, the girl explained, for keeping the sun and dust off one's neck. Grace pretended to admire the embroidery, which had been done by a novice and might have been white flowers, or possibly clouds, or even sheep.

Her basket thus loaded, Grace bade farewell to Mrs MacEwen and reiterated that she and Charlie would love to come for a meal next week. Mission accomplished, Grace headed for the exit, her thoughts already turning to the pleasure of a call on her delightful mother-in-law.

A gaggle of younger girls blocked the doorway. Grace threaded her way through them, holding her basket of cakes tightly in one hand. She was about to emerge on the other side when the shrill voice of one girl cut through the chatter.

"Who is that giant of a man coming down the road on a horse?"

Over the heads of the girls, Grace saw a flare of alarm cross the face of the older woman who was acting as chaperone. "It could be Jake Blackthorn. Quick, go inside, girls. We don't want the likes of him staring at you."

Grace pressed her back to the outside wall to avoid getting swept up in the rush. She had seconds to decide – retreat to safety or advance undaunted. As the last girl pushed past, Grace saw the silhouette of a big man on a dark horse against the glare of the late morning sun. The outline of a gun barrel jutted from the silhouette.

Before she had time to react, a sudden, shocking blow flung her backwards against the wall.

Old Miners

Charlie left town before the sun had fully risen over the horizon of dark hills. He rode towards Cromwell, following the same route Zachary Dawson would have taken when he fled Clyde with his share of the stolen gold, heading for his home in Arrowtown.

He breathed in a lung full of fresh air, perfumed with wild herbs and the natural scents of horse, rock and river, which triggered long ago happy memories. It was good to be away from town and the ridiculous rumour that he held crucial evidence about a robbery on the day he was born. Some people seemed to believe that a private investigator must have divine knowledge of all things criminal, when solving cases always came down to old-fashioned hard work.

The misty blue-green Clutha River surged below the track, which cut across a steep hillside. All around him, walls of scree and rock rose, with little vegetation to soften the harshness of the landscape. What vegetation there was had to be hardy to survive the winters, when frosts froze the land solid. The miners who had pulled shovels full of alluvial gold from the riverbed must have been hardy souls, driven by an unquenchable thirst for wealth despite the intolerable conditions.

The river would have been lower when Zachary Dawson came through in winter, its frigid waters locked away in icy glaciers and snow-capped mountain peaks. Dawson and his horse would have had to force their way through snowdrifts further up the trail. With saddlebags heavy from the weight of gold, it was no wonder the horse had foundered. If the robber had hidden the missing gold out here, it could be lost forever.

Today, the track was more benign, if the early morning sun radiating off shiny rocks could be called benign. Despite the rugged scenery, or perhaps because of it, Charlie loved this place. Even the dreaded speargrass added a certain beauty to the landscape, as long as one did not fall foul of their sharp needles.

When Charlie reached a tussock flat, he saw signs of rabbits everywhere. They'd been released in New Zealand less than two decades ago, but already rabbits had devastated this land and driven the runholders to despair. Charlie planned to cull a few to feed the dog and themselves, but first he wanted to take a moment to lie on his back in the tussock and soak up the majesty of this place.

Blaze gambolled off to chase the wildlife while Charlie soaked up the fresh warmth of the day. Duncan MacEwen prided himself on his purebred border collies but Charlie couldn't help thinking there had to be a rogue hunting dog ancestor in Blaze's past. That was his last thought before he drifted off in a daze of contentment.

He awoke with a start an hour or so later, judging from the progress of the sun. Charlie's first thought was that he ought not to be lolling around enjoying himself, when Grace was doing her best to enhance the reputation of the Pyke family. Blaze seemed worn out by her exertions, so Charlie carried her home tucked inside his coat across the front of the saddle. Nyx looked around when he mounted, but accepted the extra burden without fuss. As a police horse, Nyx had been trained to take anything in her stride.

Charlie returned to the cottage with a package from the butcher and a deep satisfaction for a morning well spent. After unsaddling Nyx and rubbing her down, he released her in the field next door with a last pat and an apple. The smell of horse and the touch of her warm muzzle in his hand felt like coming home.

Grace had already left the cottage for her morning's engagement with the ladies of the town. The frantic scattering of gowns across the bed suggested she had had trouble deciding on appropriate attire. A wave of guilt washed over him for his selfishness in seeking the delights of solitude in the hills, while leaving his new wife to brave the curiosity of local society on her own. He would have to make it up to her.

As Charlie chopped meat for Blaze, he came up with a plan. The rest of the meat went into the Dutch oven, so it could simmer all day in the herbs and spices he added to the pot. His own secret recipe, which he had devised after many a night alone or with Hamish MacEwen around a campfire deep in the hinterland. Next, he went into the overgrown garden to dig potatoes and carrots for the stew and pick luscious ripe peaches for dessert. Nyx came over to the fence for her share of carrots, just like old times.

With dinner prepared, Charlie cleaned himself up, then tackled the cottage. By the time he had finished, their bedroom was immaculate, fresh roses decorated the table, and the air smelled delicious. Grace still wasn't home, so he saddled Nyx again and headed into town to see if he could rustle up a few answers to old questions.

His first stop was the town's general store, where Charlie bought two bottles of the local wine and supplies of tea, tobacco, flour and preserves, adding a few ounces of sugar when he recalled Sylvester Healey's sweet tooth. The old miner had arrived in Clyde during the gold rush but had taken a blow to the head in a rockfall that left him feeble minded, or so folks said. Local Samaritans made sure Sylvester had enough work to make a living and enough food and fuel to see him through winter.

Sylvester might not be the sharpest nail in the shoe, but he had an instinct for survival. The old miner was a constant presence in the shadows, which meant he saw what was happening in Clyde even if nobody knew he was there. Sylvester Healey's name had been mentioned in the police report on the gold robbery, but only as one of the many men in the Clyde area at the time, all of whom were interviewed. He was not considered a strong suspect, partly because no one believed he had the brains to commit a daring robbery.

Charlie's father had often used him as a source of information about minor infringements of the law, but he'd warned Charlie that Sylvester wouldn't inform on his old friends or people he feared. Jake Blackthorn fitted both these categories, which left Charlie wondering what it would take to get Sylvester to talk. Sugar and tobacco were the obvious place to start.

Perhaps time would have mellowed his old loyalties, Charlie thought, as he brought Nyx to a halt in the old miners' camp behind the main part of the township.

Charlie was in luck. Sylvester was sitting on a rusty kerosene tin outside his home. Not that "home" was the right word for the mud-brick hut with a roof and door made of beaten-flat kerosene tins. Rose Cottage was a palace beside this hovel. It was a wonder Sylvester didn't die from the cold or choke to death on the smoke drifting out through an inadequate hole in the roof.

Sylvester pushed himself to his feet with obvious effort. "Couldn't spare an old digger a plug of tobacco, could you, young Pyke?"

"As luck would have it, I've just been to the store." Charlie chucked over a pouch of quality tobacco.

"Mighty decent of you, young fella." Sylvester filled his pipe and struck a flint to light it. After a few deep sucks to get the pipe going, he sank back onto the tin with a satisfied sigh. "Nothing like a pinch of fine tobacco to dull aches in an old body."

"I brought a few other supplies for you, too." Charlie sat down on a second tin, which creaked under his weight. Slow and steady was the way to go with a man like Sylvester, especially as he would be reluctant to talk. Charlie didn't smoke, so he got out his knife and a piece of wood to whittle. Blaze lay beside him, content to doze in the sun after her busy morning. "Took a ride out into the hills this morning. Darn rabbits are taking over the land."

Sylvester's pipe puffed. "Aye. Town's changed a bit since your day, I expect."

"Aye. Some things don't change, though." Charlie looked up from his inexpert whittling to find Sylvester grinning at him.

"Happen you took the track north," Sylvester said. "Wouldn't be looking for gold, would you?"

Sylvester must have been watching him early this morning. Not much happened around here that the old miner didn't see, which was all to the good for what Charlie needed. "Despite rumours, I'm not here to investigate the robbery."

"Oh, aye."

"But I would like to hear what you think happened." Was it Charlie's imagination or did the pipe smoke thin for a second before Sylvester resumed puffing?

"I doubt you'd care for my thoughts, young Pyke."

Sylvester puffed on in silence but his eyes had narrowed. Charlie was sure the old miner knew something, although he was no longer sure he wanted to know what it was.

"I reckon Jake Blackthorn knows something," Charlie said. "Suppose I'll have to ask him instead."

"Not your best plan, young Pyke. Black Jake likes to ask questions, but he sure don't like to answer 'em. Hope you got a rifle tucked away on that fine black mare of yours."

"Happen I do." Charlie tossed the sliver of shaped wood towards Sylvester. "Maybe you could use that to clean your pipe."

"Reckon I could." Sylvester let another few puffs pass before he spoke again. "I'm an old man, and I don't recall so well. If Jake happened to have called on Ezra Yarwood the afternoon after the robbery, sniffing around for a hint of buried treasure, I'd likely have forgotten all about it."

"Shame about that." Charlie rose and sauntered over to the saddlebags on Nyx's back. "Darned if I haven't gone and bought too much food. Reckon my memory isn't so good either." Charlie handed over a selection of tempting morsels.

Sylvester grinned wide enough to show the gaps in his rotten teeth. "Mighty thoughtful of you to help an old fella in need."

"My pleasure, Sylvester. It's a hot day to roam the countryside aimlessly. It'd sure help if I knew where Jake has his hut."

Blaze bumped the back of his knees and growled. Charlie sensed a sudden tension in the air. He had asked too much.

But Sylvester's gaze had shifted over Charlie's shoulder. The bloodshot whites of his eyes flashed with fear. "Tell him I didn't say nothing."

Jake Blackthorn was riding towards them from the direction of town on a dark bay horse. Blaze growled again. Charlie brought the collie to heel. He wished he had the advantage of Nyx's height, but if he mounted his horse now, he would look defensive. He stood his ground, while Sylvester shrunk into himself, trying to avoid being noticed.

Jake jerked on his horse's bit to stop it right in front of Charlie. "What are you doing here, Pyke? Has he been questioning you, Sy?"

"Why would I question him when he isn't right in the head?" Charlie pointed at the small pile of supplies beside Sylvester. "My mother asked me to drop off some food to the old miners as part of her charity work. Now, if you'll excuse me, I'd like to get out of this shanty town and back to my wife."

Jake watched him with the intensity of a cobra about to strike. "Think you're too good for the likes of us, don't you, Pyke, with your fancy city airs and uppity city wife. She's too much of a lady for the likes of you."

"Don't I know it," Charlie said with forced cheerfulness. "Yet here I am, the happiest man in the world, newly married to the woman of my dreams, who loves me for who I am. Must have been born lucky."

Jake urged his horse to step closer, pushing into Charlie. "You and your kin are a curse on this town, Pyke, and you always have been. The day you were born, my brother died by your grandfather's hand. I'd be watching your back if I were you."

Charlie reached into his pocket for an apple he'd been keeping for Nyx. Jake's big bay horse lowered her head into his hand to eat, while Charlie scratched between the horse's ears with his other hand. When he had let sufficient time pass, he spoke calmly. "You're wrong, Blackthorn. My grandfather had nothing to do with the robbery or your brother's death. I'm sorry for your loss, but don't you think it is time to let the past go?"

The bay snuffled against Charlie's pocket for another treat. Jake jerked his horse's head up, forcing it to step away. Blaze barred her teeth and snarled to stop the horse from moving forward again.

Jake's fists tightened on the reins. "Let the past go? You've got a nerve, Pyke, when my brother lies in a grave, and you turn up looking for your grandfather's ill-gotten gold."

"Feeling guilty about your brother's death, are you, Blackthorn? My bet is that you were involved in the robbery." Charlie watched Jake closely, but Jake didn't react except with heightened anger. He tried another tack. "Or maybe you planned to take the gold yourself and were beaten to it by someone else." Charlie noted the twitch of Jake's eyelids, which was probably about as close to an admission as he would ever get.

Jake recovered his composure quickly. "I'm no robber and nor was my brother. I deserve a share of that gold, though, for the suffering caused by the death of my brother. Where is it, Pyke? Tell me now or that scrawny little wife of yours will regret ever setting eyes on you." Jake leaned down so he could sneer into Charlie's face. "Or maybe it's already too late for that."

Charlie darted forward and grabbed Jake by one arm, pulling him off balance. "Stay away from my wife, Blackthorn." Blaze added a deep-throated growl of agreement.

Jake yanked his arm away and swung his rifle around in one seamless movement. "Or what? You'll get her to beat me up like she did to the Summerfield boy? Don't make me laugh. I'd have her on her back before she could say 'yes, please.'"

Excruciating as the insult was, Charlie couldn't afford to rise to the bait with a rifle aimed at his heart from an unmissable distance. He whistled to Nyx. Fortunately, the mare had been taught how to insert herself between fighting factions as part of her police training. Nyx didn't hesitate to step forward and push herself between Charlie and his adversary.

Charlie ran a hand down her silky neck, then mounted and took his shotgun out of its pouch, levelling it at Jake. Nyx's superior height now gave him the edge. "Don't underestimate me or my wife, Blackthorn."

Jake laughed and pulled his horse around, kicking it into a canter. The last Charlie saw of him, he was heading towards the bridge. The rage building inside him had Charlie itching to follow to see where Jake was heading, but instinct, and the "already too late" of Jake's threat, urged him to make sure Grace was safe first.

Besides, Jake Blackthorn wasn't going anywhere. Charlie would take his time and watch his back until he'd gathered the evidence needed to take the man down using the force of the law. He would have to watch Grace's back too. Jake was not a man to be underestimated. He might be a generation older than Charlie, but he was also tall, muscular, armed, and unscrupulous. Charlie would have to ensure that he wasn't caught off guard at their next meeting.

He turned to see how Sylvester had coped with the encounter, but the old fellow had vanished like a wisp of smoke. He had no time to waste tracking down the old miner, when Grace was unprotected. He clicked his tongue, urging Nyx into a fast trot, until he realised he didn't know where the morning tea was being held.

In a flash of reckless optimism, he called to his new four-legged companion, who was watching him, awaiting his command. "Blaze, find Grace."

Rustling and Other Secrets

Grace was thrown back against the wall of the community hall by the force of the blow. Only a frantic hand on a windowsill stopped her from going down in an undignified heap in the dust, as the basket of cakes she had been holding flew into the air, landing right way up.

The black and white cannonball responsible for her near fall seemed to find the situation amusing, if her lolling tongue was anything to go by. Grace put her hands on her hips and glared at the approaching horseman. "Your dog is a menace, sir."

He lifted his hat in courteous recognition of his guilt. "My apologies, milady. The dog could not contain her enthusiasm in the face of such beauty."

Grace heard intakes of breath and tittering behind her. The young ladies of the town had ventured out of the hall again, now that they knew it wasn't Jake Blackthorn on the horse.

"Who *is* that man?" a girl behind her whispered.

"Ladies, allow me to present my husband, Charlie Pyke." Grace was used to Charlie turning up with a dramatic flourish when she needed him. She didn't mind the murmurs of surprise and admiration coming from the ladies behind her. Charlie Pyke astride a tall, jet-black horse was a sight worth remembering.

Charlie nodded. "Good morning, ladies. May I steal my wife away?" He unslung the shotgun from his shoulder and slipped from Nyx's back, returning the basket to Grace with an exaggerated bow. "Mm, is that lemon cake?"

"Yes, but not for you." Grace rubbed the collie's ears. "I was about to visit your mother."

"Then I shall accompany you." He hooked her arm through his, and they strolled off as one, with Blaze and Nyx following along behind.

"My apologies for the over-zealous attentions of Blaze, Grace. I told her to find you, and she took her task a little too enthusiastically."

"On the contrary, my dear, you timed your entrance perfectly. I doubt the young ladies of the town will be gossiping about your past now. When they have finished swooning, they will be plotting to suffocate me in my bed so they can have you for themselves."

"I'm glad to find you in exuberant spirits, Grace."

"Were you looking for me for a specific reason, or did you sense there was cake to be had?"

"Isn't the desire to see my wife sufficient reason to seek her out?"

Grace had seen the relief in his eyes when he saw her. She knew that look – he had been worried about her for a reason but wasn't about to admit it, which meant subtle interrogation was called for. "How was your morning, Charlie?"

"We had a fine old time out riding, didn't we, girls? I never tire of the beauty of this place." Charlie stroked Nyx's neck, before switching his attentions to Blaze. "I think Blaze has the makings of a fine tracking dog. She's exceptionally loyal too, given our brief acquaintance."

A fine time out riding? Did her husband really think she would accept this half-truth about his morning's activities? Grace raised a single eyebrow.

He saw her raised eyebrow and responded with one of his own. "And then I went to see Sylvester Healey, who hinted that Ezra was the robber and Jake Blackthorn was trying to get a share of the gold after the robbery. Or rather, that's my rough interpretation of what little Sylvester admitted before Jake interrupted our chat. They both know more than they are admitting about the gold robbery. The best bet might be to uncover Jake's illegal activities, so we have a lever to get him to confess what he knows. Pa will know how best to achieve that."

"Is that what you call a peaceful honeymoon activity, Charlie Pyke?"

"No. To be honest, I am concerned about your safety, Grace. Jake Blackthorn threatened us both, and he is not a man to be underestimated. He was heading out of town, but he'll be back."

Grace understood the risk, but they had been drawn too far into this investigation to stop now, especially as fresh evidence was emerging. "I was planning to pay a visit to our neighbours this afternoon to buy some cheese. The Trent dairy has an excellent reputation, and I doubt I will come to any harm under Matilda Trent's care."

Charlie hesitated. "I suppose so. I'll come with you."

"As you wish, Charlie, although I suspect Matilda will talk more freely with a woman on her own."

"You're not going just to buy cheese, are you Grace?"

"I'm simply making a neighbourly visit with lemon cake to encourage Matilda to offer tea and conversation. Of course, I may mention the general interest the townsfolk are showing in the robbery, in the hope Matilda will volunteer her thoughts on the matter."

"Matilda Trent being the milkmaid who saw my grandfather on the morning of the robbery," Charlie said.

"One of the woman at the morning tea told me Matilda was sweet on her neighbour, Ezra Yarwood, when she first arrived in Clyde. It was only after Ezra's disappearance that she married Bob Trent. If rumour was to be believed, Ezra had more than one woman in his sights, including a barmaid at the Molyneux Hotel. I'd like to know more about Mrs Constance Summerfield as well, but I am far too terrified to question her."

"I don't blame you, Grace. Did you meet Connie at the morning tea?"

"I did. She likes to be called Constance or Mrs Summerfield these days, by the way, not Connie." Grace shuddered at the memory of Mrs Summerfield's glare. "Mrs MacEwen failed to introduce me with my full name, which was naughty of her. Mrs Summerfield tried to tempt me into marriage with her son, Nathaniel, before I had time to tell her who I was. I was petrified Nathaniel had told her about the fight, but he hadn't."

"I can see I am going to have to stick to you like glue, Mrs Penrose Pyke, to avoid calamity."

"And I to you, Detective Penrose Pyke." Grace pulled his head down to whisper in his ear. "Those girls at the community hall were ready to drag you from your horse and kidnap you. I can't say I blame them."

Charlie shot her a look that had Grace thinking about throwing her plans aside and returning to their cottage. But it would be impolite not to call on her in-laws when they were so close by. Their son would keep until later.

Jasmine Pyke welcomed them with open arms. The warmth of her mother-in-law's embrace, combined with the comforting aroma of fragrant food, tipped Grace into a world of simple pleasures, where she could forget about thoughts of menacing men and lust for gold.

"Charlie, could you go to the station to tell your father we're about to eat?" Jasmine asked. "You can stay with me, Grace. I'm dying to know how you found the morning tea."

"It was very kind of Mrs MacEwen to take me," Grace said. "Everyone was most welcoming, although Mrs Summerfield was rather terrifying. Thankfully, word of Nathaniel's encounter with me hadn't reached her ears. Yet."

"I'm relieved to hear it," Jasmine said. "Constance Summerfield is not a woman to cross. To be fair, she has had to battle her way into polite society with a combination of good works, large donations, and unrelenting determination. The transition from barmaid to society matron wasn't easy."

Five minutes ago, Grace had vowed to talk only of pleasant family matters with her mother-in-law, but her insatiable curiosity got the better of her. "There were hints that when she was Connie the barmaid, her reputation was not, shall we say, lily white?"

Jasmine chuckled. "No, indeed, but she was not a prostitute, if that's what you mean. Connie was determined to improve her situation and took her time to decide which of her potential suitors would best achieve her goal. She was always an attractive woman, with a certain air about her. It's hard to describe, but she held herself above her station right from the start, as if she had inborn pride or perhaps had started life under more favourable circumstances. Either that or she is a born actress."

"Is it true that Ezra Yarwood was one of her suitors?" Grace asked.

"I don't doubt it, although I couldn't say for sure, because any wooing probably happened in places a respectable woman like me wouldn't wish to be seen in. Ezra was that always dangerous mix of charmer and opportunist. But Connie wasn't stupid. She was far better off with Vern Summerfield. She married him not long after the robbery and had Nathaniel six months later. Happily for them, Vern struck riches on his gold claim soon after."

"According to her statement in the police file, Connie admitted to being outside the Molyneux Hotel 'for a breath of fresh air' at midnight on the night of the robbery, but claimed she saw nothing."

Jasmine was no fool. She saw where Grace was going with her questions. "Thomas wondered the same. Could Connie have seen the robber and found a way to get a share of the gold, perhaps by threatening to go to the police? Possibly, but there was no proof whatsoever, and the robbery must have happened well after midnight. Nothing short of Spanish Inquisition methods would get Constance Summerfield to admit otherwise. She never mentioned Vern being in town that night, for example, even though his visit would have given her an alibi."

"Unless she and Vern were in it together," Grace said. "Nothing more than speculation, of course."

"Honestly, Grace, I doubt we will ever know." Jasmine rose to see to the meal. She must have had a sixth sense because the sound of boots being kicked off at the doorstep followed a minute later.

Sergeant Pyke was carrying another file and had a rolled map under his arm. From their serious expressions, he and his son were talking about the robbery again too. Charlie and his father cleared the table to unroll the map, while continuing their conversation. Jasmine delivered cups of tea and left them to it. She must be used to such conversations after decades of marriage to a policeman.

"The miners all had secret hiding places for their finds, of course," Thomas Pyke was saying. "More than one if they were smart. Mostly in stash holes in the ground, disguised with planks and dirt." He tapped the map south of Clyde. "Ezra Yarwood's diggings were in the Conroys Gully goldfields after he moved south from his Arrowtown and Cromwell digs. He wanted to be closer to his mother after his father died."

Charlie measured off the distance on the map between thumb and forefinger. "Conroys Gully is a long way from Clyde, given the limited time he had available the morning of the robbery."

"Too far, I'd have said." Thomas choked on a gulp of hot tea but recovered quickly and continued as if he hadn't noticed. "Even if Ezra had a strong horse, and the robbery was committed at the earliest possible time, it would have been a stretch to get there, bury the gold, and return to his mother's cottage by the time Lee Hope saw him at five o'clock in the morning, especially in winter. As far as we know, he didn't have a horse. If Ezra was the robber, my guess is that he stashed the gold somewhere near Clyde, before vanishing with it the next day after swearing his innocence to the police."

"Sylvester implied Jake Blackthorn went to see Ezra on the afternoon after the robbery to extort a cut of the robbery takings. Presumably Jake didn't find the gold, because he isn't wealthy, and he has spent years searching for it. Jake had diggings up that way too, didn't he?"

"Here and here," his father said, tapping the map, "but that was years ago. Jake doesn't prospect for gold these days, and I'm not so sure he is as poor as he makes out. He has a good horse, as well as a pack pony, and plenty of money to spend buying alcohol. If Jake Blackthorn isn't the scoundrel responsible for our local problem with sheep rustling and other thefts, I'll turn my badge in."

Grace leaned over the map. "What about Vern Summerfield? Where did his lucky gold strike come from?"

Thomas Pyke's finger shifted away to the far north-east corner of the map. "Bannockburn, which is much closer to Cromwell than Clyde."

"Do you know where Jake has his hideout?" Charlie asked. "He has to have somewhere he can hide the sheep until he can sell them."

Thomas Pyke swept his hand over thousands of acres of empty area on the map. "Take your pick. Jake's slipperier than an eel and ten times as cunning. I have no proof, because the rustler is clever enough to take only a few at any one time. When the sheep are grazing the high country, it's impossible to keep track of them all. But the runholders keep an eye on stock numbers in more accessible areas, such as when they are down for shearing or lambing."

Grace leaned closer, taking in the row after row of mountains with names like Raggedy Range and Mount Difficulty. Even the names of the passes, like Duffers Saddle, sounded ominous. The marked gold workings were tiny dots within a vast system of rivers and streams, fed by creeks with names like Buster Creek and Hawks Burn, carving their way through innumerable gullies. The few markers indicating homesteads and small towns, mostly along the Clutha River, were mere dots on the map.

"Why would he only steal a few sheep at a time?" Grace asked. "You could hide a thousand sheep in that vast wilderness."

"Moving a flock can't be done without leaving traces," Charlie said. "Hoof marks on the ground, dung left on the trail. Also, you can only move a flock when the night is bright enough to see, which means the rustler risks being spotted. Sheep can be noisy when dogs are nipping at their heels. Does Jake have a sheepdog, Pa?"

"Not that I know of, but he does have a pack pony. My guess is that he takes a few ewes or lambs at a time, so he can hogtie them and carry them on the horses. I suspect him of other thefts too. Fruit missing from orchards, saddlery and supplies suddenly vanishing. I've tried to catch him in the act, but the best I've managed is to track him into this area." Thomas indicated an endless stretch of uninhabited land to the west of Clyde. "I reckon he has found a hidden gully up there somewhere. It's rough country."

"Rough country is an understatement." To Grace it seemed a vast stretch of nothing, criss-crossed by an endless series of steep gullies. "It's a wonder the miners don't get lost or perish out there."

"They do," Thomas murmured. "Thirty-five miners died out Campbell's Creek way in the great snow of '63."

"If Jake spent years roaming that area looking for miners to steal from, he probably knows it like the back of his hand," Charlie said. "I might take a ride up that way tomorrow, if you don't mind, Grace. Ma, can Grace stay with you, please? I don't want her on her own with Jake Blackthorn on the prowl."

"It would be my pleasure," Jasmine said.

Grace gave Charlie a look that said "are you mad?", but she said nothing. Instead, she gathered up the cups, which had been drained as if by magic by men used to gulping tea whenever their busy days permitted. While Charlie and his father discussed which old miners still worked the area, Grace took the cups to the sink.

When she passed the wide-open window of the sitting room, she heard a scuffle in the bushes outside. By the time her brain registered that it was too big for a rat, and it couldn't be Blaze, who was tied up on the far side of the house, the noise had stopped.

Grace poked her head out the window but saw nothing suspicious. The cottage wasn't large, so anyone close to the open window could have heard their conversation. If it was a man, he'd have had to be quick on his feet to have disappeared so fast.

Charlie joined her by the window, while his father rolled up the map and set the table.

"I thought I heard someone at the window," Grace said. "Could have been a stray dog."

They went outside, but the ground was too dry for footprints and the culprit had left no convenient traces of ripped fabric or a dropped calling card, so they went back inside.

The meal passed pleasantly, with no further discussion of the robbery or gold. It was only when they were finished that Thomas Pyke raised the subject again, and then only to caution Charlie and Grace to be careful. He said it almost apologetically, as parents do when reminding their adult children of things they already know.

"What are your plans for the afternoon?" Jasmine asked.

"I need to visit Vern Summerfield," Charlie replied, "but I don't want Grace to be alone."

"I'm only going to visit Matilda Trent to buy cheese," Grace said. "I'll be perfectly fine."

Charlie wasn't fool enough to believe that. "I'd rather you stayed here, Grace."

"Grace will come to no harm visiting Matilda," Jasmine said. "You can walk with her as far as the Trent farm and carry on to the Summerfield's house from there. You'll like her, Grace. Matilda is a stalwart of the various committees around town, and she's turned a struggling dairy farm into a great success. Old Mr Trent only had a few dairy cows when she arrived, whereas now they have pedigree animals and a contract for the local milk supply. Matilda makes the best cheese in the region, and she has turned the original cottage into a lovely home for them and their four girls."

"When did Matilda arrive in Clyde, Mrs Pyke?" Grace asked.

"Goodness me, now there's a question. It must have been a month or two before the robbery, because I recall her helping me home after I slipped on a patch of ice when I was heavily pregnant. You reach a point where you cannot see over your belly and your balance is all out of kilter." Jasmine's eyes misted with nostalgia.

"We were worried the baby had been hurt," Thomas said, "but Charlie turned out all right."

"Matilda came in for a cup of tea," Jasmine recalled. "She kept bringing the conversation back to Ezra Yarwood until I warned her off. Matilda was only sixteen and had little experience of men, as she grew up on an isolated farm. As far as I could tell, Ezra only had two missions in life. The first was to be rich. The second was to charm the drawers off any maid he met between the ages of fourteen and forty."

Charlie was still frowning. "Trust nobody, Grace, not even sweet Matilda Trent. For all we know, she could be part of the gang who robbed the gold lock-up. Women will do almost anything for a man they love, and vice versa."

"Really, Charlie, you're letting your imagination run wild," his mother said. "There's no nicer person in Clyde than Matilda Trent. She was just as lovely as a girl, and never mentioned Ezra again after I warned her off."

Grace reached over to nudge her husband's arm. "It's you who should be careful, Charlie. I wouldn't go within a mile of the Summerfield household without a loaded rifle and a pair of trained attack dogs."

"I think I can handle the likes of Vern Summerfield."

"It's not Vern who scares me. It's his wife."

"Connie may seem intimidating," Jasmine said, "but she's not so bad when you get to know her ways, as long as you don't cross her. Anyway, Charlie should be safe if he goes now. When Mrs Constance Summerfield comes to town on a charitable mission, she doesn't leave until every arm has been twisted and every role is allocated, with a full list of instructions and warnings of the dire

107

consequences of failure. I expect she has managed to extract an invitation to luncheon with the mayor's wife or someone else of similar status."

This did not sound like Grace's idea of "not so bad", but Charlie appeared undaunted. She was half-tempted to join him, if only to meet the man brave enough to marry Connie, but tea with Matilda beckoned.

Charlie escorted Grace on foot, while she rode Nyx. They swapped places outside the Trent farm. She couldn't help ruing the way she dropped out of the saddle like a sack of potatoes, while Charlie mounted in one graceful movement.

"Promise me you will go back to my parents' home when you have seen Matilda," Charlie said.

Grace promised. She watched with mixed emotions as Nyx trotted away. Blaze stopped a few yards away and looked back at Grace. While she would have been grateful for Blaze's reassuring presence, Bob Trent wouldn't appreciate a dog on his property.

"Find Charlie," she called.

Blaze gave her a last look before racing after Charlie. Her husband glanced back at the dog's arrival and waved to Grace.

Grand Pretensions

Charlie waited until Grace returned his wave. With her pretty summer gown and wicker basket, the capable medical student he knew so well appeared to have transformed into a country lass with not a care in the world. He knew it was an illusion. Regardless of how sweet and innocent she appeared, Grace had a nose for trouble. He watched her walk away – was she actually skipping? – and felt sick to the stomach.

Matilda Trent was not the problem – it was Bob Trent who worried him. Blaze obviously felt the same because she had lingered near Grace before returning to Charlie on Grace's command. Grace had made the right decision, given Bob's hostility towards stray dogs. Charlie tapped Nyx to walk on, telling himself Grace could handle the visit on her own.

The alternative was to take Grace to see Vern Summerfield, which he did not wish to do. He had no doubt that Nathaniel Summerfield would have given a one-sided version of yesterday evening's fight if his father had asked him about it. Therefore, Charlie was not likely to be a welcome visitor, and Grace would be even less welcome. Grace had no desire for another meeting with the domineering Constance Summerfield either. Charlie half-hoped Connie would not be at home, although he did want to talk to her. As a barmaid at the Molyneux Hotel at the time of the robbery, Connie knew all the local miners and their secrets, either from drunken small talk over the bar or from more intimate encounters.

Nyx didn't need any encouragement to switch to a canter when they reached the river path, heading downstream. Charlie relished the glorious sensation of the wind on his face, with its familiar smells of the countryside. Life in the city brought excitement, but he did not miss the ever-present smell of coal smoke and the press of crowds.

All too soon, he was approaching the massive stone gateposts and extensive gardens of Riverview. A gravelled driveway approached the house through an avenue of trees, giving the visitor glimpses of the grand façade of the house.

Before Charlie had announced his presence, a stable hand appeared to take Nyx and Blaze. Charlie brushed his clothes free of dog hair and dust and approached the front door. Before he could ring the bell, the door was opened by a middle-aged woman in a maid's uniform. She stood to attention, neither smiling nor asking his business, but Charlie was determined not to be intimidated.

He stepped forward as if he belonged here. "Mr Charles Penrose Pyke, here to see Mr Summerfield."

The maid led him through a wood-panelled hallway into a sitting room large enough to function as a small ballroom. The furnishings were expensive, but far too garish for Charlie's taste. Parquet floors, chandeliers, thick curtains in crimson velvet, and solid furniture with gilt-bronze fittings and mother-of-pearl inlay in the French style. From floor to ceiling, the house trumpeted its owner's success.

Through the open French doors, Charlie could see a formal garden of low clipped hedges and perfectly shaped rose bushes stretching to the riverbank beyond. Vern Summerfield sat at a dainty table on the veranda, reading through a bound sheaf of papers.

Charlie wouldn't have recognised Mr Summerfield if he had passed him in the street, as his thick brown hair was now completely grey. He was wearing spectacles, and a distinguished beard gave him the air of a refined man of business, matching his surroundings. Charlie had never known him well, given his aversion to the man's oldest son. His abiding memory of Vern came from a long-ago father and son race at the school sports day, when Vern Summerfield had been the tall, vigorous, raucously good-natured victor of the three-legged race. Charlie and his father had come third, after Duncan and Hamish MacEwen, because Thomas Pyke had stuck to the rules.

The maid stopped Charlie at the French doors. "You have a visitor, Mr Summerfield," she announced. "Mr Charles Penrose Pyke."

Vern Summerfield rose from the wicker chair and shed his glasses. Standing tall, and beaming broadly, the Mr Summerfield of memory returned. "Charlie. Good to see you, lad. Come on out."

The maid stepped aside, allowing Charlie onto the veranda. This wasn't the frosty welcome he had expected. "Good afternoon, Mr Summerfield. My apologies for interrupting your work."

"There's no need to be so formal now that you are a fellow man of business, Charlie. Call me Vern." His host cast the papers aside. "Nothing but a dull business matter. I'm glad to have the interruption." Vern turned to the maid, who was waiting by the door. "Perhaps some refreshments, Dewer?"

Charlie stood at the edge of the deck, admiring the view.

"Come and have a closer look." Vern led him to the edge of the riverbank, where they could see a gold dredge working the river bottom. The massive mechanical beast scooped gravel from the depths of the riverbed to extract the gold hidden within, leaving piles of tailings on the far bank. Functional it may be, but beautiful it was not.

"It's a beautiful sight, isn't it?" Vern said.

"Is the dredge one of yours, Mr …Vern?"

"I've got shares in her. The syndicate I belong to owns several others too. There are few things more satisfying than sitting on one's veranda, knowing that buckets of gold are being pulled from the river a stone's throw away. Some old-timers are nostalgic for the old days, but I'd sooner forget those years of toiling through rain, sleet and frost with a shovel and a tin pan." Vern slapped Charlie on the back. "Mind you, the paperwork drives me to despair. Come and join me for a cool drink. I'm eager to hear what you're up to."

They settled into comfortable chairs in the shade of the overhanging roof. Dewer brought out a jug of lemonade and two glasses on a silver tray. She poured it without spilling a drop but touched the bottom of each glass with a starched white napkin, just to be sure. Then she glided off, only to return with a tiered cake stand. Delicate finger sandwiches decorated the bottom tier, while dainty cakes graced the top. Charlie marvelled at the ability of a good maid to anticipate her employer's needs. He smiled his thanks, to her surprise.

When the maid withdrew to stand by the French doors, Charlie leaned over to his host. "Wherever did you find a marvel like Dewer in the middle of Central Otago?"

Vern took two of the little sandwiches and mashed them together, before shoving them into his mouth. "Dewer has been with us ever since we married and set up this house. She had a good reference. Lord knows what brought her to Clyde. I don't much enjoy the fancy stuff, but Constance thinks she's an angel sent by God to do her bidding."

Charlie didn't doubt it. The transformation of Connie, a barmaid at a seedy hotel, to Mrs Constance Summerfield, the wealthy doyenne of Clyde society, cannot have been easy. He held back a chuckle at the thought of the prim Miss Dewer teaching the coarse barmaid how to be a lady. Which knife to use for fish, when to dab one's mouth with a napkin, how to round one's vowels. He wasn't sure who he felt most sorry for, Connie or the maid. It cannot have been easy for Dewer either, serving a woman she undoubtedly felt was inferior to her.

"I hope you don't mind me calling on you, Vern," Charlie said.

Vern looked Charlie straight in the eyes. "I heard about your encounter with my son, of course. Nathaniel needed to be taught a hard lesson. He must learn not to hold grudges or expect success to be handed to him on a plate. My success may stem from a lucky

112

gold strike, but it came after years of hard graft. When I did make a decent find, I didn't waste it on drink or gambling – I invested it in the new business of dredging and the ever-reliable business of running a hotel." He waved a hand behind him. "All this doesn't happen by luck alone."

"No, it doesn't. You can be rightly proud of what you have achieved." Charlie knew some people looked down on the Summerfield family, but plenty of miners had struck it lucky only to squander their success. Vern and Connie were different. "You had diggings up Cromwell way, I believe."

"Bannockburn. A rich source of alluvial gold in the early days, taken over by the big sluicing companies in the end. I was lucky to arrive when the chance was still there for an ordinary man to make his fortune. I'm sure you understand what hard work is like, Charlie. I know you didn't have it easy growing up here, partly because of Nathaniel's bullying, to our shame. But you've made a success of your life, and I've heard your wife is a charming young lady, who isn't easily intimidated."

"Grace is an exceptional person and a far better wife than I ever dreamed of. I have been fortunate beyond measure."

"I know that feeling. Connie isn't everyone's cup of tea, but she's everything to me." Vern put down his empty glass. Dewer glided forward to refill it. "I expect you are here about the gold robbery. Everyone in town is talking about you being here to investigate it."

Charlie squelched the impulse to let out an exasperated sigh. "Believe me, I don't want to be investigating anything on my honeymoon."

"And yet here you are at my house." Vern took another two sandwiches and let the silence extend. When Charlie didn't answer, Vern continued. "I'm happy to answer any questions you might have. I owe you that much after my son's appalling behaviour towards you and your wife."

Charlie took a pair of sandwiches too, to give himself a moment to adjust to this unexpected offer. "It seems I cannot avoid talk of the robbery. I really wouldn't care about a quarter century old crime if it wasn't for the lingering rumours about my grandfather's involvement. I'd like to clear his name, once and for all. And, if I am honest, the £500 reward is not something a newly married man can ignore. Not that I think there's the least chance of claiming it."

"For what it is worth, I never believed your grandfather was involved, despite the gold traces on his sack-barrow. Lee Hope was a fine man. He would have been proud of what you've achieved, Charlie."

"Thank you, Vern. It's only ever a minority who judge a man by his appearance rather than his character, but they are often louder than the rest of us."

"Don't I know it. Connie too. She's had to fight prejudice to get where she is today."

Charlie began his questioning with a simple statement of fact. "Your wife was one of the few people who might have seen the robbers that night. She was outside the Molyneux Hotel taking a breath of fresh air around midnight, according to the police interview notes, but saw nothing. You were in the miners' camp at Bannockburn that night, I believe, as witnessed by a fellow miner."

Vern let out a chuckle. "Why do I have the feeling you don't believe our statements?"

"I would prefer to hear it in your own words," Charlie said. "Perhaps your wife has subsequently recalled a minor point that did not seem relevant at the time. Or perhaps she did see something but was too scared to report it, what with her being in a vulnerable position."

"Is that a delicate way of saying Connie was pregnant and frightened of what might happen to her and the baby if she admitted to seeing the robbers?" Vern sat back and sipped lemonade, his eyes never leaving Charlie. "Both true. Connie saw nothing that night, but we both feared for her safety if the robbers found out she might have seen them. In fact, she went inside around midnight, and the robbery took place between about one o'clock and four o'clock in the morning, as I understand it."

"Did she fear anyone in particular?" Charlie asked.

"I think it is fair to say that Jake Blackthorn's name was the first on everyone's lips once news of the robbery broke later that morning. He is not a man I would care to cross."

"I know the feeling."

"I suspect you already know that I was with Connie that night," Vern said. "I asked a friend to give me an alibi, because I knew how it would look if I was known to be in Clyde. In fact, I was in town to beg Connie to marry me. I had known her since her days in Cromwell and visited her regularly when she moved to Clyde to let her know I still loved her. She's a fine woman, Charlie, despite what people think. A hard worker, almost always cheerful and good fun, and able to turn her hand to anything. People are only intimidated by her because she holds them to the high standard she has set for herself."

This glowing account of Connie didn't quite match general perceptions, but Charlie got the feeling Vern meant it. Women of strong character often had more than their share of detractors, as Charlie well knew. Grace had been called "unnatural" and worse, for daring to be the first woman to train as a doctor.

"I know your wife has achieved a lot of good works for the people of this town over the years."

"She has. Connie was never, as many people imply, a woman of low virtue. Many miners and other men were pursuing her, but I knew she loved me. I had asked her to marry me many times, but this time I had struck gold. Sensible woman that she was, she wouldn't have hitched herself to a life of poverty. She's more of a lady than folk give her credit for. Better than I deserved, no doubt. I'm a lucky man."

"You struck gold before the robbery?" Charlie had been under the impression the gold strike came later.

115

"Yes, but I kept the strike quiet while I worked the find until all the gold was gone. Men like Jake Blackthorn roam the diggings looking for gold to steal. We all had secret places to stash our finds, but loose lips were still dangerous. Many a miner bragged about a find over one whisky too many, only to wake up a poor man again. Once I heard about the gold robbery, I had even more reason to keep quiet. As you can imagine, it was not the time to boast of new-found riches. Connie and I got married on the quiet and lived a simple life until Nathaniel was born. Gradually, I made it known that I had found gold. Over the next few years, we moved into a better home, bought a few pieces of furniture, invested in a gold dredging syndicate."

"Did you see anyone the night of the robbery, Vern?"

"Does it sound too trite to say I only had eyes for the woman who had finally agreed to be my wife? How did you know I was in Clyde, by the way?"

"A man staying in the Molyneux Hotel had an injury that kept him awake," Charlie said. "He saw you in the street and was supposed to report the sighting to the police, but he failed to do so."

"I'm glad he didn't. I don't mind admitting I feared Jake. The robbers had a key. If they didn't get it off the guard, then Jake was the most likely man to have access to it. Did you know the guard of the gold lock-up was Jake's brother? He died that night, poor sod."

"I did know, and Jake has certainly never forgotten it. Did you have any specific reason to suspect Jake?"

"No, and I changed my mind when I heard that both the police and Jake had visited the Yarwood cottage so soon after the robbery."

"Heard from whom?" Charlie had heard Sylvester hint at Jake's visit to Ezra, but he wanted to know if other people knew too.

"A fellow miner," Vern said.

116

"Sylvester Healey?"

Vern shot a sideways look at him. "You've been busy, Charlie."

Charlie took that as a confirmation. "What did you make of it?"

"Probably the same as you. Either Ezra Yarwood was one of the robbers or he knew something. I wondered if Jake was up to his old tricks – threatening Ezra in order to take a share of the gold rather than risking his own hide by committing the robbery. Ezra disappeared the day after. I'm sure you can put two and two together."

"You wondered if Jake had killed Ezra so he could take the gold for himself."

"Exactly right, Charlie. I'm not proud of keeping my mouth shut about the two of them, but I had Connie and our unborn child to think of. I'm glad I was silent now. Jake cannot have been involved, as he is by no means a man of wealth and still having to resort to larceny, by all accounts."

"What did Connie think of Jake and Ezra?" Charlie asked.

"Surprisingly, Connie distrusted Ezra more than Jake. Ezra was a real charmer. Women loved him, but he had the morals of a viper. He was wooing Connie, and I feared I had no chance, but she rejected him and chose me. Anyway, our fretting was all for nothing. Ezra vanished, and we later heard the robber was a stranger from another town."

"It must have been a relief when the man from Arrowtown was arrested."

"It was. I no longer had to look over my shoulder in case Jake was watching us. We built our new life and tried to ignore the ongoing whispers about the source of our wealth."

"The man arrested was Zachary Dawson," Charlie said. "Did you know he had been a partner of Ezra's in the past?"

Vern shook his head. "I don't remember, but I would have heard about it at the time, I suppose, if it was generally known about town."

"Did you know Zachary Dawson at all, Vern, either directly or by reputation? Dawson probably passed through Cromwell from time to time, because he had a sister there. He certainly passed through on the night of the robbery, Cromwell being on the route to Arrowtown."

"If I ever met the man, I don't recall him. A constant stream of men passed through the diggings. It was hard to keep track. I suppose I might have met the sister if she was married and using a different surname, but it is unlikely. I worked all the hours I could on my claim and only went into Cromwell to drink."

"Was Connie from Cromwell too? I wonder if she knew Dawson's sister?"

Vern was watching Charlie over the rim of his glass. "I doubt it. Connie moved from Cromwell to Clyde a few months before the robbery. Oh, the hours I spent traipsing back and forth to see that woman, trying to convince her to marry me. I do believe she loved me, but Connie would have been a fool to marry an impoverished miner when there were men with gold in their pockets after her. She was a looker, my Connie, and no fool. We were all after her – me, Ezra, Jake, Sylvester, and many others."

Vern dug in his pocket for a penny and flipped it to Charlie. The surface was rubbed almost flat. "I flipped that penny the morning before I struck gold to decide where to dig next. I flipped it again to decide if I would beg Connie to marry me one last time. It's my lucky penny, because it brought me a fortune and a wife. I put it in my pocket every day as a reminder that our lives turn on arbitrary twists of fate. If the coin had fallen tails rather than heads, I could be in Sylvester's shoes now."

Charlie tossed the penny back. "You were all friends once. How did the other miners take your sudden wealth and your successful wooing of Connie?"

Vern shrugged. "Every miner has to learn to deal with disappointment. Some men are lucky, others strike out. I have helped them over the years. Sylvester especially. Forgiven his bar debts, given him work where I could and supplies to see him through the hard times. Jake was a different story. He'd have spat on my charity. The rest are long gone. Gold mining is run by the big dredging and sluicing companies these days. A few men still try their luck the old way, but nobody I know."

Charlie reached over to shake Vern's hand. "Thank you for your time, Vern. I appreciate your candour."

"Sorry I couldn't be more help. Best of luck to you, lad. Watch your back."

"Always." Charlie stood up to leave.

The front door to the house banged, shaking the building.

"Vern! Where are you?"

"Connie," Vern mouthed at Charlie unnecessarily.

Her foghorn voice was moving to the sitting room, but was probably audible from across the river. "That intolerable MacEwen woman made a fool of me at my charity event. Introduced me to a new girl, implying she was a potential match for Nathaniel. The girl seemed like a proper lady but blow me down if she didn't turn out to be the wife of that Chinese boy. You know, the policeman's son."

Vern, his eyes wide with embarrassment, turned a scarlet face on his visitor. "I'm so sorry."

Charlie smiled back. "I'll just be running along, shall I? Perhaps best if I go around the side of the house."

Vern nodded his thanks before scrambling for the French doors. "Coming, Connie –" Whatever his next words were going to be, they were drowned out by his wife.

"The girl was perfectly civil, but, honestly, you can't tell me a proper lady would marry a boy like that. I never could forgive him for giving our Nathaniel that black eye at school. No surprise to me that he was drummed out of the police force last year. Dewer,

119

what are my best crystal glasses and cake stand doing on the outside table? Fetch them in at once."

"Yes, ma'am," Dewer said. "Mr Summerfield had a guest, ma'am."

Dewer must have been close by because she stepped out onto the veranda seconds later, catching sight of Charlie, who had failed to leave. Being caught eavesdropping by the help was never a good idea. Being dragged before Constance Summerfield for the offence would be completely mortifying. He put a finger to his lips and hoped for the best.

"What visitor? Why didn't you tell me we were expecting company, Vern?" Connie's steps advanced towards the French doors.

Vern stepped into the doorway, blocking her path. "Only a business associate who dropped by for a quick word. He's gone now." The doors closed behind Vern, muffling their words, especially as Connie was speaking more quietly now that she was within spitting distance of her husband.

With any chance of an informative interview with Connie Summerfield now out of the question, Charlie tried to work out how he could escape without being seen. He'd have to go all the way around the house to get the stables. Fortunately, Dewer gathered up the glasses and walked past him, giving him an almost imperceptible nod to indicate she wouldn't tell on him to her mistress.

Just when he thought he was safe, the French doors opened again, and Connie's voice came through loud and clear. "Really, Vern, why would I want the doors closed on such a fine day? What's the matter with you? Come out onto the veranda. You won't believe what I heard after Pyke's wife left."

This he had to hear. Charlie had seconds to find a hiding place. Did he have time to duck behind the low hedge? No, too far, and too mortifying if he was caught on his knees, listening. Dewer had reached another doorway further along the house. She tipped her head at him to follow, bless her. Charlie fled as fast as tiptoeing

120

allowed, ducking into the doorway as Connie stepped onto the veranda. He swallowed his pride and hid behind the door frame.

"Apparently, the Pyke boy and his wife attacked our son the very night they arrived. Outrageous. Pyke, I can understand – of course he's jealous of Nathaniel's success. But the wife? Acts like the perfect little lady in company, but word has it she fought like an alley-cat. She slashed our boy with a broken bottle, if you can believe such a thing."

Vern did his best, to his credit. "Connie, dear, you have it all wrong. Nathaniel attacked them."

"Don't be ridiculous, Vern. Who told you that?"

"There were two dozen witnesses, at least. And need I remind you, it is Charlie Pyke who has made an excellent marriage and a fine success of his career, not Nathaniel."

"Poppycock. You can't fool me. I saw right through Mrs Grace Pyke's pretty gown and city manners. It wouldn't surprise me if Julia MacEwen had dressed up the little tart as a lady just to vex me. In fact, I told Julia so to her face, in no uncertain terms. If I see that girl again, I won't be held responsible for my actions."

"Really, my dear, I do wish you would try to get along with Julia MacEwen. And I'm sure the new Mrs Pyke is perfectly lovely."

Connie ignored her husband and continued her tirade. "As for that Pyke boy, you'll do well to remember he is a detective now. If he comes sniffing around my house, I'll be sending him off with a blast of shotgun pellets in his backside. You're too naïve by half, Vern, and I don't want you talking to him."

"Enough, Connie," Vern ordered. "We need to have a serious talk with Nathaniel. He's gone too far this time, and if we don't check his behaviour, it will only get worse."

"How can you believe a bunch of drunkards against the word of our son, Vern?"

"Because he is not the saint you make him out to be. I know he's been stealing from the till at the Molyneux too. The takings haven't matched the amount of alcohol sold for months. I tackled Nathaniel about it, and I'm sure he was lying when he denied it. I tell you, Connie, one more problem with that boy and I'll disown him."

There was a moment's ominous silence, in which Charlie held his breath, before Connie exploded.

"How dare you! After all I've done for you. I've lied for you under oath, for heaven's sake. You'd be nothing without me, Vernon Summerfield."

"Don't push me, Connie. I've been loyal to you through good times and bad, no matter what. Do you think you'd have clawed your way to the top of society without my backing?"

Charlie had heard enough. He had hoped for a deeper insight into Constance Summerfield's thoughts, but the main lesson from his eavesdropping was that they had made another enemy, albeit through no fault of their own. Still, it did sound as though Connie had something to hide. Was it only that Vern had been in Clyde the night of the robbery, or had the two of them been up to more than a romantic proposal?

Dewer had deposited the tray and returned. "I'll show you another way out, Mr Pyke."

"I would very much appreciate it, Miss Dewer. Or is it Mrs Dewer?"

"Miss."

The single word carried a hint of sadness. Love lost, perhaps. Dewer's lined face indicated she must be close to fifty years old, but the fine shape of her bones suggested she might have been a beauty in her youth.

"Thank you for your discretion, Miss Dewer," Charlie said. "Mr and Mrs Summerfield are very lucky to have retained your exemplary services for so long, especially when ..." How to suggest working for Constance Summerfield must be a trial without being offensive? "... especially when a great deal of forbearance may occasionally be called for."

"The Lord tests the righteous, and we show our true worth by our response." Dewer said the words with reverence but followed them with another hint of a smile. "Besides, she pays me well, sir, especially for managing so small a household in such an idyllic location. I have saved enough to have a dignified life when I am too old to work. I can ask no more than that."

Again, Charlie reflected on the quirks of fate that had led this genteel woman to serve an ill-mannered barmaid, as Dewer guided him around a corridor and out a side door. The stable boy was already waiting with Nyx and Blaze. Perhaps he was used to guests departing soon after the lady of the house came home. Charlie left them both with a token of his thanks. It wasn't much, but it would buy a few candles for Miss Dewer to read by when her time of rest finally came.

Nyx and Blaze were rested, so he mounted and set off at a fast trot. Nyx settled into a steady canter once they reached the river path, and Charlie's thoughts turned to whether he could trust Vern's account. The truth was, he wanted to believe him. Charlie was tired of distrusting everyone he met in his old hometown. Vern had seemed genuinely open and hospitable, but was that simply clever misdirection? If the latter, he was an exceptional liar.

And then there was the formidable Mrs Constance Summerfield. Charlie hadn't failed to note that Dewer referred to being paid by Mrs Summerfield, and Connie had called it "my" house. It might mean nothing more than the unusual balance of power between Mr and Mrs Summerfield, but there was another option. Had the Summerfield's wealth come from Connie rather than Vern, and been conveniently disguised as a lucky gold strike? Not that Charlie had the least shred of evidence of either of the Summerfields being involved. In fact, he had much less cause to suspect them now that he had heard Vern's account.

Charlie left Nyx to negotiate the track while he considered his next move. His chief concern was not to leave Grace alone again – not near Jake Blackthorn, or the Yarwood property, or indeed anywhere in town. On the other hand, he needed more information

– information he could trust, instead of more hearsay and lies. Grace had promised to return to his parents' house after seeing Matilda Trent, so she ought to be safe for now, at least until Charlie had sent a couple of telegrams.

He nudged Nyx into a gallop. Blaze raced beside them, having recovered admirably from her days stuck under the cottage. A dog in its element had an unfettered joy for life that Charlie could only envy, although flying along on Nyx's back gave him a feeling of euphoria that came close, as did spending time alone with Grace. Not for the first time, he cursed himself for being drawn into this investigation when there were far more desirable ways to spend a honeymoon.

Chalk and Cheese

Grace had turned her back on Charlie's wave with firm determination, even though she was worried about how he would be received at the Summerfield's residence.

She had a sudden, unfathomable urge to skip – an activity she hadn't indulged in for over a decade. In a pretty cotton dress, holding a wicker basket covered with a checked cloth, she felt quite the country lass. The fresh air and sun had already put a glow on her cheeks, despite her straw hat. A pleasant change after her usual days spent in dim lecture theatres and hospital wards.

The Trent farmhouse was not far down the lane, which was a pleasant walk past green fields studded with wildflowers and bordered by neat dry-stone walls. The basket held the cakes she had bought to share with Matilda and her family. They could make their choice between lemon cake and Victoria sponge, and Charlie would have to settle for the leftovers, if any.

The Trent's dairy farm appeared to be flourishing. A sizeable herd of dairy cows cropped the grass, which was so green that a water race must pass nearby, unless the water came from a spring or the pond Grace could see beyond the house. The Trent's home looked similar in size to Rose Cottage from a distance, but, as Grace drew closer, she could see that it had been extended out the back to provide more space for a large family. A stone building behind the cottage presumably served as a barn, milking shed and dairy.

Grace stepped between white-painted veranda posts and pots of marigolds, and knocked on the door, her thoughts filled with the prospect of a pleasant chat to Matilda Trent. A less threatening house could scarcely be imagined.

The pretty frilled curtains in the front room shifted for a moment, then heavy footsteps stomped towards the door. Broad shoulders filled the doorframe. Bob Trent, without his shotgun.

Grace took an instinctive step back out of his reach. "Good afternoon, Mr Trent." He gave her a discouraging scowl and made no acknowledgement of their previous brief encounter. "I'm Charlie Pyke's wife. We're staying in Rose Cottage."

"Aye. I remember."

Grace tried a smile. "I'm merely paying a social call, Mr Trent. I met your wife at the fundraiser this morning and wondered if she would like to come over to our cottage for afternoon tea."

Bob's eyes narrowed as he looked her up and down. "She ain't home yet, and she'll be busy when she returns." He started to shut the door.

Grace took a deep breath and persevered out of sheer stubbornness. "I had been hoping to buy some of your famous cheese too."

"Matilda's not back from the meeting," Bob grumbled. "God knows what's taking her so long. Aways busy with charity work, my wife, when there's work to be done here."

"I know her organisational skills are valued and I expect her hard work helping to organise the horticultural show will pay off when you gain new customers. All the ladies say her cheese is delicious."

"Our dairy is already known as the best in the county," Bob said. "No need for a village trophy to prove it."

Grace forced her lips into another smile. How could the delightful Matilda have married this man? They were chalk and cheese. The thought of cheese recalled her supposed reason for the call, but Grace found herself unwilling to stay any longer. "Of course. Thank you for your time, Mr Trent. I won't keep you from your work."

"Wait. Do you want to buy cheese or not?"

Grace was not at all sure that she did. The prospect of being alone in the dairy shed with Bob Trent was not an appealing one, but he was waiting for a response. "If it's no trouble, Mr Trent."

"Come in."

Bob led the way into the kitchen, where two girls aged about twelve and fourteen were chasing each other around, throwing soap suds and squealing. They fell on the floor, giggling, when they spotted Grace.

Grace braced for Bob to start shouting, but his face crinkled into a grin. "Oi, you two little scallywags are supposed to be doing the dishes, not washing the floor. Where's Millie? I asked her to stir the pot while I answered the door."

A girl of about seventeen wandered into the room with her nose in a book. Millie cast a curious glance at Grace and threw her arms around her father. "I was stirring it, Papa, but I got to a good part in the story."

Bob Trent gave Grace a helpless shrug. "Right. You two finish the dishes. Millie, stir that pot or the dinner will burn. And tell Etta that she's on milking tonight. I'm taking Mrs Pyke to buy cheese, and I don't want to return to Armageddon."

"Yes, Papa," they chorused, flashing a trio of identical grins.

Grace followed Bob around to the dairy shed, feeling a new respect for this outwardly gruff man with a soft heart.

The interior of the solid stone dairy was cool and spotless. A glance into the milking shed had told Grace that it was spotless too, or as near spotless as one could make a shed where dairy cows stood every day.

"You'll be wanting cheddar," Bob said, going to a large square block of cheese on the shelf. "Keeps better than the other muck." He waved a knife toward little rounds of white cheese in the corner of the shelf, before waving the knife at Grace. "How much do you want?"

"What type is the other cheese? It's always nice to try something new."

127

"Some type of French cheese my Matilda heard about from a foreigner. Gooey in the middle and smells like armpits on wash day. It's expensive."

A laugh interrupted his unappetising sales pitch. "Bob, my darling, how many times have I told you not to put customers off my award-winning cheese?" Matilda Trent shuffled in and leaned against the wall with an audible sigh of relief. "Hello again, Mrs Pyke."

Bob took out a clean handkerchief and dabbed the sweat off his wife's brow. "Matilda, you oughtn't be walking in the heat in your condition. I said I'd come to get you in the buggy."

Grace suddenly realised her visit had delayed Bob from this vital duty. No wonder he had been surly. "Hello again, Mrs Trent. I'm afraid I distracted your husband by dropping in unannounced to buy cheese, after hearing it praised as the best in the region."

Matilda brushed aside her husband's ministrations with a peck on the cheek. "In that case, perhaps I could interest you in both types of cheese, Mrs Pyke? I'll take over here, Bob. You deal with the girls. I hope they've been behaving."

"Little angels, as ever," her husband said.

"Definitely some of each type, Mrs Trent. How could I resist?" Grace was willing to bet that Matilda's infectious smile had been responsible for more cheese sales than any number of awards.

Grace bought a Charlie-sized hunk of hard cheddar and a small round of gooey goodness, tucking them into her basket. Bob had gone about his work, so she asked Matilda if she could have a word. "Come next door for tea if you'd like. I bought a delicious cake at the fundraiser."

"Can we talk here, Mrs Pyke? I feel as if I cannot walk another step. I'd invite you to the house, but everyone says your husband is investigating the old gold robbery and Bob gets cross when the subject comes up."

"Of course, Mrs Trent. I really would like to have you over for tea when you feel up to it, although I must admit I intended to ask a few questions as well. My husband has been pushed into the investigation against his better judgement. It seems some people refuse to let the robbery be forgotten."

"Don't I know it." Matilda plopped down onto a stool and gestured for Grace to do the same. "Lord knows, I'll be happy when this baby is born. I'm sure it must be a boy. None of my girls kicked this hard." She brushed a hand over her round belly, her smile so wide it lit up her entire face. "Ask whatever you wish and please call me Matilda."

"The offer of cake is still there." Grace flipped the cloth from the basket. "Lemon cake or Victoria sponge."

"I've gone off cake for some weird reason, and cheese too. My dear husband is worried about me, but that's the way I always am when I'm with child." Matilda crossed her hands on the baby bulge and waited with the patience of a Madonna.

Grace felt a twinge of envy at her serenity. "Charlie's grandfather saw you taking the cows in for milking the morning of the robbery, I understand."

"That's right. I wouldn't have noticed Mr Hope if he hadn't called out to wish me a good morning. I was only sixteen and fairly new to the Trent farm at the time, so my attention was firmly fixed on my job. Bob's father was a stickler for everything being done just right. I'm afraid I didn't see anyone else or anything out of the ordinary that morning."

"Mr Trent must have had great faith in you to leave the herd in your hands at such a young age," Grace said.

Matilda waved the compliment away. "I grew up on a farm up the valley, the oldest of seven children. The farm couldn't support us all, which was why I came here to work for wages. I couldn't afford to lose my position by making mistakes, because my earnings helped keep my family going."

"They must be proud of you, Matilda. I hope that time improved their situation."

"It has, especially when Bob offered to marry me when I turned eighteen. He's a good man, my Bob, once you get past his tough shell."

Grace weighed her next words carefully, treading a fine line between upsetting Matilda and finding out about her relationship with Ezra Yarwood. "Your husband is lovely with the girls. He's a better man than your neighbour was, by all accounts."

Matilda's grimace spoke volumes. "Ezra Yarwood was nice to me when I first arrived. I thought him quite charming and was sorry he didn't come to visit his mother more often. But it wasn't long before I dreaded his visits. Not that he did anything wrong – he just kept watching me and creeping up on me when I was busy, until I feared what he was after. It wasn't only my youthful imagination, because Bob noticed too and warned him off with a pitchfork. Ezra got the message, and I didn't see him again."

"Horrible for you."

"It's a terrible thing to say, but I was relieved when he disappeared," Matilda said. "I was sorry for his mother, of course, but she told me once that Ezra had left her enough money to live in comfort. The least he could do when he hightailed it out of town with a fortune, but more than I expected of him all the same."

"It sounds as though you are sure Ezra was one of the robbers."

"Not entirely sure, Grace. But the police dug up his garden, didn't they? And sometimes Mrs Yarwood would say things that made me think he was guilty. Little comments, like she hoped Ezra was enjoying a wonderful life, implying he was rich."

"Do you think Mrs Yarwood ever heard from her son, Matilda?"

"I honestly don't know. Mrs Yarwood is prone to rambling, and it's been getting steadily worse. Sometimes I think she lives in a world of her own imagining. I fear what will happen to her if

130

Ezra doesn't return soon. We help her out where we can, as a neighbour ought to, but I fear she may have to come and live with us, eventually." Matilda gave Grace a despairing shake of her head. "Bob would have a fit if I suggested it. We've little enough room for the six of us, without a baby on the way. I may have to turn into one of those dreadful matrons who seeks out worthy sons-in-law for my girls as soon as they are old enough to wed. Etta is twenty-one and drawing plenty of looks from the young men. As long as she doesn't wed Nathaniel Summerfield, I'll be happy."

Grace couldn't help the chuckle that escaped her lips. "I expect you heard of my encounter with him."

Matilda grinned back. "I salute your triumph, Grace. I only wish you'd kicked the little toad harder."

"I'm sure your Etta can do better than Nathaniel Summerfield. Julia MacEwen is after a wife for her oldest son, Hamish." Grace wished she'd left the thought unspoken when she saw the horror on Matilda's face. "I'm sorry, Matilda. That was terribly presumptuous of me."

Matilda recovered her good humour in a flash. "Oh, Grace, you are a breath of fresh air. I can tell you're not a country girl. Mr MacEwen owns thousands of acres of land. His wife will be searching for a daughter-in-law amongst their own kind."

Grace opened her mouth and shut it again, rather than argue that the Trent family were landowners too, even if only a few acres.

Matilda picked up on her confusion. "Lovely as Mr and Mrs MacEwen are, Grace, they're *gentry*. It's like asking the Prince of Wales to marry the daughter of a shopkeeper."

"Oh. I'm sorry if I offended you, Matilda. I'm not sure what came over me. I usually abhor matchmakers."

Matilda patted her hand. "I'm not in the least offended, only amused. One of the afflictions of newlyweds is the desire to see others as happy as you are. Just wait until you have a baby. Whether you mean to or not, I guarantee you will find yourself extolling the glories of motherhood to your childless friends."

Grace knew what she meant. Her friend Molly had had her first baby only a few days ago, and she had already forgotten the pain of childbirth in favour of singing the praises of the most adorable baby in the world.

"Please come for tea another day, Grace. I'd love to chat with you, but I am feeling exhausted after walking in the heat. Not that I'd admit it to Bob. At least I have all my girls to help with the chores this time."

Grace helped her new friend to her feet and across the cobbles to the cottage, before she went on her way, feeling revived by Matilda's cheerful attitude to life. Grace would take pleasure in telling her own husband that she had come to no harm on her visit to the Trent farm, against his better judgement.

At the gate, her feet turned back to town. She had promised Charlie she would return to the Pyke's cottage after visiting the dairy farm and she was happy to comply. A pleasant afternoon interrogating Jasmine about Charlie's boyhood deeds and misdeeds appealed far more than being alone, especially as Jasmine Pyke was the type of woman to have a jug of freshly squeezed lemonade wrapped in a damp cloth in the coolest part of the house.

A few minutes later, her daydream of cool drinks and laughter was interrupted by the sound of a spade making slow thrusts into the earth behind the thick hawthorn hedge in front of the Yarwood's property. Grace looked back down the road to see if anyone was coming, before kneeling down to look through a gap in the hedge.

The old woman digging in the vegetable patch reminded Grace a little of her Great-Aunt Anne. Not by looks, for Anne was thin and this woman was stout, but by her resolute determination to do a task that was clearly beyond her physical capabilities. As Grace watched, her fingers tingling with the desire to rush to the woman's aid, Mrs Yarwood plunged the spade in at an awkward angle and fell. She lay in the dirt, cursing up a storm.

Grace rushed to the gate and climbed over, rubbing a long streak of grime onto her pretty summer dress. If her mother was here, she would be rolling her eyes at her daughter's inability to get through a day without ruining her nice clothes. Grace had long ago given up any hope of achieving this simple goal. She raced across the uneven ground, adding a layer of grass seeds and pollen to the dirt. The property must have been beautiful once, with a large garden and fruit trees, but it had regressed towards a wilderness over the years.

Mrs Yarwood lay on the ground, still writhing and cursing. Which was fine by Grace, who knew that still and silent accident victims were the ones to worry about. When she stumbled to the woman's side, Grace saw that the hem of Mrs Yarwood's dress had been caught by the spade, pinning her to the ground. Grace removed the spade and helped the old woman upright.

Mrs Yarwood sagged in her arms. "Ezra? Is that you? Have you finished mending the wall?"

"My name is Grace, Mrs Yarwood. I'll take you back to your house."

Grace withheld her surname, as Charlie had said Mrs Yarwood held a grudge against Charlie's grandfather and therefore the entire Pyke family, because Lee Hope's statement to the police made Ezra the chief suspect in the robbery. Lee Hope had simply spoken the truth – that he saw Ezra in the garden with a spade early on the morning of the robbery. However, that wouldn't stop Mrs Yarwood from blaming Lee Hope's testimony for her son's disappearance.

Mrs Yarwood appeared to be startled by her voice. She thrust her face close to Grace and frowned, which left her heavy forehead jutting forward over cloudy blue eyes. "Are you Ezra's girl?"

Grace tried not to flinch at her proximity, realising the cloudy eyes meant the old woman's eyesight was failing. "I'm a neighbour. Ezra's not here, but I can help you."

"Ezra's out fixing the wall," Mrs Yarwood repeated with disconcerting certainty. "He'll be in soon."

133

Grace resisted the temptation to ask about Mrs Yarwood's son while she was still dazed. Instead, she assessed her quickly to ensure her patient had no injuries, before helping her along an overgrown path to the cottage, where the veranda roof sagged under the weight of climbing roses run rampant.

The boards of the deck showed signs of rot, but they held the weight of the two women as Grace heaved Mrs Yarwood up the steps and into the house. Inside, the cottage was not as bad as Grace had feared. The sitting room was clean, although it was filled with a jumble of furniture, crocheted blankets, ancient crockery, trinkets, and baskets of wool. Pride in one's home lingered long in a wife's mindset, especially as the cottage represented her husband's rise from poverty to become the owner of a plot of land through his gold mining success.

Grace sat her patient on an armchair and noted the kettle was already simmering on the stove. "Would you like a cup of tea and a slice of lemon cake, Mrs Yarwood? Or would you prefer Victoria sponge?"

The old woman looked at her, puzzled. "Ezra likes lemon cake. So does my husband."

"Mine too," Grace said. "Lemon cake it is."

"Cut big slices for the men."

Grace found a plate and cut several slices, although she knew Mrs Yarwood's son hadn't been seen in almost a quarter of a century and her husband had died even longer ago. Jasmine Pyke had warned Grace it would be a waste of time to talk to the old woman, as her mind was addled. But Grace also knew that old folks with memory problems often recalled long-ago events with more clarity than recent events. She hoped the old lady might also have a diminishing capacity to censor the truth, such as the need to leave out incriminating evidence.

While the tea was brewing and her hostess was busy settling herself in an armchair with what was obviously a favourite blanket over her knees, Grace took the opportunity to peek in the two small rooms off the hall. The two rooms were bedrooms. One of the rooms had a shelf of men's clothes, and various manly accessories, such as a knapsack and shaving kit. All neatly dusted, but clearly unused. Ezra's room, Grace assumed, preserved as it had been all those years ago. She didn't have time to examine the contents, as Mrs Yarwood was waiting for the promised tea and cake.

Mrs Yarwood accepted the offerings without commenting on Grace's brief absence. The old woman reached out a hand to pat Grace's arm. "He loves you, dear."

"Who loves me, Mrs Yarwood?"

"Ezra, of course. He'll be back soon. I'm going to make a cake for your wedding."

Grace waited to see if Mrs Yarwood would continue, but the old woman was staring at the cake in her hand as if unsure how it had got there. Grace tried another tack. "Has Ezra gone away?"

"He'll be back soon." Mrs Yarwood bit into the lemon cake and didn't say anything else until she had finished the slice. Then she took up the cup of tea and leaned in close to Grace to whisper a secret. "The Chinaman saw him."

"Is that why Ezra went away, Mrs Yarwood?"

The cup trembled in Mrs Yarwood's hand, spilling tea into the saucer. "I … I don't know."

Her eyes narrowed as she squinted at Grace. "Ezra was scared of him. He wanted the gold. All because that Chinaman saw my boy with a spade." Her sudden burst of anger turned into a sob.

Grace dared not move in case she distracted the old woman from the past. "Which man was Ezra scared of? The Chinaman or another man?"

Mrs Yarwood's face crumpled. "The other man. Blackjack."

"Black Jake? Jake Blackthorn? Is that who you mean, Mrs Yarwood?"

The old woman turned on her with a fierce intensity. "Who are you? You're one of them, aren't you? After the gold. How many times do I have to tell you, it's not here!" She pushed herself out of the chair and stumbled to a cupboard, wrenching it open to

135

reveal a shotgun. Her voice rose to a screech. "Get out! Get out of my house! The gold's not here."

Grace grabbed her basket and fled. Her spine tingled, knowing the shotgun was pointing in her direction, but trusting to her greater speed and the poor eyesight that would hinder Mrs Yarwood's aim. The shotgun never fired. Grace tumbled over the gate, tearing the hem of her dress, and threw herself down behind the hawthorn hedge to regain her breath.

She had no idea how much time had passed in agonising silence, but as Grace crouched there, ready to run if necessary, she had the prickling feeling of eyes watching her. She pretended to be winded, but her eyes flicked back and forth along the road. There! A branch swaying more than the gentle breeze could stir. A darker shadow crouched within the greenery, reminding Grace of her impression that there had been an eavesdropper at the Pyke's cottage this morning. It seemed she was out of the frying pan and into the fire. How she wished Charlie was with her, or Blaze or Nyx, or anyone.

Grace rose from the ground and brushed herself down. The shadow was between her and the Pyke's house. The only option was to go onwards, towards Rose Cottage, and pray that Charlie was there. If not, she would lock herself in and arm herself, if only she could make it that far.

She started walking, keeping a firm grip on the basket, her only weapon. A light wicker basket and a Victoria sponge were not even close to her weapons of choice, but she had foolishly left behind her leg holster, where she kept her knife, thinking it inappropriate when attending a ladies' morning tea. When would she learn?

Glancing back, Grace saw the shadow moving down the tree. He was following. The watcher was the wrong shape to be Jake Blackthorn. Could it be that slightly creepy old miner, Sylvester Healey, who always seemed to be lurking? He had been in the crowd watching the fight last night, and Grace thought she had seen him for a moment outside the community hall this morning as well, although he had slipped away quickly into the shadows. Or was it Nathaniel Summerfield, intent on revenge for his humiliation? Grace picked up her pace, wondering how she had gained so many enemies in such a short time in a small country town.

She willed herself to walk without looking back, relying on the crunch of gravel to warn her of a person approaching. Unless the watcher snuck up on her through the fields. She whirled around, but the only person in sight was Bob Trent, tending to a water trough.

Grace was almost at the track to Rose Cottage when she heard hoofbeats on the road behind her.

In a Stew

Charlie returned directly to town after his visit to Vern Summerfield. His first stop was the post office, where he sent two telegrams. One was to Cromwell and the other was to Alistair Stewart, his partner in the detective agency in Dunedin. In his desperation for new leads, Charlie threw caution, and pennies, to the wind by including a list of all persons of interest, whether probable or not. Alistair had access to police resources in Dunedin and a remarkable number of informants scattered around the countryside from his days as a detective inspector in the police force. It was a faint hope, but one never knew what shaking the trees would reveal.

After he left the post office, Charlie nudged Nyx into a trot. He was eager to get back to his parents' house, where he would collect Grace and borrow the equipment he would need for his trip into the hills tomorrow. He wanted to warn his parents about Jake Blackthorn as well.

Grace hadn't returned from her social call on Matilda Trent. Jasmine assumed Grace must have become engrossed in conversation with Matilda or had returned to Rose Cottage. Charlie didn't want to alarm his parents, so he said goodbye and walked Nyx to the corner. Once out of sight, he urged the mare into a fast trot, with Blaze running beside them.

A sixth sense warned Charlie to approach Rose Cottage as if it was a crime scene with the offender still present. Blaze sensed it too, because her nose sniffed at the ground. She growled and dashed past him towards a peach tree, circling its base and whining. The tree was a perfect place to watch the cottage unseen, which added to Charlie's uneasiness. Blaze headed off again, moving in a darting arc back towards the road. Charlie called her back, assuming the watcher had left when he heard them coming.

The cottage was unnaturally quiet. On such a fine day, Grace should have been outside, lazing under the trees. Even if she was inside, the windows should have been open to let the breeze in. Instead, the door and windows were closed, with the curtains drawn.

Charlie slid from Nyx's back and ran to the cottage, yelling, "Grace!"

The curtain on the front window twitched. The front door crashed open, and there she was, grasping a knife in one hand, her face drained of colour. She dropped the knife and ran into his arms, squeezing the fear out of him.

Charlie lifted her and carried her into the cottage, where he set her on the sofa and held her, promising he would not leave her alone again. They sat for a long time, entwined, until their pulse rates returned to normal.

Finally, Charlie got up to get them both a glass of water. Blaze had settled near the door, reassuring Charlie that the watcher hadn't sneaked back. Grace seemed to have returned to her usual self too, so Charlie pulled the curtains and opened the windows, flooding the room with light and fresh air.

He sat down and took her hand. "What happened, Grace?"

"Someone was watching me. Not Jake Blackthorn. I wondered if it was Nathaniel, coming to seek revenge, or perhaps Sylvester. Mrs MacEwen nearly gave me a heart attack when she drove her buggy up behind me just as I reached the track to the cottage. I was fortunate she stopped by to see me on her way home. Actually, Mrs MacEwen's arrival served a dual purpose, since I wanted to ask her about Matilda Trent."

Charlie would ask for more details about the watcher later, but for now, he was interested in hearing what Mrs MacEwen had to say. "I can't say I was happy with you going to see Matilda alone, no matter how sweet she appears. We oughtn't forget that she was rumoured to have a connection to Ezra."

"That can definitely be ruled out," Grace said. "Well before the robbery, Matilda was actively avoiding Ezra, who had behaved in an ungentlemanly manner towards her. Bob Trent had to scare Ezra off with a pitchfork. Mrs MacEwen confirmed that Matilda refused to have anything to do with Ezra within a short time of her arrival in Clyde, and he avoided her too. Matilda hadn't seen Ezra since Bob scared him off and she saw nothing on the morning of the robbery apart from your grandfather passing by."

"I'm pleased Matilda gave Ezra short shrift. Not that she was ever a likely suspect, even as an accessory." Charlie removed the empty glass Grace was toying with and pulled her into his arms again. "I trust you didn't run into the irascible Bob Trent."

"I did, actually, and it was a revelation. Bob Trent might not be the most charming of men to strangers with misbehaving dogs, but he was a sweetheart with his wife and girls." Grace paused to reflect on her encounter. "I believe he is one of those men who is totally content with his work and family, not seeing the need to seek company outside his own household. I very much doubt he would pursue wealth by criminal means, which suggests he is unlikely to have had anything to do with the robbery either. In fact, Matilda had strong grounds to believe Ezra was one of the robbers, based on her conversations with Ezra's mother."

"I wish we could talk to Mrs Yarwood." Charlie felt a slight movement beside him – no more than a faint flinch, but enough to reveal his wife's reaction. "You did go to see Mrs Yarwood, didn't you, Grace?"

"I didn't mean to, honestly, but she fell over in her garden as I was passing."

"Naturally, you had to see if she was injured."

"Of course. I plied her with lemon cake to get her to talk. She mistook me for 'Ezra's girl' and said Ezra would be back soon to marry me, as he'd promised. Mrs Yarwood mixes up the past and present and has a tenuous grasp on reality. At first, she said Ezra was out mending the wall, but later she implied Ezra had left town in a hurry after being harassed by Jake Blackthorn, who was after the gold. I'm guessing Jake knew Ezra was one of the robbers and pressed him for a share of the fortune, in exchange for not informing on him to the police. Matilda seemed certain that Ezra had fled town with the gold."

Yet again, Charlie marvelled at Grace's ability to extract information from people who would never talk to a detective or the police. "Excellent work, Grace. That version of events matches Sylvester Healey's hint that Jake visited Ezra after the robbery, which Vern Summerfield had also heard. Did Mrs Yarwood say anything else?"

Grace plucked at her dirty, ripped gown. "Right about then, she snapped out of the past and chased me off the property with a shotgun. After an ignominious tumble over the gate, I spotted the man watching me."

Charlie drew her head into his chest. "I'm sorry, Grace. I never should have left you alone. It must have been terrifying."

"It wasn't so bad once I got to the cottage. Mrs MacEwen's arrival probably scared off the watcher. After she left, I locked the door and found a weapon." Her lip trembled, but the moment of vulnerability passed quickly. She smiled up at him. "I almost cried when I saw what you had done – the dinner cooking, the flowers, my mess tidied away – and all I wanted was to have you beside me and forget the world outside."

They shared a quiet moment together, while Charlie struggled to find the right words.

Grace got in first. "Dinner smells wonderful, my darling. I suggest we eat early so we can get an early start tomorrow on our wilderness expedition. I don't want to be riding in the midday sun."

Charlie took one of those long, deep breaths he so often needed to take before confronting one of his wife's wilder notions. "*We*, Grace? If I go out into the hills at all, it will be alone. You will be safe staying with my parents."

Grace crossed her arms. "You promised me you wouldn't leave me again."

He crossed his arms too. "Then I shall stay in Clyde too. Going out there on the off chance of finding an old miner who knew Jake's and Ezra's secrets was always a longshot."

Grace gave him one of those innocent smiles, which he knew would precede an innocent statement he would be incapable of countering. Marriage to a clever woman certainly had its downsides. She uncrossed her arms and leaned up against him, which only made him more suspicious.

"A dear friend of mine has waxed lyrical, repeatedly, about big skies and dramatic landscapes," Grace said. "You wouldn't have me come all this way only to miss out on such rare delights, would you, my love? Besides, it's Sunday tomorrow and I cannot bear the thought of being hounded by a curious church congregation or staying around to risk someone taking potshots at us."

Charlie considered putting his foot down, but he had seen that look on Grace's face too many times to fight it. In fact, he had secretly counted on her stubbornness. He had wanted to take Grace into the hills around Clyde ever since he met her. His favourite person in his favourite place. She was right that she was in more danger in town. But he would have to ensure they were not followed, which meant leaving before daylight to avoid watching eyes.

"I'll get the gear ready." Charlie said the words with feigned resignation and didn't add that he had brought two saddlebags and two sleeping rolls back from his parents' house. As he went out, he gave Blaze her orders. "Stay. Guard Grace."

Charlie returned from the tack shed half an hour later to find that Grace had moved the table out onto the veranda and set it with candles and the least chipped plates. The sun sinking below the western hills, the flickering candles, and the scent of ripe fruit gave him the sensation of being transported to the Garden of Eden. This

142

was the honeymoon he had imagined. Trust Grace to overcome her frightening encounter and rise to the occasion.

Charlie went inside to draw the cork on the wine. When he went to look for his wife to offer her a glass, he found her putting on one of her beautiful new gowns, which had been a wedding present from her parents.

Grace smiled at his lack of words. "We are here to celebrate our new life, husband, and celebrate we will. The water in the washbowl is still hot, but don't be too long. I tasted your delicious stew, and I haven't the resolve to wait much longer for dinner."

He reappeared in his finery and caught Grace up in a slow waltz around the sitting room, to Blaze's bemusement. Tonight would be a night to forget the investigation and enjoy the moment.

That vow lasted only as long as the meal.

Grace drifted into silence, while Charlie thought about what had happened to Ezra Yarwood. Specifically, he was worried by Mrs Yarwood saying Ezra would be back from mending the wall soon. Was that Mrs Yarwood's last memory of her son? If so, it was all the more reason to think Ezra never left town, despite what Matilda believed. The police had found all of his possessions still in his boyhood bedroom, including his knapsack, which lent further weight to the theory. Had Jake Blackthorn lost his temper at Ezra's refusal to divulge where the gold was hidden and killed the golden goose by mistake?

Grace swallowed the mouthful she had been chewing for the past minute or so. "I wonder which woman Ezra intended to marry. Could it have been Connie?"

"Connie agreed to marry Vern Summerfield the night of the robbery. None of the women in Clyde disappeared with Ezra."

"Perhaps Connie agreed to marry Vern because Ezra left her for another woman. You know the old saying – Hell hath no fury like a woman scorned. Especially if Ezra had promised her marriage and a share of the gold, but then reneged."

"Connie must have given up on Ezra before the robbery, because she was already pregnant with Vern's child. From what I overheard at the Summerfield's house, Connie and Vern both have secrets. A word of warning. Connie is angry with us for hurting her sweet, innocent son."

"I know. Connie was furious at Mrs MacEwen for tricking her over my identity. Mrs MacEwen was still shaking when she visited me." Grace paused to slip Blaze a piece of meat. "Did Vern Summerfield tell you anything useful?"

"Vern was surprisingly amenable. He even apologised for his son's appalling behaviour. Vern admitted he was in town the night of the robbery but saw nothing. His gold strike was before the robbery, but he kept it quiet because he feared Jake would come after him or Connie if Jake got wind of sudden riches."

"Can't say I blame him."

"If only we had some hard evidence rather than rumour and hearsay." Charlie pushed his plate away, unable to stomach more food after hearing of the distress he'd unwittingly caused to both Grace and Mrs MacEwen by his return to his hometown. "I fear my presence in town has set a spark to a tinder-dry forest of old resentments."

"It's probably best to have it out in the open, rather than festering like an infected wound. The only remedy is to scrape the wound clean and cauterise the skin." With that less than appealing analogy, Grace gathered up the plates and scraped the leftovers into the dog bowl. The collie snaffled the food up as fast as Grace could scrape. "It seems Blaze appreciates your excellent cooking as much as I do."

She refilled their wine glasses and took hers to the bench seat on the veranda, patting the space beside her. "It's too nice a night to go inside." Grace leaned into her favourite spot, with her head tucked in the hollow of his shoulder. "Where to from here, Detective Pyke?"

"I've sent a telegram to Alistair to gather information on various suspects. If Ezra fled Clyde with a fortune, as Matilda Trent believes, then we need to know where he went."

"And if Ezra was killed here?"

"Then there are two lines of inquiry: the location of his body and the location of the missing gold. I need to make a list of suggestions for my father, starting with another search of the area around the wall Ezra was fixing, as that seems to have been the last task he did before he disappeared. I also want to ask Pa about 'Ezra's girl' and have him request the case files from Cromwell and Arrowtown."

Charlie went inside to make a list of questions for his father, intending to drop it off at his parents' place early the next morning on their way out of town.

Grace was staring out into the gathering darkness when he returned. "Is it possible that your grandfather did see something that hinted at the location of the gold, perhaps without realising what he had seen? I wouldn't ask, except that it strikes me that the rumour your grandfather knew where the gold was hidden seems remarkably persistent."

"Every idea is worth exploring, Grace. But what could Lee Hope have seen that he wouldn't have reported to the police?"

"Maybe he did tell the police, but his observation was considered irrelevant."

"If so, there is no record of it. I'll add it to the list of questions for my father."

"It's hopeless, isn't it? How can we gather evidence and check alibis when the events occurred twenty-four years ago?"

Charlie sighed. "A shame you had to sacrifice the lemon cake to loosen Mrs Yarwood's tongue. Serious contemplation of impossible cases ought to end with something sweet. On the other hand, you did mention an early night, which sounds sweet to me."

"Charlie dearest, would I let you go without? I bought two cakes. The lemon cake worked its magic on Mrs Yarwood, but I'm sure you will condescend to force down a slice of Victoria sponge instead. It's only slightly squashed from its encounter with a hedge."

"Victoria sponge? Mm, perfect. A pity we cannot combine the pleasures."

"Cake in bed? Really, husband, how shockingly decadent." Grace rose from the bench. "I'll get the cake. You see to the dog and lock the door."

Big Sky

The next morning, Grace was woken in what felt like the middle of the night by a rustling sound in the main room of the cottage. Blaze hadn't warned them of an intruder, but nor had the collie lit the candle she could see flickering through the open door of the bedroom. She leaned over to wake Charlie, but his side of the bed was cold.

Grace peeked through the doorway. What on earth was her husband doing up when it was pitch dark outside? She emerged from the bedroom, rubbing her eyes and yawning. "Charlie, I know you are eager to be away, but isn't it the middle of the night?"

"Almost dawn, my love."

How could he be so darn cheerful at this hour? She peered at the saddlebags he was packing by the light of a candle. "There's enough food here to feed us for a week."

"You're not the only one who can swap food for information, my sweet."

Her husband had paused long enough to flash a charming grin in her direction, but Grace refused to be placated by his charms at this hour of the morning. "But what's all the rest of this equipment? Are we going for a ride in the nearby hills or are we mounting an expedition to the interior of deepest, darkest Africa?"

"Bedrolls, billy, shotgun, knife, stove and flint to light it, spare kerosene, water flasks, food for us, feed sacks for the horses, dog food, medical kit, rope." Charlie noted her frown. "Did I explain we will be camping out, not staying in a hotel?"

"Not exactly. I suppose I never thought about it. You did mention stars, but I assumed they were for looking at, not sleeping under." Grace nudged her bare foot into the bedroll, which seemed no thicker than a blanket or two.

"There's nothing more romantic than camping out under the stars, Grace."

"If you say so." Grace could think of ten things more romantic off the top of her head. Starting with a warm, soft bed. But she had insisted on joining the expedition, and it was too late now for regret. "Am I allowed to have breakfast first?"

"Of course. How about you do that while I saddle the horses. I want to get away without the whole town watching."

Quarter of an hour later, they were ready to go. Charlie made one last inspection of the saddlebags and girths and then boosted Grace into Nyx's saddle. She draped a shawl over her shoulders to ward off the early morning chill and said a prayer for a sudden rainstorm of sufficient intensity to end this foolishness.

"It's going to be a lovely day," Charlie said with hearty disregard for the silent prayer. "You'll need a hat when the sun comes up."

Charlie passed her a broad-brimmed hat, which slipped down her forehead and smelled of dust. He stepped back to admire the effect. "Perfect. With you in that dark hat and shawl on a jet-black horse, you'd be hard to spot from a distance in this light."

What light, Grace thought? But her annoyingly perky husband was right. The night had edged from pitch black to ink blue. She could see a yard or two in front of her now. Charlie mounted up and they were off, with Blaze running alongside, looking as eager for adventure as Charlie was. Grace sat upright in the cursed saddle and tried to look serene rather than resigned.

Charlie took the long way into town, along the top of the riverbank, stopping in a grove of trees overlooking the bridge. "It'll only take a moment to deliver the list of matters I'd like my father to investigate. I want my parents to know you're coming with me into the hills too, so they won't worry when you don't arrive."

"Should I come? We ought to apologise for missing church."

"No need." Charlie handed her the shotgun and a cartridge. "Do you know how to use this?"

Grace held it upside down and away from her body. "Point the long end at a bad guy and say 'bang'?"

Before he could reply, she flipped it over, broke it open, inserted the cartridge, clicked it shut, and brought it to her shoulder with her cheek pressed to the stock so she could check the sight line – all in the blink of an eye. "I may not be a country girl, but I am not entirely without skills."

"You terrify me sometimes, my darling."

Grace shrugged with feigned nonchalance. He didn't need to know that she had watched him clean and test the shotgun last night. She had never held a shotgun before, let alone pulled the trigger, and wasn't about to start now, because the chances of misfiring and shooting a loved one were far too high. Her faithful knife, strapped inside her boot, was all the weapon she wanted. All the same, she would keep the gun loaded until Charlie returned.

His teeth flashed white in the growing light, and then he was gone. Grace swept her gaze from side to side, seeking the slightest hint of movement and listening for the tiniest crack of a twig under a boot. Even so, Charlie's return caught her by surprise. If Nyx and Blaze hadn't perked up their ears, she wouldn't have detected his arrival.

Charlie stowed a parcel with a deliciously yeasty aroma into the bulging saddlebags, remounted Erebus, and guided their party down to the Clyde bridge. Nyx took it in her stride, but Erebus snorted and skittered at the sound of his hooves on the bridge above the rush of fast flowing water below. Charlie didn't appear to notice.

The road followed a terrace of high ground down the river. In the distance, a rooster crowed. Then the world was silent, apart from the steady clop of hooves.

Dawn unfolded gradually. At first, only the jagged mountain tops flared red and orange in the rising sun, but slowly the light swept downwards, revealing golden folds of land running alongside the valley floor. Grace's mood soared. Perhaps her crazy husband was right after all about the beauty of this rugged land. She decided not to comment without further evidence, collected after several gruelling hours in the saddle. For now, she was content to sit on Nyx's swaying back and enjoy nature's show.

From time to time, they passed by homesteads, surrounded by farm animals and orchards and the human bustle at the start of a farmer's day. Familiar birds flittered through hedges and darted over stone walls, their gentle twittering a counterpoint to the clink of milk churns and barking dogs. Sunlight edged its way down the hillside until it reached the valley floor, warming her left side. Charlie rode on her right, their knees almost touching.

The Cobb & Co coach had come this way, but it had seemed a different place then. The bone-rattling discomfort and noise of the coach, and the cloud of dust it threw up, had made the countryside fade into the background. On horseback, Grace felt as one with her surroundings, and free to enjoy the sights and sounds, and the smell – so fresh and delightful after the city. She drew in a breath and closed her eyes. When she opened them again, Charlie was watching her with a knowing smile. She laughed and blew him a kiss, which he replied to with a touch of his fingers to his lips and then to his heart.

The superficial resemblance to civilisation did not last long. Stone walls gave way to outcrops of jagged rock, trees gave way to stunted bushes, green grass gave way to the lumpy tufts of golden tussock. No more houses, no more well-tended road. The horses moved apart as the ruts grew deeper. No wonder the coach had jerked and lurched.

Eventually, even that remnant of civilisation dropped behind them when they turned off the road onto a track into the hills. The morning freshness ebbed away with the relentless rise of the sun. Grace swapped the shawl for the buttercup-yellow neckerchief she had been persuaded to purchase at the charity fundraiser. Goodness knows she would have little use for it in the city.

Charlie took the lead on the single file track. Nyx's gentle swaying rhythm turned into an irregular jiggling as the mare picked a route around rocks and dips, leaving Grace clutching the pommel of the saddle to keep her balance.

As they moved further into the hinterland, Grace felt herself growing smaller within a vast, desolate landscape. Gradually, she became aware that they were not the only living beings out here in the wilderness. The thrill of an unseen bird echoed down the valley. Dainty butterflies flittered close to the ground, their dull hues signalling that this was not the place for showy colours. Tiny feet scampered over sharp rocks as fat lizards, warming their striped bodies in the sun, noticed their presence and fled to safety. Even the vegetation, which had seemed so monotonous at first glance, was not without beauty. Clumps of plants with white and purple flowers held on for grim life in hollows in the rock. Patches of green moss and lush foliage hid within wet seepages. But mostly, the plants warned of the harsh land – some with vicious spikes and others with a twisted, defensive crouch, close to the ground and pushed to one side by the prevailing wind.

At one point, Grace caught sight of several sheep, which fled at the sound of hoofbeats. "Look, Charlie, some sheep have escaped from a farm."

Charlie laughed. "They haven't escaped, Grace. This is the farm. Earnscleugh Station."

"Where?" Grace stood up in the stirrups to get a better look. "I don't see any fences."

His hand swept around in an arc, encompassing the entire landscape. "High country stations are thousands of acres – far too large to fence. Hence the value of experienced sheepdogs."

Blaze looked up at him, then went back to sniffing out a rabbit trail, ignoring the flock of sheep as if they weren't worthy of her attention.

When they reached the head of the valley, the land spread out for miles on all sides, clothed in clumps of golden tussock, folding into a myriad of deep gullies, and rising into dark, craggy mountains. Heaps of schist rock rose in all directions, an army emerging from the ground to guard the land against intruders. Grace shivered. Despite the sunshine, it was cooler up here.

Charlie pulled Erebus to a halt to allow Grace to come alongside him. "Beautiful, isn't it?"

"Dramatic, certainly." But her husband was right. The longer one looked, the more a sort of rugged beauty became apparent. Not that Grace would care to live out here, but the enormous emptiness lent the land a majesty and peace that made the soul soar. "Beautiful it may be, but I hope you know where we are, Charlie, because I haven't the faintest idea."

"We're heading over there," he said, pointing past a particularly high crag of rock.

Soon they were descending into a steep gully where the sun deserted them. A stream burbled along the bottom between sharp rocks, which had fallen from the steep sides around them. Grace feared to talk in case her words set off a rockslide. When Charlie spoke, his voice echoed around the rock face, making Grace cringe.

"You can see where the miners have worked the area over the years. Pa said there's still an old timer trying his luck further along."

Grace took his word for it.

"Don't look so worried, Grace. I used to come out here all the time with my father. Pa tells stories about carrying me in a sling when I was a baby, to give my mother a break. Apparently, the rocking motion of the horse sent me to sleep. When I was bigger, I used to sit on the saddle in front of him and we would camp out overnight. Happy days."

Charlie pulled to a halt. "Hello? Anyone home?"

Grace looked around but couldn't see who he was calling to, until a ragged figure appeared from within a pile of stone under an overhanging shelf of solid rock. When her eyes adjusted, she realised it was a crude stone hut rather than a pile of stones. The

152

old miner didn't move from the entrance to the hut, perhaps fearing what they wanted from him.

Charlie dismounted and repeated the greeting in Cantonese. The miner came forward, sliding down the slope with practiced ease, and greeted Charlie like an old friend in their shared language.

Charlie gestured for Grace to come forward. "This is my wife, Grace Penrose Pyke. Grace, this is Jim Ah Ping."

The old man bowed his head to her. Grace wasn't sure of the correct greeting, so she dipped her head in reply. She was taller than the old man by a head and felt pale and delicate next to his sun-darkened skin and stringy muscles. Charlie took a packet of tea, apricots from the orchard, another package labelled with Chinese characters, and several tins from his saddlebag. Then they settled down on a flat-topped rock to pass the time of day with talk of old acquaintances, the weather, gold won and lost, and the people who had passed by, both now and during that long-ago winter.

Grace let the words flow over her, not knowing most of the people or the places mentioned. She heard Charlie mention his father, Jake Blackthorn, Ezra Yarwood, and others, with varying degrees of response from Jim Ah Ping. After a final exchange of what Grace took to be pleasantries in Cantonese, the two men shook hands.

Charlie helped Grace to mount Nyx. The hour or so they had spent off the horses came back to bite Grace. Her legs felt stiff and her thighs chafed as she settled into the saddle again, leaving her wondering how long their day would be. She was determined to get through it without complaining. Her husband was enjoying their excursion, and she would too, even if it killed her.

"Blaze is looking a little footsore," Charlie said, as he rearranged the bedrolls behind her into a bowl shape. He called the collie and hoisted her up onto Nyx's back, telling her to lie and stay. Blaze cocked her head to one side, as if uncertain what he meant. Nyx looked around with exactly the same question in her sweet eyes. Then Blaze settled into the soft bowl of blankets with what Grace was sure was the equivalent of a human shrug. Grace gave Nyx a reassuring pat, while Charlie rewarded her with half an apple. Erebus was quick to snaffle the other half.

Charlie mounted, and they were off again, up and down and around, criss-crossing streams and popping up on high plateaux with views for miles, until Grace couldn't tell which way they had come, let alone which way they were going. She could only hope her husband knew where on earth they were.

They visited two other old-timers, stopped for a long meal break under a towering schist tor, and all the while the sun moved steadily in an arc from east to west, towards a horizon of bald mountain tops. Grace learned to spot the signs of gold diggings: the piles of tailings, the remains of water races, and the occasional stone hut tucked under the surrounding rocks. One fellow continued to shovel gravel into a cradle as they talked, before shaking the rock through with water. He grinned with his few remaining teeth when showing her the tiny flecks of gold left behind. She couldn't imagine how they had the patience and fortitude for the hours of back-breaking work for so little reward.

At one point, they had an extended stop at one site, while Charlie scoured the area for stash holes. Ezra Yarwood's old diggings, he explained. They found nothing, except for signs that others had been there before them, long ago.

Finally, after a long uphill ascent, Charlie pulled Erebus to a halt beside a stack of rocks with a deep overhang, forming a cave-like shelter underneath. From here, the land spread out before them like a wrinkled cloth of brown and gold, extending for miles to the Clutha River and beyond. The tussock was sparser here, leaving the ground covered by lichen-speckled rocks and occasional mats of vegetation no higher than Nyx's hoof. A few scattered pockets of alpine herbs and flowers clung to cervices in the rocks.

Grace hoped they wouldn't linger too long in this inhospitable place.

"You'll be pleased to hear we've reached our campsite," Charlie said. "You've been incredible, Grace. You must be exhausted after such a long day in the saddle."

Grace didn't have the energy to question his choice of campsite. She dropped to the ground on unsteady legs, which felt like a curious combination of lead, gelatine, and fire – the latter being her chafed thighs and calves. "Well, I did insist on coming on this mad jaunt, which means any exhaustion is my own fault."

Charlie spread out the blankets on an area of vegetation. "Why don't you lie down for a bit on this cushion plant, while I see to the horses and camp."

Grace was happy to oblige. The so-called cushion plant was a firm and lumpy mattress, but it was vastly better than the sharp-edge scree around it. "Why aren't we camping right on the top?" she asked, pointing to the ridgeline a few hundred feet away. An enormous upright slab of rock dominated the skyline, almost as if had been deliberately placed there to mark a giant's waypoint.

"We'll be glad of the shelter of the overhang, especially if the wind comes up. Besides, there's no water up there."

Grace looked around at what seemed like a desolate landscape. "Is there water anywhere?"

"There's a small tarn in that dip over yonder," Charlie said, "with the tiny beginnings of a stream flowing out of it over a low waterfall and down into the valley."

Grace lay back on the blanket and felt her back click as she stretched out and took the weight off the sore bits of her anatomy. She sighed at the bliss of it and doubted she could get up again even if she wanted to. Blaze, who had walked most of the afternoon, plopped down beside her. Charlie bustled around, seeing to the horses first – putting feed sacks around their heads, unsaddling them, rubbing them down – before setting them loose to find their own shelter and grazing amongst the tussock down in the valley. Grace was by no means sure that it was a good idea to let their only means of transport roam freely, but she kept her doubts to herself.

155

Meanwhile, Charlie put their saddlebags deep under the overhang, returning with a bundle of food, a bowl, the small kerosene stove, and a fire-blackened billy. He disappeared over the hill and returned with a full billy and bowl. Blaze hauled herself up from her cozy spot beside Grace and padded over to him. Soon, the collie was slurping water and chewing on dried meat, while Charlie set the billy to boil.

Grace knew she ought to offer to help, but her limbs refused to move. Besides, she'd only get in the way, especially as her husband's brisk efficiency indicated he had done this many, many times in the past. She rolled onto her side, suppressing a groan. "You seem as home out here as you are in Dunedin city, Charlie. Which do you prefer?"

Charlie glanced up from making an adjustment to the stove. "I love it out here. When I first moved to the city, I hated it. All the buildings and people crowding in until I couldn't think straight. The noise, the bustle, the stench, the filth ..."

"Says the man with horse dung on his boots."

"I was about to ask for a transfer back to inland Otago when I meet you and Alistair. It terrifies me to look back and realise how close I came to not meeting you. I wouldn't change anything now, because I am happier than I ever imagined it was possible to be. As long as we are together, I don't care where I am." Charlie said the words matter-of-factly, as if his feelings on the matter were self-evident.

His answer warmed Grace to the core. "Hey, mountain man, have I ever told you that I love you?"

"I believe you may have mentioned it once or twice, city woman. Cup of tea, milady?"

"I'd kill for a cup of tea. An apricot too, if there are any left. In fact, I'd eat anything right now, even that disgusting dried meat Blaze is gnawing." A sudden awful thought crossed her mind. "That's not what we are eating tonight, is it?"

156

Charlie laughed but failed to reassure her. He brought over the tea in a chunky enamel mug and propped her upright against a rock with a blanket behind her. He was treating her like an invalid, but she didn't have the strength or the will to protest. A short while later, Charlie delivered a plate piled with hunks of Matilda's gooey cheese, which Grace had forgotten about, slices of bread, apricots, and other unexpected but extremely welcome treats.

"Have I ever told you that I love you?" Grace repeated, as she crammed food into her mouth with unladylike haste. As she bit through a crispy crust into the soft centre, Grace realised the bread must have been freshly baked that morning. "I adore your parents too. Your dear mother must have been up very early to bake the bread."

"Mm," Charlie mumbled through a mouthful of cheese and bread. "Fresh air does wonders for the appetite. Sorry it's been such a long day with little to show for our efforts."

"We learned Ezra hasn't been seen out at his diggings, or anywhere else, by any of the old-timers since before the robbery. Not even to clear his possessions out of his hut. Not a single person had heard so much as a rumour that Ezra might be alive somewhere."

"No surprise there," Charlie said, "but it's good to have confirmation. Everyone knew Jake Blackthorn and kept out of his way when he was about, but it seems he hasn't been seen around these parts for years either."

"I thought it was interesting that they saw a lot of him in the months after the robbery, poking around. That fits with our theory that Jake wasn't the robber himself, but he knew that Ezra or someone else had hidden the missing gold. If Jake kept hunting for it, presumably he thought Ezra wasn't able to get it himself, which suggests Jake believed Ezra was dead."

"I agree, Grace. If Jake hasn't been seen out here lately, I reckon he must have his hidden camp to the north of here, back towards Clyde. Plenty of steep, gnarly country out there. Makes this place look like a walk in the park." Charlie put down his plate

157

and stretched, stifling a yawn. "We'll go home that way tomorrow."

Sounds delightful, Grace thought. "How many hours of daylight do we have left? I feel as if I could sleep for a week."

Charlie checked the sky. "Several hours until it's fully dark. These long days of summer don't leave us many hours of darkness, but there is no reason we cannot take a nap before dusk. I hope it hasn't been too awful for you, Grace."

She settled back on the blanket again, feeling more cheerful with a full stomach. The sky formed a brilliant blue dome with no buildings or trees to break the outline. "Someone once told me the skies are bigger out here and I didn't believe him. I confess I was wrong – they really are bigger. It's as if I'm lying on a cloud, looking up at the entirety of heaven."

Charlie stretched out next to her. "Don't tell me my city wife is actually coming around to my way of thinking?"

She nudged him in the ribs. "Don't push it, Pyke. The euphoria brought on by resting and gooey cheese might be clouding my judgement. I expect Connie or Jake to ride up any minute and shatter any illusions that I am in heaven."

Grace wished she hadn't mentioned it when she felt his body tense beside her.

He sat up and looked around. "I haven't seen anyone following us and Blaze hasn't either. I'd like to think we are safe out here, but I keep coming back to the possible eavesdropper who knows where we are heading. Or rather, where I am heading, because I talked about going out on my own. Hopefully, if anyone does find us, they'll only be expecting me. In that case, I want you to hide, Grace. I mean it."

Grace took the point. It would be better if any attacker didn't know they had a second person to deal with. The knife tucked in her boot gave her some reassurance, but she wished she had learned to handle the shotgun properly. Not that she believed it would come to that. "Charlie, my sweet, surely there isn't the slightest chance anyone could find us out here in the middle of nowhere, even knowing the general direction we were heading at the start of the day."

"You'd be surprised, Grace. The miners saw us, not that any of them would talk to the likes of Jake. I've tried to be careful, but we cannot avoid leaving tracks. Crushed plants, the occasional hoofprint in the soft mud by streams – plenty for an experienced tracker to follow. Despite what it may look like, there are not many feasible routes we could take. People and horses can be easy to spot out here, especially on a ridgeline."

Charlie rose to his feet. "But you're right. The chances are slim, and we are here to enjoy our time alone, not fret about the idiocy of the rest of the population. I'm going to have a wash before I cook dinner."

"Is there a natural hot spring?" Grace asked hopefully.

"Cool, bracing mountain water does wonders for a tired body," her cruel husband replied.

"If you like heart attacks," Grace muttered. She closed her eyes and soaked up the sun, knowing that a cold night out on an open hilltop would be on its way soon enough.

Grace must have dozed off for a moment. When she awoke, she could hear splashing, laughing, and barking. This she had to see. Down in the bottom of a dip in the land, a pond had lingered through the summer within a boggy area squelching with mosses. At the far end, a trickle of water fell over a steep rocky drop, forming a small waterfall. Charlie and Blaze were cavorting in the shallow water, splashing each other and having a grand old time.

Blaze lifted her nose into the air and barked, warning Charlie of an interloper. His reaction time was impressive. Charlie glanced at his clothes, which no doubt concealed a weapon, but they were a few yards up the slope above the splash zone. He had grabbed a rock before realising who the interloper was.

Grace had taken a grandstand seat on a rock. "Don't stop, Charlie. I was enjoying the show."

Charlie dropped the rock. "Come on in, Grace. The water's not so bad once you're numb." When Grace showed no signs of moving, he smiled a slow, deliberate smile. "Shall we get her, Blaze?"

The collie raced up the bank towards Grace. Blaze looked back at Charlie for his approval and then shook the water from her coat before Grace could jump out of the way. Charlie reached them and grabbed his wife, carrying her kicking and laughing to the edge of the pond. He swung her back and then out towards the water.

"Wait! At least let me take my clothes off."

"An excellent idea, wife. I'd be happy to oblige." Charlie stripped her bare, despite Grace's pleas that she'd never live it down if someone was watching, then waded into the water carrying her.

"Don't get my hair wet," she squealed.

Charlie dunked her in water that was not far short of freezing, but held her head up, obviously recalling the tedious hours it took for her long hair to dry after washing it.

"Get me out of here, Pyke," Grace gasped, "before I turn into an iceberg."

Charlie pulled her out of the water and waded out of the tarn, holding her close to his body warmth. "At least we're both clean." He flung her over his shoulder and clambered back to their campsite, depositing her in the cave under the overhanging rock and stealing a long kiss while he was at it. Not too long a kiss though, as they were both shivering. "I'll get our clothes."

Grace rubbed herself down with a cloth and dressed quickly. "Can we have a fire? Oh, I suppose not, since there is nothing to burn but rock."

"I did bring the makings of a small fire, because the weather at this altitude can turn bad at any time. I wasn't planning to light one, because of the danger of being seen, but we are safe enough if I light it under the overhang. If my wife died from hypothermia on her honeymoon, I'd never live it down."

Grace watched him extract kindling and a flint from his bottomless bag of tricks. The sun wasn't close to setting yet, but the air was already chilling down quickly. She'd always thought Dunedin was cold, but that would be nothing compared to the extremes of temperatures up here at high altitude, even in summer. The tiny fire was surprisingly warming, although that might have been partly because of the comforting sight of flickering flames.

Grace held her hands close to the heat. "This place must be absolutely bone-chilling in winter."

"Up here, it is bitter beyond imagining. An unprepared traveller can die before he's even aware of the peril. Even the towns in the valleys can get deep snow. There are compensations, though. Skating on ice-covered ponds is always a good lark, and you should see the hoarfrost. It turns the branches and twigs of trees into a starburst of icicles. Beautiful."

There it was again, her husband's strange concept of beauty. Perhaps, like this place, one had to experience it to understand. Charlie disappeared up to the ridgeline for one last scouting expedition before they settled in for the evening. The rock shelter seemed empty without him. She was glad she wasn't here on her own, for all that her husband raved about the peace to be found in solitude.

Grace was starving again, which made little sense, since she had sat on her bottom all day, letting Nyx do the work, and made a pig of herself not much more than an hour ago. She contented herself with another cup of tea, safe in the knowledge that Charlie always packed plenty of food.

He arrived back after about twenty minutes and set the billy on the kerosene stove. "You're in luck, Grace. My mother made a meal for us this morning, so you won't be forced to have Blaze's dried meat after all."

"God bless her thoughtfulness." Already the shelter was filling with the aroma. "Your mother's cooking always smells so heavenly, like your Aunt Lily's. Perhaps I should ask her to give me lessons."

Blaze sneaked in beside them and whined. Charlie ruffled her ears. "Ma didn't forget you, Blaze." Charlie pulled the saddlebag towards him, extracting a parcel for Blaze and a bottle of wine.

"Good heavens, Charlie. I've no idea how you managed to bring so much, but I beg your forgiveness for doubting your packing excesses."

Charlie popped the cork and poured into the enamel mugs. "Your crystal goblet, milady."

They clinked mugs and settled back into companionable silence.

Charlie doused the fire once they had eaten, as the daylight was turning to dusk and the fire would soon be visible from a distance. He rustled around, packing their things back in the saddlebags and gathering their bedding. "We'll be warm enough sleeping under the overhang, especially if we share body warmth. But first, I want to show you what the stars look like out here, away from the gaslights of the city. We're fortunate to have a still night. The wind can be ferocious up here."

They passed the time curled up together, chatting about nothing and everything, until Charlie deemed the time right for gazing at stars. He covered her eyes and led her out into the night. From their uphill direction, she realised he was taking her to the top of the ridge.

When he removed his hands, Grace was ready with an appreciative gasp for his benefit. Stars were stars, she'd reasoned, wherever you are. How wrong she'd been. The gasp never made it past her paralysed jaw. The sky was not simply filled with dots of light – it was smeared with broad swathes of dense lights, clouds of brightness, and diamond dots on a dark blue background – an indescribably glorious palette of light and dark beyond imagining.

All she could do was cling to her husband and gape.

"Magical, isn't it?" he whispered. "Out here is as close to heaven as a person can get."

"We have to sleep up here under the stars, Charlie. We simply have to."

Charlie went back down to the overhang to gather up their bedrolls, while she sat and stared up at the sky, scarcely believing that it could be the same sky as the one she thought she knew. When Charlie returned, he cleared the rocks as best he could on the far side of the upright slab of rock and made them a nest of bedding.

Grace lay in his arms under the blankets with tears in her eyes. "This is the most romantic honeymoon imaginable. Thank you, my love, for bringing me up here. Tired as I am, I don't think I'll get a wink of sleep tonight."

"Who said anything about sleeping?" Charlie replied.

An Empty Land

Grace didn't wake until the sun crept around the side of the rock slab. She stretched her limbs with the languid pleasure of a woman on her honeymoon without a care in the world, but soon realised that every inch of her body ached, despite being numb from the cold.

Her face burned from the aftermath of yesterday's intense sun, which had defied the protection of her wide-brimmed hat. Her arms and legs ached from the long ride, with a particularly sharp sting in her tortured thighs, which had been pushed unnaturally wide and relentlessly chafed by the stirrup straps. And then there was her back, which was a symphony of bruises from the wind-blasted sheets of rock on which she lay. Lovemaking under a blanket of stars had seemed the very epitome of romance last night, but it was not without consequences.

Her first lucid thought was that she must have dozed off again after Charlie rose around dawn. Her second was that dawn had long since passed, and the promised cup of coffee had failed to appear. With fingers stiff from gripping reins, Grace pushed herself up to a seated position, shooting a new set of pains through her posterior.

The pain vanished as soon as she saw the breathtaking view. The land dropped away gradually below her on all sides, before dipping into the steeper valleys where the goldminers worked, giving her the sensation of being on top of the world. An undulating sea of tussock, turned red gold by the morning sun, stretched out before her, broken by the long shadows of tall rocky tors, which dotted the landscape like ancient monuments. In the distance, an endless chain of mountain peaks still wore a cap of snow.

She rose and bundled the bedding, eager to share her newfound love of the wilderness with Charlie. After the first few agonising steps, the stiffness in her body seeped away to a dull ache. The prospect of another day in the saddle wasn't exactly joyous, but a hot breakfast would help. Grace sniffed the breeze for the aroma of coffee and bacon, but the only smell she detected was fresh air laced with vegetation and dirt. She wobbled down the slope on shaky legs towards the overhanging rock, where there was no sign of activity. No husband waving to her. No dog dashing up to share her joy for life.

At the overhanging rock, Grace found Charlie's bedroll and one of the saddlebags beside the unlit kerosene stove. The two saddles, shotgun, and all the other equipment were still tucked away at the back of the cave under the overhang, out of sight. The only place he could be was at the tarn, getting water or washing. She went to the edge of the dip but couldn't see him.

"Charlie! Blaze!"

Her cries drifted in the wind, unanswered apart from the distant trill of a bird, which sounded like a skylark to Grace but could have been a circling bird of prey for all she knew of mountain avifauna.

Concern turned to fear when Grace saw the billy lying abandoned by the tarn. She ran down the slope, risking a twisted ankle in her haste. The damp ground by the pool showed marks of a scuffle. Two sets of footsteps close to each other, two knee dents in the ground, two handprints in front of the knees, and a couple of paw prints. Grace checked a wider area, fearing a pool of blood, but found nothing but drag marks and footsteps that petered out once she left the soft earth around the water.

The breeze whined through the jumble of rocks, taunting her. She listened again as the whine trailed off to a whimper. "Blaze?"

A bark this time, beyond the point where the water dropped over the steep edge into a short waterfall. Grace forced herself to look over the edge, fearing what she would see on the rocks below.

Blaze was down there, upside down, wedged in a narrow crevice between two rocks. The fact that she could still whimper and wiggle her legs was a good sign, Grace told herself, as she scrambled down. Poor Blaze must have been kicked or thrown with considerable force to have become so firmly wedged in place, because it took Grace a few minutes of gentle heaving to extract the collie.

A quick examination showed no broken bones, miraculously, but Blaze was tender in the area around a boot-shaped mark of mud on her side. When Grace set her on the ground, Blaze gave her a sloppy lick, before taking a few tentative steps. Whoever had kicked their dog over the side of that waterfall had better be prepared for a furious reception when Grace caught up with him. But first, she had to find Charlie.

Grace picked up Blaze and scrambled back up to the tarn. Blaze seemed to be walking with no problem, so Grace pointed to the scene of the scuffle. "Find Charlie, Blaze."

The black-and-white head bent, sniffing. Blaze followed the drag marks up to the top of the dip, but not back towards the overhanging rock. Instead, she turned downhill and headed off with her nose to the ground. Grace crossed her fingers and followed behind, praying that she wouldn't find a corpse. Blaze started running when the drag-marks started again, only stopping when she reached a dip in the land trampled by horses and boots. She went around in a circle, before heading off to the north.

"Wait, Blaze. Come, girl."

There was no point heading off into the wilderness without thinking through the options first. Grace studied the mass of prints. Two horses, she guessed, and a smaller pony. Another sweep of the area showed only departing hoofprints, and no more footprints, heading in the direction Blaze had taken. A flash of bright yellow caught her attention. Up close, she saw it was a strip of buttercup yellow, with half an embroidered flower, or cloud, or possibly a sheep. Charlie must have picked up the neckerchief she dropped yesterday, not that she cared about a scrap of cloth when her husband was missing.

She racked her brain for a logical explanation, but she kept coming back to the one scenario that fitted the facts – Charlie had been kidnapped by two men and taken away on horseback. Grace had a vague memory of Charlie getting up around dawn, which meant the kidnappers had around an hour's head start.

Grace had never felt so alone as she did standing there, looking out over thousands of acres of emptiness, with no idea what to do next. Fear gripped her intestines, but she knew the one thing she couldn't afford to do was panic. She would take one logical step at a time and find Charlie. If she couldn't find him, she would go back to Clyde for help. Quite how she would do either of these things was beyond her at this moment, when she didn't know which direction to go or whether she had any means of transport other than her own two legs.

Instead, Grace bent down and hugged Blaze to calm her own shaking. Then she returned to the tarn to take a long drink and fill the billy. Back at the overhang, she filled the flasks, not knowing when she might find water again. By the time she and Blaze had had a quick breakfast, Grace had a plan. Not much of a plan, but a plan.

Step One of the plan was based on the optimistic assumption that the kidnappers had not found Nyx and Erebus, wherever they were, and the equally optimistic assumption that she could find the horses. Because she didn't trust herself not to get lost looking for them, Grace was reliant on Blaze's exceptional nose.

"Find Nyx, Blaze. Find Erebus."

Blaze ran around in a circle, before heading downhill in a wide zig, followed by a zag, until she disappeared in a dip. Now and then, Grace saw flashes of black and white as Blaze sniffed an erratic route into the distance, before vanishing entirely. Grace trusted the collie to the job she was born to do. Meanwhile, she stowed their gear in the saddlebags and prepared herself for the day ahead. When the silence grew too oppressive, she pulled

Charlie's spare shirt over her own clothes, for no good reason other than the comfort of his familiar scent.

She was lugging the heavy saddles to a flat-topped rock when Nyx and Blaze appeared, with Erebus trailing behind. Nyx came right up beside her to drink from the bowl of water Grace had put out for her. Grace wanted to fling her arms around her glossy black neck, but didn't want to frighten her off. Gently, she reached for Nyx's halter and tied a rope to it. The relief had her quaking at the knees. Grace tied off the rope around a slab of rock, hitching rails being in short supply in this wilderness, with not so much as a shrub in sight. Only then did she sink against the mare's warm neck and stroke her.

Erebus was standing a few yards away, shuffling restlessly. Grace only needed one horse, so she focused on keeping Nyx happy by fastening a feed bag around her head. Nyx munched into the mix of oats and chopped apple with evident pleasure. Erebus extended his head towards the other bag, his nostrils flaring at the smell. Grace shook the feed bag to encourage him closer. He edged forward until she could grasp his halter. Step One of the plan completed.

Step Two of the plan required her to lift heavy saddles and saddlebags onto two extremely large moving targets and secure them with whatever belts and buckles she could find. Grace took a deep breath and stood on top of the flat-topped rock, encouraging Nyx closer. Nyx eyed her from under long lashes, blew a puff of breath out of her soft nostrils, and walked up beside the rock. Grace could have cried. She heaved and shoved and adjusted the saddle until it appeared to be in the right place and not in danger of slipping under the horse's belly. The mare shook her head at the lack of finesse, but stood still, sweetheart that she was.

Now for Erebus. Grace managed that feat by putting him between the rock and Nyx, so he couldn't move out of reach. The saddle and saddlebags looked as if they had been put on by a blind drunkard with a severe case of the shakes, but at least they were on. If … when … they found Charlie, he would be pleased she hadn't had to leave the extra horse and saddle behind.

"Good boy, Erebus." Grace patted the giant horse with heartfelt thanks.

After that, she only had to remove the empty feed bags and put the bridle on Nyx, apologising for clanking the bit against her teeth twice when she got the bridle in a tangle, before juggling the horses again so she could mount Nyx from the top of the rock. By the time her aching posterior hit the saddle, which miraculously remained in place, Grace was feeling physically and mentally drained.

Time for Step Three – finding her husband within thousands of acres of hills and gullies. First, she took the horses to the tarn to drink, then she turned to Blaze, whose entire body quivered in readiness for her next command.

"Find Charlie, Blaze."

Blaze ran back to the drag-marks and hoofprints, and put her nose to the ground, moving back and forth across the area, before heading off into the vast wilderness. The angle of the sun told Grace they were going roughly north, into unknown territory. She didn't know where she was going, beyond the vague memory she had of locations on the map, but she trusted her black-and-white guide to get her there.

Step Four of the plan – rescuing Charlie – was far too daunting to contemplate right now. Only because there was not yet enough information to devise a solid rescue plan, she assured herself.

Grace focused her full attention on following Blaze. The route descended gently at first on a clear track, but, in her mind, those first few miles were the worst. Abject terror at the possibility of losing Charlie forever threatened to tip her into a panic. If she'd have had anyone to help her, other than a dog and two horses, she'd have given in to the panic, but Charlie's life might depend on her. Instead, Grace recited her blessings over and over – it's lucky I was with him, Blaze will find him, Charlie will escape and find us, everything will turn out fine in the end …

Slowly, panic died away and recriminations set in, as the downward slope steepened and the enormity of the task sunk in. Why had she insisted on a fire last night? Why hadn't she got up earlier? And why in the name of all things holy had she not put her foot down before they got dragged into an investigation on their honeymoon?

Finally, an aching dread crept over her. How could Blaze follow a fading scent out here with a relentless breeze skimming the ridge top? Was the dog simply following hoof prints, which may or may not belong to the kidnappers' horses?

At a junction where one faint path met another even fainter trail, both heading towards nothing in particular, Grace stopped for a drink of water. Her hand shook so badly, she spilt precious drops onto the parched land. A flash of colour caught her eye near the fallen drops. Buttercup yellow again. Grace laughed – she hoped not too hysterically, not that there was anyone to hear. Charlie was leaving them a trail using strips of neckerchief, and she hadn't been paying attention.

She rode on with renewed determination and an apology to their faithful border collie, who had been right all along. Her thoughts drifted to what she would do to the kidnappers when Blaze found them. Her first notion was to take to them with her knife and performing cardiac surgery to rip out their heinous hearts, but she soon progressed to more subtle and inventive forms of torture, such as consigning them to the dim light of a prison cell for the rest of their miserable lives, spending twelve-hour days embroidering handkerchiefs with flower-clouds.

Nyx stumbled on a rock, jerking Grace into the here and now. She came close to catapulting over Nyx's withers and tumbling down a steep slope, but grabbed Nyx's mane just in time.

Even when Nyx recovered, Grace kept hold of the saddle, channelling all her energy into staying aloft and moving forward. The route narrowed to a sharper ridge, with the land dropping away in front and on both sides. Finally, Blaze turned to the east, leading them down a steep descent into a maze of gullies, where the faint trail vanished completely.

Grace held on with grim determination and prayed that Nyx didn't trip again and plunge them both into oblivion.

Revenge

Charlie had woken that morning with an overwhelming feeling that life did not get any better than this. He left Grace to sleep, while he went down to the overhanging rock with Blaze at his side to get breakfast underway. The collie sniffed the air, whining softly.

"Hungry, are you? Me too." Charlie gave Blaze some meat, which she gulped before he had the stove set up. She licked her chops and went off to investigate a scent trail.

Charlie left Blaze to her wanderings, while he went down to the tarn, billy in hand. The embroidered yellow neck scarf Grace had been wearing yesterday lay discarded near the water. Charlie picked it up and held it to his nose. He was squatting by the water, neckerchief in hand, daydreaming about splashing in the pool yesterday and making love under the stars, when he heard Grace coming down the slope behind him. Foolishly, being too deep in blissful memories to recognise potential danger, he didn't turn to check it was her.

A second later, a bag went over his head. Instinct kicked in, but it was too late. The muscular attacker forced him onto his knees, dazed him with a powerful punch, and had him bound hand and foot before Charlie could fight back.

Behind them, an angry snarl warned him that Blaze was back. Charlie yelled at her to stay, but the faithful collie dashed down the slope and must have launched herself at the attacker, because Charlie heard a curse, then the thud of a boot against flesh. Blaze's pitiful yelp faded into the distance. Charlie fought against the bindings and the sack over his head, but there was nothing he could do. A whimpering sound from below told him Blaze had been booted over the waterfall.

"You despicable lowlife," Charlie snarled. "Don't think I'll forget this."

His attacker laughed. "Seems to me you're in no position to make threats, young Pyke. I've trussed lambs with more fight in them than you. Missus done worn you out, has she?"

Jake Blackthorn, and he wasn't attempting to disguise his voice. Charlie would worry about Jake's ultimate intentions later. Right now, he had to protect Grace. "My wife is back in Clyde, safe from the likes of you."

"Is that so? That's not what my informant said. In fact, I could swear I saw two horses on the ridge above Conroys Gully yesterday. Led us on a right dance, you did. We were about to give up when we saw the fire from the other side of the valley. The city's making you soft, boy, if you're risking a fire in summer."

The "we" didn't escape Charlie's notice. Had Jake recruited Sylvester to his cause? The good news was that Grace hadn't been seen beyond Conroys Gully and the fire had been spotted only from a distance. Very likely, Jake and his accomplice had camped across the valley to avoid risking their horses in the rough terrain at night. If Charlie could persuade Jake that Grace had gone home, she might be saved from capture.

"My wife's the one who's soft from city life. I had to pay a miner to show her the way to the road back to Clyde. Couldn't have her ruining my trip by complaining every five minutes about how miserable she was."

"Not very gentlemanly behaviour on your honeymoon, Pyke."

"A man's got to take charge from the start," Charlie grumbled, "or he'll be henpecked for the rest of his life."

Jake grunted his approval. "We'll see if you're telling the truth soon enough."

Jake dragged Charlie away from the tarn, bumping him over rocks and rough ground, into the shelter of the valley below. Charlie heard horses moving around and the sound of another set of boots approaching.

"Couldn't find the hellcat. There's one bedroll by that overhanging rock up there and one set of saddlebags." The speaker walked up to Charlie and booted him in the stomach.

"Nathaniel Summerfield, I presume." Charlie attempted nonchalance, to cover his shock at hearing his old school bully's voice. Not easy to achieve, when he was gagging from the unprovoked attack. Had Nathaniel really come all this way to seek revenge for a minor insult to his dignity? "I was just telling your accomplice that my wife got tired of riding and went home."

Nathaniel let out a string of curses. "I was looking forward to teaching that harpy a lesson. Has he told you where his grandfather hid the gold yet?"

"I haven't asked," Jake replied. "We should get him away from here. Someone else could have seen that fire and decided to check it out. Besides, it'll take more than a polite question or two to get information out of this one. I want to have him where nobody will hear his screams."

Nathaniel sniggered. "What about the wife?"

"Pyke's right about one thing. His wife's a city girl. If she's out here, she'll be helpless without him. When Sergeant Pyke and his search party finally find her, if ever, she'll be half starved and totally out of her mind, or dead."

Nathaniel's snigger turned to a vicious laugh. "Revenge has never sounded sweeter. Let's get going."

They heaved Charlie over the back of a pony and tied him down. This was going to be a long and uncomfortable day.

The only thing worse than the prospect of being at the mercy of the gold-lust of Jake Blackthorn and the vengeance of Nathaniel Summerfield was the terrifying thought they might be right about Grace. Not that she would be helpless, because Grace was the most resourceful person he knew, but the odds were certainly stacked against her in a place that was as unfamiliar to her as the surface of the moon. Charlie prayed Blaze was still alive, because the dog's death would surely crush whatever was left of Grace's spirit.

Charlie wished he hadn't put her in this position. It was entirely his fault for dragging her out into the wilderness on a whim, and not keeping his wits about him.

His stomach rumbled, but it was just as well he hadn't had breakfast, because bouncing around awkwardly on the pony's back would have made him throw up a meal. Not an enticing prospect while wearing a sack around his head. His one sensible decision this morning had been to have a drink of water before filling the billy. He would need it out here as the sun rose higher, and the day heated up.

Having made a fool of himself, Charlie wasn't about to dig himself in deeper by wasting time on recriminations. Instead, he focused on the direction of the sun, and the ups and downs of their route, trying to match the information to the map in his head. It wasn't too hard, because they travelled north and downhill for a long time, presumably following the old prospector's route along the ridgeline. The number of hours was harder to judge, but Charlie guessed they had been travelling for over two hours when Jake called a rest stop. Needless to say, neither Jake nor Nathaniel shared their water bottles with Charlie, or even gave him a break from his uncomfortable position.

His one small triumph was in fumbling Grace's bright yellow scarf from his sleeve and ripping it into strips, being careful not to let it fall from his bound hands. Charlie dropped the pieces at intervals, especially when he sensed a change of direction. In all likelihood, the wind would blow the light fabric away, but anything was better than straddling the pony, as helpless as a sack of unwanted kittens destined for the river.

Jake and Nathaniel soon mounted up and descended to the east. Before another hour had passed, they dropped deep into a valley, where the sun didn't reach. The air was damp here, from the many streams joining the valley from both sides. The tinkle of running water was driving Charlie mad, both from thirst and from the need to relieve his bladder.

He was beginning to think they were heading back to Clyde, when the pony turned sharply, crunching over shingle and pushing through spiky bushes. The dull echo of the horses' hooves told him they'd entered a narrow, steep gorge. Within a few minutes, the oppressive sensation of being hemmed in eased, and light filtered through the sack around his head again.

"Wait here," Jake said. "No talking."

The horses stopped and Jake's footsteps echoed back down the short gorge.

Charlie turned towards the sound of a horse shuffling its hooves off to the right. "What are you doing here, Nathaniel? You don't want to end your years in prison for the sake of an old grudge against me. Jake Blackthorn is using you, and it won't end well."

"Shows how little you know, Pyke," Nathaniel said. "You strut into town touting yourself as a famous detective and crowing about clearing your grandfather's name, but you're wrong about everything."

"It's you who's wrong, Nathaniel," Charlie said, with more confidence than he felt. "Jake has dragged you into this by telling you a pack of lies."

Nathaniel booted his horse forward until Charlie could feel them inches away. "I'm the one in charge, Pyke. Jake Blackthorn is no more than hired muscle doing my bidding."

Even through the sack, Charlie sensed the barely suppressed rage in Nathaniel's tone. He also knew the truth when he heard it. Nathaniel really did think he was in charge, like the arrogant fool he was. "Why are you doing this, Nathaniel?"

"Because you will try to spread the lie that my parents took the gold. Do you know what it was like to grow up being the butt of jokes about the rich boy whose parents robbed the town's wealth for their own gain? Having the likes of that haughty Julia MacEwen looking down on my mother like she was muck?"

Charlie reeled at the venom in the tirade. He wanted to fling the venom back at Nathaniel, who had made Charlie's life wretched by taunting him about his mixed-race parentage and his grandfather's supposed crimes. However, there was no point in flinging insults when Jake would be back any second. Charlie's best bet would be to divide and conquer.

"I don't think your parents were involved in the robbery, Nathaniel. Nobody does. The police investigation ruled them out at the time, for heaven's sake. Your father wasn't even in Clyde." Charlie heard the crunch of boots returning. He lowered his voice. "Jake Blackthorn and Ezra Yarwood are my main suspects. Jake will double cross you and leave you to take the blame, like he always does. Let me loose and we can work this out together."

The boots stomped up before Nathaniel could reply. "I told you not to talk to him, Summerfield," Jake said.

"I don't take orders from you," Nathaniel replied, in a voice too soft for Jake to hear.

The pony jerked forward. They walked in silence for another few minutes, the horses' hooves muffled by softer soil after miles of clattering over rocky, unstable ground. Charlie detected the smell of sheep dung. Jake's hidden lair for sheep-rustling, presumably.

They halted. Hands grabbed Charlie's feet and untied them. One rough shove and he was grovelling on the ground in front of his captors.

Nathaniel wrenched the sack off. "Welcome to Jake's palace."

Charlie figured the sack had been intended to stop him from seeing the route to Jake's hidden valley, which was a hopeful thought. If they intended to kill him, they wouldn't have bothered. On the other hand, they had made no attempt to disguise their identities, which meant they could not risk letting him go. Perhaps logic wasn't their strong suit. Either way, he could use a breath of fresh air after three hours of smelling mouldy old potatoes and half-rotten sacking.

"For the love of God, Summerfield," Jake said, "don't tell him what he don't need to know. Get inside, Pyke."

"Jake's palace" merged into the walls of the gully as if its rough-hewn walls were part of the surrounding rocks. Although bigger than the usual miner's hut, it was far from a palace, having been designed for hiding in the shadows rather than standing proudly in the light for all to see. The chimney vented through a crevice in the rock above, which would filter the smoke along its length to make it harder to see. Beyond the far wall, a smaller building probably housed a stable and storage, judging by the scatter of hay and coal around the door. Hoof marks of sheep dotted the ground as far as Charlie could see.

Admiration for Jake's cunning came a poor second to the topmost thought in Charlie's mind. Jake had been right – in this place, nobody would hear him scream. If they kept him bound hand and foot with these heavy cords, which they surely would, there was almost no chance of escape.

Precious little chance of rescue either, come to that. Charlie knew roughly which catchment he was in and knew it to be a wild and uninhabited place, where few had a reason or desire to venture. He had two options: wait it out, hoping for a miracle, or double down on the age-old tactic of turning his adversaries against each other, hoping one of them would make a mistake.

"Unless you want a wet patch on the Persian rugs in your palace, Blackthorn," Charlie said, "I suggest you let me relieve myself before we go inside."

Jake loosened the bindings around Charlie's wrists just enough for him to answer the call of nature. Jake redid the knots, but Charlie kept his hands as far apart as he could to give himself the best chance of escape. It wasn't much, but it was something.

"Take him inside, Summerfield," Jake said, "while I see to the horses. Make sure you bind his ankles tight and don't talk to him until I come back or I'll be forced to knock your head against a rock to beat some sense into you. Pyke and his scrap of a wife made a fool of you once – don't let him do it again."

178

Nathaniel bristled, but did as he was told. He pushed Charlie into the stone cabin and forced him onto the floor by the back wall, before binding Charlie's ankles too tight for comfort.

Inside, the cabin displayed the success of Jake's criminal enterprises. Instead of the dirt floor and meagre furnishings Charlie had expected, he saw a comfortable armchair, a thick rug on the wooden plank floors, and a sturdy table in the sitting area, with a kerosene stove and well-stocked set of shelves in the cooking alcove. Jake probably did most of his cooking on the pot-belly stove in the centre of the room, which also heated the cabin.

Through the opening to another alcove in the wall nearest Charlie, he could see a single bunk, which had been made to the rigorous standards of a former militia man. All the more reason not to underestimate Jake Blackthorn. More promisingly, the wall above the bed had a narrow, shuttered window. The window looked far too narrow for Charlie to squeeze through, but he'd give it a darn good try if he could only get the chance.

First, he needed to find a way to cut the ties on his limbs. Jake had taken his knife, of course, and no other options presented themselves in the immediate vicinity. The interior walls of the cabin had been crudely plastered, leaving no sharp edges of stone, and the floorboards had no loose nails. Short of Nathaniel handing him a knife, or Charlie crawling to the kitchen, he was trussed as helplessly as a Christmas goose. The best he could hope for at this point was to delay the Christmas feast.

Nathaniel sat down in the only armchair and waited, as ordered. Was Nathaniel really so sure he was in charge, or did he merely assume that he was because he was paying Jake for his help?

"Come here often, do you, Nathaniel?" Charlie asked.

"None of your business, Pyke."

"My father reckons Jake must have an accomplice to have kept his thievery hidden for so long. Do you bring Jake his supplies, so the police have less chance of tracking him coming in and out of town?" Charlie saw Nathaniel's momentary smirk, confirming his speculation. "Or do you help him steal and sell the stock as well?" No reaction. "I guess that explains why the MacEwen's farm has so often been the target of sheep rustling. Always hated the MacEwen family, didn't you, Nathaniel?"

"They're arrogant two-bit sheep shaggers who pass themselves off as landed gentry. Hamish MacEwen has treated me like scum my entire life, just like his parents. I can't imagine why Hamish took up with a lowly half-breed like you."

"Is that why you tried to take your anger out on me? Because I was Hamish's friend and you weren't? Or was it because I was smarter than you?" Charlie tensed for another kick in the gut, but his captor only rose a few inches off the armchair before plopping back down.

Nathaniel eyed him up like a lizard about to kill a fly. "I've plenty of reason to despise you, Pyke, not least because your father is a liar."

"What? Come on now, Nathaniel, you cannot believe that. My father is a respected officer of the law."

Nathaniel's snort said otherwise. "Yeah, and pigs might fly. Sergeant Pyke lied when he said Lee Hope was at his house that day. Just as you are lying when you pretend you are here for nothing more than a honeymoon. You don't fool me, Pyke. Always have to be the hero, don't you? What happened to bring you back here to a place you aren't wanted? My guess is that it has to be solid evidence about where Lee Hope hid the gold. Maybe an old diary of your grandfather's has come to light, or your mother finally admitted what her father had done."

Charlie struggled to stop fury from clouding his judgement. Nathaniel obviously believed what he was saying, and Charlie had to find out why. "You're wrong, Nathaniel. I came back to Clyde for nothing more than a peaceful honeymoon and a chance for my wife to get to know my parents. If it hadn't been for the grudges held for so long by people like you and the lies you are still spreading after all these years, I would never have looked into the old gold robbery. But, since we are here, why don't you enlighten

180

me as to why you think my grandfather was involved in the robbery."

"As if you didn't know, Pyke. You ought to have taken my advice and gotten the hell out of my town while you could."

"*Your* town?"

"It will be." Nathaniel smiled the superior smile of a man very sure of himself. "Times are changing. The era of bowing and scraping to the big runholders is over. It's time for the man of business to rule. By the time this socialist government is finished, the so-called landed gentry will be licking my boots. All I need is enough money to take advantage of the new era."

Nathaniel had a point, to the extent that the Liberal government was committed to breaking up a few of the large estates into smallholdings to give ordinary men a chance to work the land, but Nathaniel was vastly overstating the extent of change. The new government was rebalancing the scales, not advocating wholesale revolution. Besides, Nathaniel was hardly in need of a financial leg up, given the Summerfield's wealth.

"Why don't you ask your father for whatever money you need?"

"Because he believes a man should work his way up in the world," Nathaniel snapped. "I haven't the patience to wait for my inheritance when there's a pot of gold out there just waiting to be plundered."

"Maybe your father isn't as wealthy as he makes out?"

"Of course he is, you dimwit. My family own shares in one of the most successful gold dredging syndicates in the country, as well as three hotels and a stake in other businesses. My father will be elected mayor soon. He has the miners and the gold syndicates behind him and a few free ales should convince the rest of the town to vote for him too."

"And how would that help you?"

"I will ensure that one of the new mayor's first jobs will be to oust the disgraced police sergeant. That's if your father hasn't

181

already crawled away with his tail between his legs. The shock of your death won't help, of course. A fall from a horse over the edge of a bluff can cause terrible injuries, should your body be found. Out here, I'd be willing to bet your mortal remains never get a Christian burial. Your heathen Mama will be heartbroken."

If Charlie hadn't believed the danger of his situation before, he certainly did now. Nathaniel was not simply bragging – he meant it. "Be reasonable, Nathaniel. I won't tell you what you want to hear if I know I am going to die."

"Oh, I'm sure you will, Pyke, because if you don't tell me where your grandfather hid the gold, I will find your wife and do things to her in front of you that will have you both begging for mercy."

And there it was – Charlie's Achilles heel. He would give his life to protect Grace from harm, and Nathaniel knew it. The problem was, he did not know where the gold was hidden, and he was certain his grandfather hadn't either. However, now was not the time to mention that fact. As far as he could tell, his only remaining option was to bluff by pretending to know the location of the gold, if only to get out of this isolated death trap.

Charlie didn't have much longer alone with Nathaniel, so he decided on one last attempt to unsettle his captor. This time, he went straight for the jugular. "You appear to be under the misapprehension that you will inherit your family's wealth. If I don't make it home, my father will ensure that never happens."

"Your father has nothing on me, Pyke. Every time he's tried to charge me with a crime, it turns out the evidence has been lost, or the witnesses retract their statements. If you think you can turn Blackthorn against me, you're an imbecile. When money speaks, Jake clams up and listens."

Charlie noted Nathaniel's smirk and tried one of his own. "My father can have you disinherited in the blink of an eye."

"How?"

"He has proof that you're not Vern Summerfield's son." Charlie was making it up as he went along, but he doubted Nathaniel could tell, especially as his captor had leapt out of the comfortable armchair and was glaring at Charlie with all the calm, rational poise of a man about to have an apoplectic fit.

"How dare you? Of course I'm his son. I'm his oldest son and thus his heir."

Nathaniel was right, but the truth wouldn't help Charlie. "You must know you weren't conceived in wedlock, Nathaniel, and I know you've always been the butt of jokes about your mother's loose morals when she was a barmaid at the most notorious hotel in Central Otago."

Nathaniel stormed across the two yards of space separating them, giving Charlie just enough time to clench his stomach muscles before the incoming boot landed. Ever so, the vicious kick knocked the wind out of him. Much more of this and he'd end up with a ruptured organ.

"I apologise for putting it so bluntly, but the fact is that my father has undeniable proof Vern is not your father. You won't inherit so much as a bottle of bootleg rum from the Molyneux Hotel if I don't come home alive and well or if Grace is hurt in any way."

Nathaniel clenched his fists but kept them by his sides, for now. "You're a liar, just like your father."

"At least I'm legitimate. Don't you want to know who your real father is?"

Nathaniel didn't reply, but the sound of heavy boots stomping towards the cabin sparked a perfect, if improbable, twist to his lie.

Charlie looked towards the door and said, "Well, well, speak of the devil. Guess that explains why a notorious crook let you in on his secret sheep rustling operation. Say hello to your papa, Nate."

183

Hidden Valley

Without the dog and horses, and the occasional glimpse of buttercup yellow, Grace would have been utterly lost. Even so, she was clinging to hope with her fingernails.

Blaze had seemed certain of her direction until they descended into a steep valley off the track. Dozens of narrow gullies, each with a stream, descended on either side. Whatever was left of Charlie's scent was probably masked by the water and smells of wildlife and vegetation. The fragments of neckerchief had become progressively smaller until no more remained. At several points, even the faintest hints of previous travellers disappeared entirely, leaving Blaze to sniff her way up a series of sharp ridges and down again through a jumble of jagged rocks to spots beyond the reach of the sun.

Grace knew they were on a hopeless quest when Blaze circled one spot for five minutes. She sagged in the saddle and hung her head, watching idly as the horses drank from the stream. After five minutes of staring at the ground, Grace realised that there were other hoofprints in the silt around the stream.

Blaze let out a quiet yip and raced ahead. Grace was watching her like a hawk, but one minute the collie was there, the next she had disappeared. She hurried after Blaze, calling her name and praying the dog hadn't fallen into a mine shaft. In a rising panic, she kicked Nyx into a trot.

Nyx refused. In fact, she stopped dead and tossed her head. Grace was urging her on when she heard Blaze give a single quiet bark behind her. It took Grace another minute or so to spot the opening to a narrow gully. If there hadn't been a broken twig on a spiky branch and half a hoofprint in the shingle, she would have missed it. Looking closer, she realised that the shingle had been swept over with a branch to remove signs that people had passed this way. A rockfall hid the shape of the narrow gorge behind it, with the bushes further disguising the entrance.

Blaze sprung out from behind the bushes, giving her heart palpitations. "Quiet, Blaze," Grace said, sensing they must be near their destination. She urged Nyx through the bushes.

Beyond the narrow gorge, the gully widened out and Grace saw hoof marks made by horses and sheep in the soft ground by the edge of the stream. Further up the gully, a stone cabin was all but invisible within the rocks. If she hadn't been searching so desperately for it, she'd have missed it.

Grace retreated around the bend until she came to a bush strong enough to tether the horses to, leaving them on long halter ropes so they could reach the stream to drink. As there was little grass to be had, she added apples from the saddlebags to revive the horses' lagging energy. Blaze got dried meat and a swift hug for her life-saving tracking skills.

The first thing to do was to reconnoitre in case there was a safe way to rescue Charlie. With luck, the kidnappers might have abandoned him, but Grace doubted his rescue would be so easy. She loosened the strap holding her knife in the top of her boot and pulled the shotgun from its pouch. A quick look in the saddlebags failed to find any cartridges, and she didn't want to waste any more time. If it came to a confrontation, which she prayed it didn't, she'd just have to bluff her way out of it.

Grace told Blaze to stay, before setting off alone on her rescue mission.

As she got closer, the sound of two men arguing drifted down the valley. Since neither voice belonged to Charlie, she assumed he'd successfully turned the kidnappers against each other. The thought gave her courage a much-needed boost. She approached the stone cabin by sticking as close to the rocky edge of the gully as she could, out of sight of the front entrance.

A simple wooden shutter, made from a packing case by the look of it, covered the window on the end wall nearest her. Grace stuck her knife into the flimsy wood and carved a spyhole. The first quick peek told her the window belonged to an empty alcove off the main room. She looked again, but the only man she could see was Charlie, trussed up and sitting against a wall. Her heart leapt to see he was alive and conscious.

This close to the cabin, the jabber of voices became audible.

"You'd have to be stupider than a headless chicken to believe that codswallop. God almighty, boy, can't you see Pyke is playing with your head?"

Grace was sure she knew the voice, but she couldn't place it. The second man replied, but she couldn't make out what he was saying. There was no denying the fury in his tone, though. The argument was as good a diversion as she was going to get. There was only one problem – the window was little more than a narrow ventilation slit in the thick stone wall. Should she risk getting stuck and making their situation worse? Or was there another way to get her knife to Charlie, so he could cut the cords binding his limbs? Grace eased the shutter out from the wall for a better look, but there were no other windows close to her husband.

The volume of the argument went up a notch. "I'm not asking you to believe me," the first man yelled. "Hell's fury, Summerfield. If you can't trust your own mother, you're a damn disgrace."

Jake Blackthorn and Nathaniel Summerfield, Grace's least favourite residents of Clyde. She threw caution to the wind and wriggled her way into the slit. It was a tight squeeze for her, even after breathing in and twisting her head sideways. Charlie's broad shoulders would make an exit impossible.

Halfway through, the hem of her skirt caught on a sharp protrusion in the stone wall. Grace tried to wriggle backwards to unhook it, but reversing was even harder than going forward.

"Of course, I trust my mother," Nathaniel shrieked, "but Pyke said his father had proof."

186

Grace used his shrill retort to cover the sound of her ripping hem. With one almighty heave, she tumbled out of the window onto the bunk below, rolling onto the floor with a thump. Charlie glanced sideways for an instant, before quickly turning away. She could see the sudden tension in the set of his shoulders, but only because she knew him well.

Despite the thump, the argument continued unabated, to her relief.

"Connie is one fine woman, who'd be well justified in walloping your backside black and blue for believing those disgusting rumours about her being free with her favours."

She waited until Jake was shouting at peak volume before shoving her open knife across the floor. The knife spun around twice on the uneven floor before coming to a rest against Charlie's heel. He kept his gaze forward, but she caught the quirk of his lips in her direction as he scooped up the knife. Grace stayed to ensure that Charlie had sliced through the bindings on his ankles. She was about to leave when she realised he wouldn't be able to cut his hands free with such tightly bound wrists.

Nathaniel was now so furious he probably wouldn't have noticed if Grace walked into the room and sliced the rope. "Of course, I never believed those rumours about my mother, you dullard. But maybe you attacked her and took liberties against her will. I wouldn't trust you as far as I could spit, Blackthorn."

Before Grace could decide what to do, Charlie slid the knife into his boot laces to hold it steady while he sawed the wrist ties. That's my husband, she thought proudly, always thinking his way out of a pickle.

"I never touched Connie," Jake was yelling. "And I've never taken any woman against her will, least of all Connie. She's a better person than you will ever be, you arrogant little guttersnipe."

Grace blew her husband a kiss. He held up five fingers. In the absence of more precise information, Grace assumed he was asking her to give him five minutes to get loose. Then he flicked his hand at her and gave her a meaningful look. Go away? Surely

187

not. Perhaps he meant for her to create a diversion after five minutes, so that he could take his kidnappers by surprise – if they ever stopped arguing.

The diversion would have to be loud and terrifying, she decided, as she exited the window with a single desperate thrust, losing two buttons on the way. Grace raced down to the horses, determined not to waste a second.

As she yanked at the loosely tied halter ropes, she recalled where Charlie had put the shotgun cartridges. Time being short, she flung open the saddlebag, startling Erebus, and rummaged under the enamel plates and cups to the bottom of the bag. Cartridges in hand, Grace hauled herself up onto Nyx's back using whatever straps and protrusions came to hand. Elegant horsemanship it was not, but she was in the saddle, and that was all that mattered right now.

Grace jammed her hat on her head, loaded the shotgun, tied the reins to the pommel, and tapped Nyx in the sides. "I hope you're ready for the Charge of the Light Brigade, old girl," she whispered in the mare's ear, as she leaned low and urged Nyx into a full gallop.

The animals caught her frenzied excitement. Blaze raced ahead, barking, while Nyx charged with her neck at full stretch, with Erebus galloping beside her. Grace let out a series of war whoops and fired the gun once she was sure that the noise of pounding of hooves would have reached the cabin. The blast echoed around the rocky gully, making it sound like a dozen shots. Erebus shied and bucked at the noise, loosening the poorly fastened saddlebags. Plates, mugs, stove, and various other bits of gear jangled and clattered, adding a whole new level of clamour to the distraction. If that didn't capture the kidnappers' attention, nothing would.

Grace kept her eyes on the cabin, expecting Jake and Nathaniel to burst out at any moment. What was wrong with these people that they hadn't come out to fight off the cavalry?

As they galloped up to the cabin, Grace heard crashing and cursing inside. When a broken chair flew out the doorway, landing a yard away, Nyx slid to a stop, almost tipping Grace from her back. Nathaniel's flailing body followed close behind, landing with a whump of expelled air right by Nyx's hooves. Fortunately for him, Nyx's police training stopped her from rearing or lashing out. Nathaniel took one look at the giant horse looming over him and curled into a whimpering ball.

Grace trained the shotgun on him, making sure he heard the click of the barrel engaging. "Nathaniel Summerfield, you are under arrest for kidnapping my husband. I'd advise you not to resist, because I would take great pleasure in putting a round of shot into your vile hide. In fact, I might be tempted to –"

Her words were interrupted by a roar from within the cabin. Charlie and Jake burst outside in a tangle of limbs, with Blaze hanging onto Jake's leg and Jake spewing curses. Jake lifted a fist to beat the dog off, but Charlie landed a bone-rattling blow first, sending Jake sprawling onto the veranda.

Charlie dropped a knee onto Jake's back and yanked his hands behind him. "Lay a finger on my dog again and you'll wish you were never born." He glanced around to check what Nathaniel was up to. "Hello, Grace. Nice of you to drop by."

"It would have been rude not to visit when I was in the neighbourhood." Grace unhitched the rope attached to her saddle and threw it to him.

Within minutes, their captives were trussed. Charlie leaned on the door frame, with one eyebrow raised over a crooked grin. Blaze had her front paws on his thigh and was attempting to lick any part of his flesh she could reach. "What the blue blazes was all that noise, Grace?"

Grace made the five-finger hand-wiggling gesture. "I presumed you meant me to mount a distraction in five minutes to befuddle the kidnappers, leaving you free to subdue them."

"Befuddle? They were terrified the entire armed constabulary had come to arrest them. Most impressive as a distraction, my sweet, but the hand gesture was only meant to tell you to get to safety while I dealt with them."

"Oh. We really must work on our hand signals, Charlie. Are you hurt?"

"A few bruises and damaged pride at having to be rescued, but extremely glad to see you."

Grace broke open the gun and slipped off Nyx's back. "And your captives? Do I need my medical kit?"

"My captives have learnt that I don't tolerate anyone threatening my wife and kicking my dog, but are otherwise unharmed, more or less. They're as stunned as I am that you managed to track us down."

"Blaze followed your trail. Without her, and Nyx and Erebus, I would never have found you. The pieces of yellow cloth helped too. Honestly, I felt like I'd been dragged into one of those evil fairy tales that give little children nightmares."

Charlie ruffled the fur around the collie's neck. "We'll definitely have to keep you now, Blaze. A good tracking dog is worth her weight in gold to a detective, especially one with the brains to help rescue me from a desperate situation."

As if there had ever been any doubt that they would keep Blaze, rescue or not. Grace glanced over at their captives, but they did not appear to be suffering any serious injuries. Apart from the seeping blood on Nathaniel's arm at the site of his self-inflicted bottle wound and a few bruises, they seemed miraculously intact. Neither said a word, but if looks could kill, she and Charlie would be knocking at the pearly gates twice over.

She resisted the urge to take her fury out on these despicable scoundrels, but only because they couldn't fight back. Even a vengeful wife had to maintain certain standards of decorum, after all. Besides, Grace doubted she could have shot at them, however evil they were, unless there was no other choice. With the blast of the shotgun still ringing in her ears, and her shoulder throbbing from the recoil, she hoped never to fire a gun again.

Grace switched her attention to her husband, but he showed no signs of major injury either. The way Charlie was leaning against the door frame concerned her though. It wasn't hard to diagnose fatigue and dehydration, at the very least. She retrieved a water flask and the last two apricots from Nyx's saddlebag and handed them to her husband.

"Seems you've caught yourself a couple of kidnappers, Detective Pyke. Probably a murderer and a sheep rustler too. Perhaps now we might finally find out what happened after the gold robbery."

"Reckon so," Charlie mumbled between gulps of water. He pulled her to his side and put wet lips to her ear. "Hey, mountain woman, have I ever told you that I love you?"

"I believe you may have mentioned it once or twice." Grace dropped Charlie's hat on his head and dotted a kiss on his lips. "Delightful as this ramble through the countryside has been, my love, I would like to go home now."

Unwelcome Evidence

A fair proportion of the town turned out to watch the spectacle of their return. Six stolen sheep led the way in tight formation, under the expert control of a border collie who had previously feigned incompetence at herding. Duncan MacEwen stood agog at the return of his sheep and former dog. All other eyes were fixed on the two bound captives and the man and woman behind them.

Charlie could have done without a reception committee, but he was not surprised by the crowd, their return having been spotted in the distance by a small boy in a tree. The same lad was now approaching the end of the Clyde bridge with Sergeant Thomas Pyke in tow. Charlie's father stopped to wait for them, hands on his hips and pride in his posture. As the procession approached the bridge on the other side, Thomas turned to herd the crowd back to the top of the slope, so the sheep wouldn't panic and run amok.

Duncan MacEwen had two of his own border collies with him, who took over from Blaze once the sheep were off the bridge. After a quick discussion with Thomas Pyke, Duncan proved the sheep were his by the marks he'd put on their hides when he'd become fed up with rustling. After promising to return to make a statement to that effect, Duncan strode past Blaze with a rueful shake of his head, stomped past Jake and Nathaniel with a glare, and stopped beside Charlie to shake his hand.

"I won't keep you from your prisoners, Charlie," Duncan said, "but you can be sure we will be throwing a celebratory meal of epic proportions for you and Grace very soon. Julia and I will look forward to hearing your tale then." Duncan tipped his hat at Grace, then strode back to his sheep, whistling to the dogs to take them home.

Sergeant Pyke came forward and gave Erebus a pat. "What am I arresting these rogues for, Charlie?"

"Kidnapping me and threatening Grace, for starters. Sheep rustling in Jake's case, aided and abetted by Nathaniel."

Thomas raised an eyebrow at the kidnapping charge but maintained the outer calm of an experienced policeman. He dropped his voice to a whisper. "I followed your suggestion of searching the Yarwood property and surrounding area again, Charlie. We found the remains of a body. Hopefully, we can prove it is Ezra Yarwood. It would be a relief to everyone if Jake confesses to killing him."

Charlie had his doubts about their chances of getting Jake to confess, but time would tell. They continued their march to the police station, where Thomas and his constable took charge of Jake and Nathaniel. Charlie and Grace took the four horses and the pack pony to the field behind the station, where he suggested Grace should go inside and reassure his mother that all was well. Grace complied without arguing, which told him all he needed to know about her state.

It was only mid-afternoon by the angle of the sun, but to Charlie it seemed an eternity since he had woken on a mountain top next to his wife. He let the horses drink their fill at the trough, then he unsaddled them and rubbed them down with aching arms.

Grace returned with an armful of hay and a bag of oats slung over her shoulder. With her broad-brimmed hat, suntanned skin, and dusty riding skirt, Charlie could only marvel at his wife's transformation in a few short days.

His mother walked beside her carrying apples and a large, meaty bone. She shook her head at her son in despair. "Grace tells me you were kidnapped, Charlie, leaving her abandoned. I swear my heart cannot stand any more of your escapades. It's a wonder my hair hasn't gone completely grey."

"Would you rather I took up a sensible occupation, Ma? I hear there's an opening for a bartender in the Molyneux Hotel."

While Charlie took the saddles to the shed, his two favourite women fed and praised the horses. Blaze curled up under the shade of a tree, gnawing on her bone as if she hadn't been fed in a week. Charlie knew how Blaze felt. His stomach was an empty cavern.

But food would have to wait. "Go inside and rest, Grace," Charlie said. "I'll make a statement at the police station and return as soon as I can. My father can't interview and charge them until he knows the facts."

His mother glared at him. "You will come into the house, Charlie Pyke, and wash the filth off your face and hands, before sitting down to a proper meal. Those two scoundrels can cool off in a cell for half an hour."

"Perhaps we can do both, Mrs Pyke," Grace said. "We can wash and eat while Sergeant Pyke takes our statements."

An hour later, all objectives having been met, Charlie and Grace signed their statements. His father was champing at the bit to interview the prisoners, while his mother seemed remarkably stoic in the face of the perils he and Grace had overcome. However, there was an angry flush to her complexion that did not bode well for Nathaniel and Jake, should Jasmine ever be allowed alone with them. She looked ready to explode when Charlie pulled up his shirt to show his bruises.

His father's jaw tightened, but all he said was, "we'll get the local doctor to certify your injuries for the record."

Charlie knew he could rely on his father to follow police procedure to the letter. He had already assured Charlie that the constable would be present at all times, so Sergeant Thomas Pyke could not be accused of bias against his son's attackers when the charges came before the court. Unfortunately, that meant Charlie could not be present at the interviews. In fact, his father told them to go back to Rose Cottage and try to forget about the investigation for the rest of the day.

"What about the body you found, Sergeant Pyke?" Grace asked.

"The local doctor should be here soon with Ezra Yarwood's medical records, if any exist."

"Does the doctor have much experience in gathering forensic evidence from a long-deceased corpse?"

Grace asked the question with wide-eyed innocence, which didn't fool any of them, especially Charlie. "Grace has worked for the Dunedin police surgeon for several years, Pa. She ought to look at the remains, alongside the local doctor."

Sergeant Pyke, to his credit, did not question her competence. After exchanging a quick glance with his wife, he said, "the corpse is in the hospital mortuary. Let me know what you find as soon as possible. I should warn you that all that remains is a skeleton and a rotting pair of leather boots. I've little doubt that it is Ezra Yarwood, because I found the body in an abandoned well shaft on the Trent's farm, not far from the boundary with the Yarwood's place. The type of tools that would be used to mend a stone wall were found around the body, and a layer of rocks had been thrown on top. The cause of death is not in doubt, as the skull had been struck with considerable force by a sharp, jagged object. A rock from the stone wall, presumably."

"It must have been quite a mission to extract the body from a well shaft," Grace said. "No wonder his body wasn't found for so long."

"We dredged the farm pond at the time of Ezra's disappearance," his father said, "but old Mr Trent didn't mention the well shaft back then. Bob Trent's father, I mean, who is now deceased."

"Was failing to mention the well a suspicious oversight, do you think?" Charlie asked.

"Not really. I had to get Bob Trent's permission to search the property again. It wasn't until we had hunted high and low that Bob recalled the old well. His father had had the shaft sunk when they first took over the farm, because of a dispute over the use of the water in the water race. The dispute had been resolved before the shaft was deep enough to strike water. Bob says the well was capped at ground level to prevent accidents, years before the robbery, and nobody gave another thought to it. It was completely overgrown."

"Bob Trent must have been appalled at the thought of the body hidden on their farm all these years," Grace said. "How did he react, Sergeant Pyke?"

"Bob was genuinely shocked, I think, although he took it with his usual stoicism. Matilda was horrified and distraught, as you'd expect. Both of them assumed the body belonged to Ezra Yarwood, which is hardly surprising in the circumstances. Matilda's first thought was for poor Mrs Yarwood. I felt dreadful telling Matilda that she must not talk to her neighbour until the body had been formally identified by the doctor."

"If Ezra was buried with his tools," Charlie said, "he must have been killed the afternoon following the robbery. We know Jake Blackthorn visited Ezra that afternoon to persuade Ezra to tell him where the gold was hidden. Presumably, Ezra wouldn't tell Jake, or perhaps he gave Jake false information about the gold's location, after which Jake killed him."

"Sounds reasonable to me," his father said. "Now all I have to do is get Jake to admit it, and this deplorable saga will be over."

"What about the missing gold?" Grace asked.

"If Jake hasn't found it after all these years of searching, I doubt we'll ever find it. Unless there was a third party who took the gold and suddenly develops a guilty conscience after twenty-four years of silence."

A knock at the door interrupted further speculation. The local doctor had arrived to view the remains of the murdered man found in the well.

After the doctor examined and recorded Charlie's injuries, he offered them a lift to the mortuary in his buggy. Charlie helped Grace into the seat beside the doctor, while he took the cramped rear seat of the buggy. Grace and the doctor swapped anecdotes about unusual causes of death, leaving Charlie to consider the evidence. He hoped they could solve the case for Mrs Yarwood's sake. A man murdered for stolen gold was still a victim who deserved justice, in Charlie's view, although the town would likely spare little sympathy for Ezra Yarwood.

At the hospital, Grace set to work without turning a hair at the stomach-churning sight of the grisly remains. As Charlie's father had said, the cause of death was clear from the crushed skull. Grace was able to confirm the body was a young man, based on bone structure and teeth. She found an irregularity in the smaller bone of the forearm, which matched a break recorded in Ezra Yarwood's medical records. If nothing else, Mrs Yarwood would finally know the fate of her only son.

Charlie examined Ezra's boots while Grace completed a minute examination of the skeleton. The leather uppers of the boots were badly decayed, but the thick soles were largely intact. Charlie used one of the hospital's sharp instruments to pick out the soil clinging to the treads of the boots. The outermost layer was the type of soil one would expect on a farm, but underneath there was a fine layer of another type of dirt, studded with a few finely crushed stones. It was probably nothing more than the dust and stones of the road Ezra walked from the gold lock-up back to the farm, but Charlie scraped a sample into an empty medicine bottle for a closer look later.

Once the post-mortem notes were completed and signed by Grace and the local doctor, they returned to the Pyke's cottage in the doctor's buggy.

Grace went to help Charlie's mother, who must have been out somewhere, as she arrived back at the cottage in the Pyke's buggy at the same time as them. Charlie went to the police station to let his father know Grace had confirmed the body's identity.

Sergeant Pyke took him into his office and shut the door behind him. "I can't tell you how grateful I am to you both for making progress on this case after all these years, Charlie. Knowing that Ezra was the second robber and having an explanation for his disappearance will allow me to retire in peace.

If we can pin Ezra's murder on Jake Blackthorn, I'll retire in glory."

This was the second time his father had mentioned retirement. To Charlie, his father was ageless, but the truth was that Thomas Pyke was in his fifties now, and policing a large rural area was a young man's job. For all his father's robust good health, his face was scored by deep lines and his gait was noticeably stiffer these days.

"If you do retire, Grace and I would love to see more of you and Ma in Dunedin."

"We'd like that," his father said. "At your wedding, I realised just how much Jasmine misses her sister too. You never know, we might surprise you by moving to the big city. To be honest, I doubt I could stop Jasmine moving if there was ever a grandchild on the way."

"Eventually, we hope to be blessed with a house full of them," Charlie said, "once Grace graduates as a doctor."

"Delighted to hear it, Charlie. Grace really is the most extraordinary woman. Listening to your account earlier made me realise how much we owe her for rescuing you. I don't doubt that Jake and Nathaniel would have killed you once they realised you knew nothing."

Charlie nodded. It had frightened him too. Grace's arrival at the hidden cabin had seemed like a miracle at the time, and even more so in retrospect. "What have you got out of them so far, Pa? No, let me guess. Nathaniel whined about how the townsfolk suspected his parents of stealing a fortune, leading to unwarranted persecution of him during his miserable but pampered childhood. I expect he blamed Jake for forcing him to be party to a kidnapping he knew nothing about."

"Exactly so. I told Nathaniel that you had made a sworn statement that he admitted being in charge of the kidnapping plan, while Jake was simply hired muscle – a statement which Jake corroborated. Nathaniel denied it, naturally, but the money to pay

Jake must have come from somewhere. Gambling, possibly, or illegal alcohol sales after hours."

Charlie recalled the conversation between Connie and Vern. "I overheard Vern Summerfield saying his son was stealing from the till at the Molyneux Hotel. He's fed up with Nathaniel's behaviour and wanted to do something about it. Vern was so angry he was ready to disown Nathaniel."

"That may be true, Charlie, but Vern won't give evidence against his own son at trial."

"Vern's integrity might surprise you. Either way, you might shake Nathaniel's confidence using what I overheard. He's an easy man to goad and nowhere near as clever as either of his parents."

Sergeant Pyke leaned back on his chair until it was in danger of tipping. "The details are neither here nor there. Nathaniel and Jake will both be convicted of kidnapping, without doubt, and Jake will be convicted of stealing sheep as well. Jake has vehemently denied killing Ezra, though."

"He went to see Ezra on the afternoon of the robbery," Charlie pointed out. "Sylvester Healey saw him."

"Jake admits that much, but he says he left Ezra alive that day and Sylvester will vouch for him. I'll have to interview Sylvester, of course, but I have to admit that Jake gave the impression he was telling the truth. His eyes tend to flick to the side when he lies, but his eyes stayed on me when he denied the murder charge."

"Did Jake say what he talked to Ezra about?" Charlie asked.

"Jake said when he heard about the robbery, he visited all the people he suspected, to see if he could get a slice of the fortune in return for his silence. I asked him whether he was only after the gold or did he also plan to avenge his brother's death. Jake denied revenge was his intention, but his eyes flicked to the side when he said it."

"Meaning Jake could have gone to see Ezra seeking both revenge and easy wealth. No surprise there. He certainly had the strongest motive to kill Ezra."

199

"According to Jake, Ezra told him the police had already made a thorough search of the house and property and found nothing, because there was nothing to find. Ezra convinced Jake he was telling the truth, which Jake accepted because he had no evidence to link Ezra to the robbery. I got the impression Jake really did walk away from Ezra that day believing he wasn't the robber."

If his father was correct, that left a killer still on the loose. Charlie knew his father was worried for the same reason he was, and it was time to put the issue into the open. "Nathaniel and Jake are both convinced my grandfather took the gold from Ezra, which also makes my grandfather the most likely murderer, if they are to be believed. Sylvester Healey hinted at it too. In fact, I think Sylvester is the source of everyone's suspicions against Lee Hope. Sylvester was keeping an eye on Ezra, hoping Ezra would lead him to the gold."

His father looked down and fiddled with the edge of a police file, but his slumped shoulders gave his thoughts away. "There's more, Charlie. Ezra told Jake that he had seen Lee Hope with the gold on his cart early that morning as he passed the Yarwood's house. When Jake heard that the police found gold dust on the sack-barrow, he was furious at the police for letting Lee Hope go, thinking that I had stepped in to protect my father-in-law by giving him a false alibi. Jake felt there was no point coming to the police with what Ezra told him, especially not when the news broke the next morning that Ezra had disappeared."

There it was at last – the reason Jake was so convinced Charlie's grandfather knew where the gold was. No wonder the rumours had persisted for so long, if Ezra claimed he had actually seen the gold on Lee Hope's cart.

His father hadn't finished the sorry tale. "It was only weeks later, when Ezra's former gold mining partner was arrested, that Jake realised he might have been tricked. At that point, he conceded Ezra was probably the robber after all, but Jake still believed Lee Hope was involved. Jake thought your grandfather had seen where Ezra had hidden the gold and killed Ezra to silence him. It's plausible, of course, because Lee Hope did see him soon after the robbery, when nobody else was out and about."

"But we all know my grandparents weren't rich," Charlie said.

"Jake had an explanation for that, too. He thought Lee must have panicked after he killed Ezra and hidden the gold until the fuss died down. Better to forfeit a fortune than swing on a scaffold. I suppose it was not an unreasonable assumption, especially given the number of people harassing your grandparents, looking for buried treasure."

"But why was Jake so sure that my grandfather killed Ezra?"

"Because Sylvester Healey saw Lee with Ezra late that afternoon, after Jake had left."

Charlie felt the bedrock of his life shift under his feet. He didn't know what to say, other than the obvious. "Sylvester could be lying. We'll have to find someone who can provide an alibi for my grandfather that afternoon."

"We already have a witness, Charlie. After he was released from arrest, your grandfather was left under my care. I wasn't at home after the robbery, because I was helping with the interviews of other suspects, but your mother assured the police that her father was at our cottage all that day and night."

"Well, then," Charlie began. He stopped when he saw the anguish in his father's face.

"God help me, Charlie, I wondered if Jasmine wasn't telling the truth at the time, but I chose to ignore my gut feeling. I didn't believe – or perhaps I just didn't want to believe – my father-in-law could be involved in such an unthinkable crime on the day his first grandson was born." Thomas Pyke's voice broke and he had to look away to hide the tears in his eyes.

Dashed Hope

Charlie had never seen his father so distraught. He didn't know how to comfort him, so he did what Pyke men did best – he placed a reassuring hand on his father's arm and took the burden on his own shoulders. "Stay here, Pa. I'll go talk to Ma. After that, we'll take a formal statement from Sylvester Healey. My grandfather is innocent, and I'll prove it."

Charlie closed the office door behind him and told the constable his father needed time alone to complete paperwork.

The short walk next door to his parents' cottage was one of the longest of his life. The irony of his position was not lost on him. He had been scathing of Connie's denial of her son's wrongdoing in the face of the evidence, and now he was doing the same in protecting his grandfather.

Charlie heard laughter drifting out the open window. He hesitated at the door, but putting the moment off would help no one. Grace and his mother fell silent at the grim expression on his face.

"I need a few minutes with my mother, Grace. Alone."

Grace stiffened at the unexpected request. They were, after all, a team who shared everything. Then she rose. "I'll check on Blaze. She's had a long day." She grasped his fingers briefly as she left, signalling her support.

His mother patted the vacated seat at the table with a shaking hand.

Charlie could see no point in drawing out the pain. "Jake is sure my grandfather killed Ezra and hid the gold, Ma. We know he is innocent, of course, but Jake says he knows Lee Hope went to see Ezra late in the afternoon after the robbery."

His mother didn't hesitate for an instant. "That's true, he did."

202

Charlie had expected an outraged denial. He was still stunned and unsure how to proceed when his father came into the room and sat beside him.

"Perhaps you will tell me why you lied to the police, Jasmine," Thomas said.

Jasmine reached her hand across the table to her husband, but she withdrew it when he didn't meet her halfway. "I'm sorry, my darling. I've been torn with guilt at not telling you, but I feared for my father. The man who was the local sergeant at the time wasn't a fair-minded policeman like you, Thomas. He had already interviewed me, and I could see he was the type of man who despised my people. If the sergeant knew my father had gone back to see Ezra, he would have jumped at the chance to arrest a Chinese man. I was going to tell the police inspector when he arrived the next day, but he was just as bad."

Charlie tried to speak, but his father stopped him.

"I understand, Jasmine," Thomas said. "You were protecting my reputation and career as well. But the fact is, we need to know why your father went to see Ezra."

"He suspected Ezra of trying to set him up to take the blame for the robbery by using his sack-barrow to move the gold. My father wanted to judge Ezra's reaction to the accusation for himself. Ezra denied the robbery and accused my father of telling tales to the police to implicate him. Ezra was mending a wall when my father arrived. He grabbed a mattock and threatened my father, who was sensible enough to run away. Lee Hope left Ezra alive. He swore it to me and my mother on his own life and ours. I believed him, Thomas, truly. I believed him with both my heart and my mind. My father was a fool to visit Ezra, but he did not kill him, and he never laid eyes on that cursed gold."

Thomas reached out across the table to wipe his wife's tears away. "I know he is innocent, Jasmine. Lee Hope was one of the best men I have ever known. Unfortunately, we are now back in the same position of defending his honour with the weight of evidence against him." He pushed his chair back. "Perhaps you could give us a moment alone, Charlie. Then I'll go to see Sylvester Healey."

"Sure, Pa. I'll check on the dog."

When Charlie left, his parents were heading into each other's arms. Like his father, Charlie believed his mother was speaking the truth – or what her father had convinced her was the truth. Charlie found Grace under a tree, with Blaze's head in her lap, soaking up the affection Grace was lavishing on her. Charlie would have given anything to swap places with the collie.

"I'm off to talk to Sylvester Healey, Grace. I'll come back for you soon."

Grace got to her feet. "Can I come?" She asked tentatively, which wasn't like her.

Charlie pulled her into his arms. "Of course you can, my love. You should know that events have taken a turn for the worse. My grandfather went to see Ezra Yarwood after Jake left. As far as we know, Lee Hope was the last person to see Ezra alive."

"Apart from the murderer," Grace said.

"Apart from the murderer," Charlie agreed, crushing her closer in gratitude for her support. "And maybe Sylvester Healey. I'm beginning to wonder if Sylvester is the harmless simpleton he makes out."

"He is like a shadow, don't you think, Charlie? Moving around town doing his odd jobs, seeing everything, but with no one noticing him, except to feel sorry for him."

"Sylvester seems to have Vern Summerfield wrapped around his little finger, and I know other folks give him food and supplies as well. Rightly so, given his impoverished circumstances. And yet Sylvester was clever enough to realise that Ezra was one of the robbers."

"Perhaps he saw the robbery happening and knew it was Ezra," Grace suggested.

"Either way, Sylvester was watching the Yarwood's house after news of the robbery broke. He admitted seeing Jake visit

Ezra, but I'd like to know just how long he was watching and whether watching turned to an argument with Ezra over the location of the gold."

Another memory tugged at Charlie's brain, reminding him of a detail he had overlooked. "Vern said all the miners were chasing Connie, including Sylvester. He's easy to overlook now because of his infirmities, but we don't know what Sylvester was like then. He must have thought he had a chance with Connie, which means the head injury that affected his brain could have occurred after the robbery."

"Then let's talk to him. We can't rest until we have this case solved, Charlie."

They had to run to catch Charlie's father, who was already striding at a brisk pace towards Sylvester's shack.

Charlie caught up with his father at the end of the road. "Calm down, Pa. We both know my grandfather was honest through and through. On the other hand, I'm inclined to believe Jake too, at least to the extent that Ezra fooled Jake into thinking that my grandfather had the gold. Jake would not have walked away from a fortune otherwise. He and Nathaniel must have felt certain of my grandfather's involvement, or they wouldn't have resorted to kidnapping me."

"I don't know what to think anymore, Charlie. Nothing about this case makes sense."

"That's because it was never your case to investigate, Sergeant Pyke," Grace said. "You were busy looking after adorable little baby Charlie and his mother. All you have seen is what was recorded in the police file, which is full of holes because nobody was telling the whole truth. Let's find out what Sylvester knows and go from there."

"Thank you for your support, Grace, and yours, Charlie." Thomas said. "Sylvester was always scared of Jake and now we know why."

They found Sylvester leaning on his shack, smoking his pipe. "Heard you've arrested Black Jake. Reckoned you'd be wanting to speak with me sooner or later."

"Jake won't be getting out of gaol anytime soon, Sylvester," Thomas Pyke said. "You need not fear him now. Jake said you saw him visiting Ezra after the robbery. Can you tell us everything you recall about that day?"

Sylvester took a deep puff on his pipe and let the smoke drift into the otherwise cloudless sky. "Ain't much to tell, but I couldn't blab to the police back then, 'cos Jake woulda killed me. After Ezra disappeared, there seemed no point in telling what I knew."

"We understand your actions at the time, Sylvester," Charlie said, "but now we need to know everything you saw during the entire time you were watching the Yarwood's house."

Sylvester switched his red-eyed gaze to Charlie. "Are you sure you want to hear the truth, young Pyke?"

"Just tell us what you saw, honestly and in as much detail as you can recall," Thomas said. He took out his notebook to underscore that this was an official inquiry.

"If you say so, Sarge. I reckoned Jake or Ezra might've done the robbery as soon as I got word of it. Reckoned a reward would be posted, sooner rather than later, and I aimed to get it. Well, I couldn't watch both, but they made it easy for me. Jake called on Ezra the afternoon after the robbery. They were in the garden, and I was in the hedge, listening to them argue."

Charlie and his father both leaned in, eager to hear. Grace hung back, but still within hearing distance.

"Ezra said it wasn't him what robbed the lock-up. He was angry that Lee Hope told the coppers about him being out in the garden early that morning."

"Did Ezra say who he suspected of the crime?" Charlie asked.

Sylvester fiddled with his pipe, sucking the end until the tobacco glowed hot. He did not meet their eyes. "It's a long time past an' me noggin ain't what it used to be."

"Sylvester, we want the truth."

"Ezra said Lee Hope done it." Sylvester cringed away from them. "Not saying I believed him, mind, just saying what he said."

"Did Jake believe Ezra?" Charlie was hoping Jake had lied about being fooled by Ezra's version of events. If so, Jake might have returned later, after Lee Hope had left, to force Ezra to tell him where he had stashed the gold. Sylvester would have been too scared to admit it then, but now that Jake was behind bars, the truth could be told.

"Oh, aye, Jake believed him. He left and didn't come back."

"What?" Charlie wasn't sure if he had heard right, but Sylvester had said the words with such certainty that Charlie was forced to relinquish his hope. Sylvester might not always tell the full truth, but he was a poor liar. Right now, his expression was as untroubled as if he'd said it was nice weather today, with none of the expected twitches and mumbles.

"Jake left," Sylvester repeated. "Ezra said he had a wall to fix, and he wanted to get on with it, unless Jake wanted to help him. Jake left and Ezra got his tools. I kept watch in case Ezra were burying the gold, but he really did work on the wall, until another man arrived. They argued something fierce. I feared being seen, so I snuck back to the hedge by the house, waiting for Ezra to come back. But Ezra never did. Nobody else came or went from the house while I sat there fretting, 'til I got the jitters and scarpered in case someone saw me."

"Did you go to find Ezra, Sylvester?" Thomas asked. "Did you tire of waiting to see where Ezra had hidden the gold and try to force it out of him?"

The old-timer's weather-beaten face crumpled with fear. "No, I swear, I never touched him. I never even went near him. I only wanted the reward."

Charlie would have felt sorry for Sylvester at that moment if he hadn't been so deep in a fear of his own. "Who was the man you saw after Jake left?"

"I can't tell you. Please don't make me."

Sergeant Pyke pulled handcuffs from his belt. "Sylvester Healey, don't –"

"It was the Chinaman." Sylvester shrunk away from the two Pyke men as if expecting a beating, leaving no doubt which Chinese man he meant.

Sylvester took hope from their lack of reaction. "I'm sorry, but it's the God-honest truth. Ezra told Jake the Chinaman was the robber. Ezra said he was digging his garden early in the morning and he saw Lee Hope go past in his cart with the sacks of gold on the back. Ezra tried to pretend he hadn't seen him, but the Chinaman weren't fooled. Ezra were scared stiff 'cos Hope went to the police and put the blame on him, knowing …"

Sergeant Pyke supplied the words Sylvester feared to say. "Knowing I was his son-in-law and would believe him? Sylvester, I appreciate your honesty in telling us what Ezra said, but I can assure you my father-in-law was with my wife and I at the time of the robbery. His grandson was about to be born and he wouldn't have missed that for the world."

"I believe you, Sergeant Pyke," Sylvester said. "You're an honest copper, I know. I didn't trust Ezra's word neither. But when Jake left, Ezra was alive. Lee Hope came to see Ezra after that, and I heard them arguing up a storm, like I said. Ezra weren't never seen again, not be me nor anyone else."

Charlie heard his father thank Sylvester for his statement in a voice as dead as a man going to the gallows, which was precisely how Charlie felt inside.

They turned for home on leaden feet. Even the soft touch of Grace's hand on his arm failed to drag Charlie from his despair. She was being kind, but she must be shocked at the idea of being married to the grandson of a murderer.

Grace broke the silence with forced cheeriness. "Well, that's good news. Sylvester didn't actually see Lee Hope kill Ezra, and of course we know he didn't. All we need to do is find the person who did."

"Your support is appreciated, Grace," Thomas said, "even if it turns out to be misplaced."

Charlie clutched Grace's hand and put his other hand on his father's shoulder. "Sylvester could be a better liar than we think, or another person could have come over the fields to kill Ezra after my grandfather left. We've got this far, Pa. We can still solve this dratted case."

"How in the name of heaven are we going to do that, Charlie?" his father said. "Please tell me you two have a plan to clear Lee's name. Any plan will do, no matter how crazy, so I can take a glimmer of hope back to Jasmine."

"I have an idea," Grace said, "but I can't promise it will come to anything. It will have to wait until tomorrow, though, because right now I don't have an ounce of strength left. I'll need to see Mrs Yarwood again. I know it is unfair to ask, Sergeant Pyke, but could you hold off telling her about the discovery of Ezra's body until I have talked to her tomorrow morning?"

"After twenty-four years of not knowing her son's fate, another day won't make any difference," Thomas replied. "I doubt Mrs Yarwood will comprehend the tragic news, anyway."

They returned to the Pyke's cottage in a sombre mood to collect the horses and dog. The sight that met their weary eyes was almost more than Charlie could bear.

Mrs Constance Summerfield was outside the cottage, towering over Charlie's tiny mother, tongue-lashing her like a demented fishwife. "No, I won't listen to you, Mrs Pyke. Your husband had no right to arrest my son on the say-so of your son and his wife. They've already attacked Nathaniel once before. It's them who ought to be locked up."

The police constable was trying to get between the two women, while Vern Summerfield was attempting to drag his wife away by the arm.

Jasmine Pyke wasn't about to be rescued by anyone. "Your no-good son can rot in gaol for all I care. I'm fed up with you both. Nathaniel kidnapped Charlie and threatened to kill him. He left my daughter-in-law alone to die in the middle of nowhere, for the love of God. What kind of heartless scoundrel would do such an evil thing?"

Thomas Pyke had always impressed Charlie with his calm and rational approach to even the most obstreperous of villains. But today, his father had reached the end of his tether. Thomas broke into a run and waded into the fray. "Enough!" he bellowed.

The shock froze all the participants in place.

Vern was the first to react. "My apologies, Thomas. We only wanted to visit Nathaniel. My wife is rather upset."

"Take your wife home, Vern," Thomas ordered. "I don't want to see her back here until she can behave with decorum." Connie opened her mouth, but Thomas cut her off. "Now, Vern, or I swear I will arrest her for breach of the peace."

Vern and the constable escorted Connie to the waiting buggy. Charlie clung to Grace, wondering what she must be thinking of this dreadful place he had dragged her to for their honeymoon.

"Go home, Charlie," his father ordered. "Let's put this abysmal day behind us and try to remember that there is nothing love cannot overcome." Thomas put an arm around his wife and steered her into their cottage.

Charlie wondered if his father was talking about himself or them. Either way, Charlie knew that he and Grace needed to be alone as much as his parents did.

When they arrived back at Rose Cottage, Charlie saw that his mother had dropped off a meal and lit the stove under an enormous pot of hot water, presumably while he and Grace were at the hospital. A hip bath sat in the middle of the floor.

Grace shed tears at the welcome sight of hot water, which made Charlie realise just how close to exhaustion she was. She must have had the worst day of her life, waking up to find him gone, then mustering her resources so capably to rescue him. Despite that, she hadn't hesitated to volunteer to examine the remains of Ezra Yarwood and had stood by the Pyke family throughout the ensuing drama.

Charlie lifted her in his arms and laid her on the sofa. When he had the bath ready, he helped her to undress and wash away the grime of a brutal day. By the time he tucked her into bed, she was yawning.

Grace ran her fingers through his hair. "You still haven't told me what Nathaniel and Jake were arguing over at the cabin. It must have been important to distract them so thoroughly."

"I cruelly played on Nathaniel's sensitivity about his mother's loose reputation by telling him that Jake was his real father."

"Thank goodness for stupid criminals and smart detectives," Grace said. "I need to sleep now."

Charlie pulled the covers up to her chin and kissed her forehead.

"We'll crack this case, Charlie," Grace whispered, right before her eyes closed.

I'm glad one of us thinks so, Charlie thought, as he tiptoed to the door.

Charlie washed away his own layer of filth in the steaming water. Blaze got the last turn in the grubby bath. The old cloth he used to dry the dog with was beyond salvation by the time he'd finished. After checking her for bruises and cuts, Charlie and Blaze devoured the meal in silence, before they retired to their respective beds and slipped into an uneasy sleep.

Ezra's Girl

Grace woke in a state of panic, convinced that Connie Summerfield had tracked her down in the night and beaten her with a parasol for arresting Nathaniel. When her heart rate dropped back to normal, Grace realised the imagined pain was real. Her body ached in so many places she had to peek under her nightdress to check whether there were fresh bruises. There weren't. Two days in the saddle as a novice horse rider had simply tested her muscles in ways she had never experienced before.

She waddled with her thighs apart to the sitting room for her medical kit to apply salve to chafed skin and arnica cream to stiff muscles. Blaze came over and sniffed, her wrinkled muzzle showing her disgust at this new perfume. Grace splashed on rosewater, but Blaze remained unimpressed. She gave up and filled the dog's bowl with pungent dried meat, which met with the collie's wholehearted approval.

Charlie and Blaze had demolished the dinner Jasmine Pyke had left for them, so Grace set about making breakfast from their remaining supplies, which left her a choice between fresh fruit, porridge, three-day-old Victoria sponge, or corned beef and pickles. She went with porridge and stewed apricots, which was so delicious she warmed the remaining sponge and drenched it with apricot sauce. Charlie ambled out of the bedroom at the sound of spoon against plate, and roundly approved the concept of dessert for breakfast.

Feeding time over, Charlie looked out the window and declared the day half over, although the sun was still low in the sky. "What's this plan of yours, Grace?" he asked, when the dishes were done.

"A last attempt to get information out of Mrs Yarwood. I thought you could search Ezra's belongings while I engaged her in conversation, assuming she doesn't take to us with her shotgun."

"Should I be looking for anything in particular?"

"Anything that might give away what he was up to on the day of the robbery. When I was there last time, I noticed Mrs Yarwood had kept Ezra's room as it was all those years ago, or so it seemed. The police would have searched it, of course, but there is always a chance they missed something, especially as we know more about what happened now."

They tied the dog up, to Blaze's disgust, and walked down the road to the Yarwood's property.

Grace was oblivious to her surroundings, trying to recall what it was about her nightmare that was nagging at the back of her brain. Finally, she had it. "Charlie, why did you tell Nathaniel that Jake was his real father?"

"Only because I needed a way to set them against each other. I told him my father had evidence, which he would use to disinherit Nathaniel if he didn't let me go."

"But they look nothing alike. Jake is dark, brown-eyed, and brawny, while Nathaniel is fair, blue-eyed, and reasonably handsome when he isn't flourishing a broken bottle. Why did you think Nathaniel would believe it?"

"Because Nathaniel is an idiot with a foul temper, and his mother had a reputation as a loose woman when she was a barmaid. Nathaniel must know he was born out of wedlock, unless his parents haven't told him he was born six months after they married. Why do you ask?"

Grace stopped by the hawthorn hedge that ran along the edge of the Yarwood's property. "I hadn't met Vern Summerfield before yesterday. He seems quite different to Nathaniel, in temperament at least. He remained calm yesterday, even when his wife was furious, and appears to have a grasp of right and wrong.

In terms of appearance, he could be Nathaniel's father, although Vern has brown eyes. Was his hair dark before he went grey?"

"Vern had light brown hair. Nathaniel takes after Connie in temper and looks, I'll grant you, but that doesn't mean he isn't Vern's son."

Grace knew he was right, but proving Lee Hope's innocence meant grasping at whatever straws fluttered vaguely in the breeze. "Nathaniel has a prominent forehead, which Vern and Connie haven't. And he has been rotten to the core since he was old enough to bully children at school, despite Vern's influence. Even Connie, for all her determination to rise to the top of local society, strikes me as good at heart. Her anger was directed at saving her son, which is understandable. Didn't your parents stick by you when you were accused of murder?"

"My mother was ready to gallop to Dunedin with her rolling pin swinging," Charlie recalled. "Fortunately, your steadfast belief in me saved me first, for which I am ever grateful. You're not suggesting that Nathaniel really is Jake's son, are you, Grace?"

"Not at all, but he might be somebody else's. Mrs Yarwood must have been blonde once, and she has blue eyes and a prominent forehead. Ezra's skeleton was heavy browed too. I'm only speculating, but if Connie's baby was fathered by Ezra Yarwood, and he jilted her for another woman, Connie might be more than a little angry, don't you think?"

"And when Connie is angry, anything can happen," Charlie concluded. He paused, then added, "I did overhear Vern say he would disown Nathaniel if he got into any more trouble, which is a strange thing to say of your own son, no matter how bad they are."

"Interesting, although hardly conclusive. How did Connie react?"

Charlie cringed at the memory. "She screamed, 'How dare you, after all I've done for you. I lied for you under oath. You'd be nothing without me, Vern Summerfield.' Which, in retrospect, is rather damning to both of them. We need to tread carefully with Mrs Yarwood on this one."

"We might not be welcome regardless of our reasons for calling," Grace said. "I think our only hope will be if Mrs Yarwood mistakes me for Ezra's girl again. I hate to deceive her, especially now that we know her son is dead, but I cannot think of any other way to find out what happened that day."

They continued along beside the hawthorn hedge, meeting Matilda Trent coming out of the Yarwood's gate. Grace suffered a twinge of embarrassment at the thought that Matilda might have overhead their conversation, but knew it was unlikely from a distance when they had been talking in low voices.

Charlie ran ahead to help Matilda, who was struggling with the gate latch. "Morning, Mrs Trent. Let me get that for you."

"Thank you, Charlie. Nice to see you again after all these years." Matilda suddenly blanched. "Oh, dear, you must think I've gone back on my word to your father. I didn't mention anything to Mrs Yarwood about the ... about your father's discovery in the well. I always deliver fresh milk on a Tuesday, you see, and I didn't want the old dear to think I'd forgotten her." She leaned back on the gate for support as she struggled to find the right words. "Was it ... you know?"

Charlie took her arm. "Let us see you home, Mrs Trent. I shouldn't say anything, but I may as well tell you my father will pay an official visit to Mrs Yarwood this afternoon."

Matilda sagged against Charlie's arm. Grace took her other arm to help support her, but Matilda didn't seem to notice. "Poor Mrs Yarwood. I didn't like her son, but nobody deserves to die like that. Do you know how it happened?"

"Unfortunately, we're running around in circles on this case," Charlie said. "I'm not sure we'll ever know what happened. Mrs Trent, I hate to ask you this in the circumstances, but it is difficult to find people I trust who can tell me what Ezra was like. I don't even know what he looked like."

"Ezra could turn a girl's eye, that's for sure. It wasn't just that he was fair of face, it was his charm. The charm was only skin deep, though. He had a temper on him too." Matilda thrust her forehead forward and scowled under lowered eyebrows, probably without realising she was mimicking him. "He could turn nasty on the flip of a coin. He even yelled at his mother, which shows you the kind of man he was. But he was good to her too, coming home to help her out and suchlike. That was the problem with him – all kindness until he wasn't. Give me a consistent, trustworthy man like my Bob any day."

Grace exchanged a glance with Charlie. Matilda might have been describing Nathaniel Summerfield. "Do you know if Ezra argued with anyone in particular in the days before or after the robbery?"

Matilda shook her head. "We avoided Ezra, and his mother's house is far enough away from ours that we wouldn't hear anything. Ezra wasn't known for his sweet temper. He had a reputation for gambling and drinking as well as chasing women."

"I only ask because Ezra was out fixing the stone wall next to your property during the late afternoon or evening after the robbery. I realise it isn't close to your house, but a person in the field might have overheard an argument."

"Bob's brother usually brought the cows in for evening milking back then, whereas I was usually inside the dairy, which is solid stone. Old Mr Trent was quite the taskmaster, and I had little free time. But now you mention it, I do recall the police inspector asking the same question when he visited us after Ezra disappeared. Bob's brother mentioned overhearing raised voices more than once during that day. He couldn't recall when, and he didn't know who was arguing, although he was sure all the voices were male. He would have investigated if he thought there was a serious altercation."

"More than one argument?" Charlie said. "I know it is a long time ago, Mrs Trent, but can you remember if Bob's brother said how many arguments he heard?"

216

"I don't think he could recall. He had no reason to pay attention to Ezra's bad temper, as long as Ezra stayed away from us."

"Does Bob's brother still live in Clyde?" Charlie asked.

Matilda shook her head. "He got a job at a piggery up-country when Bob and I started filling the house with children. He passed away a few years back when a tiny scratch became infected. A terrible tragedy."

They had reached the lane down to the Trent's farm. "You've been most kind, but I can manage from here," Matilda said. "I apologise for my moment of weakness. Pregnancy does make one rather prone to being emotional."

"You don't need to apologise," Grace said, "especially not in the circumstances. You've been a saint looking out for Mrs Yarwood all these years. It can't be easy. I went to visit her the other day, and she mistook me for the girl Ezra was planning to marry."

Matilda let out a puff of air that was half laugh, half dismissal. "Mrs Yarwood does that to every woman between the ages of sixteen and sixty. The old dear is no different to all mothers of men who enjoy the pleasures of a single life – ever hopeful and always disappointed. I don't mean to be unkind, but Ezra's mother lives in her own world of make-believe these days."

That was one theory blown apart. Grace had to agree with Matilda, especially as she knew Mrs Yarwood better than anyone. It had always been a stretch to think that the old woman's ramblings meant anything.

"Take care, Matilda," Grace said. "I would still love to have you over for tea if you can spare the time."

"That would be lovely, Grace."

Grace watched her waddle down the lane. "Matilda should be putting her feet up in her condition, not looking after her elderly neighbour as well as her own family."

217

They turned in the opposite direction, back towards the Yarwood's house, each deep in thought.

They had almost reached the Yarwood's gate when Charlie spoke. "The most likely time for Bob's brother to have heard Ezra arguing with two or more men was when he brought the cows in for the evening milking. My grandfather could have been one of the men, but who was the other? Sylvester didn't see another man come or go, if he was to be believed."

"It helps to know he heard a man, rather than a woman," Grace said. "A shame Bob's brother isn't alive, not that he'd recall any more than he did at the time. We can't be sure the arguments he overheard were late in the day though, as he might have been out on the farm at any time. In fact, the Trent house is not so far from the wall that Bob's brother couldn't have heard an angry altercation from the farmyard. Or Bob Trent, for that matter. I know he is not the most talkative of men, but Matilda did mention that Bob didn't like to talk about the robbery."

Grace knocked on Mrs Yarwood's door. Fortunately, the lady of the house answered the knock in a state of confusion rather than belligerence.

"Good morning, Mrs Yarwood. Do you remember me?"

"Ezra's girl?" Mrs Yarwood squinted at her uncertainly, before switching her focus to Charlie, but struggling to come up with a name. "Is this your brother? I thought he died." She wagged a finger in his face. "You were a fool to get caught, boy. Caused my son no end of problems, you did. They thought Ezra did the robbery just because he knew you, but my son was a good boy."

Grace could see from Charlie's shocked expression that he had jumped to the same conclusion as she had. Ezra's girl, who they had just concluded was non-existent, had now been given an unexpected identity. Ezra's girl was not a local lass – she was the sister of Zachary Dawson, the robber who had been caught. The sister had lived near Cromwell, Grace recalled. If the shotgun came out now, at least they had moved a step forward in their

218

understanding, assuming this wasn't another of the old woman's fantasies.

Charlie reacted quickly. "I'm sorry I got caught too, Mrs Yarwood. Ezra was a great friend to me. He always spoke highly of you."

"And so he ought," Mrs Yarwood said. "Ezra is a good boy who loves his mother. He'll be back soon."

"Ezra left his knapsack here, didn't he?" Grace said. "He'd never go far without that. I wondered if we could look at it, Mrs Yarwood. For old time's sake."

"It's in his room, dear. You," she said, pointing at Charlie, "you can stay here and tell me what Ezra says about me."

Grace whispered "magnifying glass" in Charlie's ear.

"What was that?" Mrs Yarwood demanded.

"My sister was reminding me to tell you about how much Ezra enjoyed coming home to see you." Charlie passed Grace his notebook, which had a pocket for a slim magnifying glass inside it. "When we were panning for gold together, Ezra was always busy thinking up jobs he had to do as an excuse to come home to see you, Mrs Yarwood. Like mending the dry-stone wall."

Grace went into Ezra's room, leaving the door open so she could hear their conversation. It wasn't hard, as Mrs Yarwood was so deaf that she spoke at a shout.

The old woman cackled her delight. "Oh, aye, he loves a nice straight line of stones, does Ezra. Cross as a badger he was when old Trent's cows pushed over part of his wall."

"Did old Trent come over to help when Ezra was fixing the wall, Mrs Yarwood? Or one of the Trent boys, Bob or his brother? Or somebody else?"

Grace smiled. Charlie was clutching at straws, but one never knew if an old memory could be sparked. He was giving her time too. Grace went about her task with a recklessness that would have had the police surgeon tutting. She rifled quickly through Ezra's old possessions but found nothing linking him to any woman.

Either Ezra didn't have a sentimental bone in his body, or he had destroyed whatever love letters and mementos he had had. Perhaps he wasn't the love letter type of man. In fact, he may have been illiterate, as many people of his generation were.

Mrs Yarwood snorted. "Old Trent never gave a rat's arse about the wall, especially when his cows were eating our grass instead of his. Bob is just the same. Never a man to talk to his neighbours if he could talk to his cows instead, let alone help fix the wall."

Charlie tried again. "Ezra must have been angry about the damaged wall. Perhaps you heard him arguing with someone that day?"

"You'll have to stop mumbling, boy. My hearing ain't so good. Did you bring lemon cake?"

"Not today. I know Ezra loved lemon cake. Did he like to argue too?"

"Oh aye, my Ezra was always having a barney with someone or other, especially when he had the drink in him. But he's a good boy. He'll be home soon."

There was a momentary silence, in which Grace imagined Mrs Yarwood nodding happily and Charlie beating his head against the wall.

Grace moved on to Ezra's old knapsack, taking it over to the window to study it in the light. The police would have gone through everything at the time, Grace reasoned, but they might have missed an insignificant detail or two. Specifically, had Ezra used the knapsack to carry a portion of the gold from his hiding place back to the cottage to give to his mother. She was hoping Ezra might have carried a clue about the hiding place away with him, unnoticed in the darkness of the early morning. She took out the magnifying glass and set to work.

Charlie's voice was sounding a little strained as he sought to prolong the conversation and gather information, without making any mistakes that would give away his identity. "It's so long ago," he said. "I think my sister was worried your son might marry someone else for a while there. That barmaid was always keen on Ezra, wasn't she?"

"Ezra never cared for no tuppeny-bit tramp of a barmaid," Mrs Yarwood declared. "Not to marry her, anyway."

There was a long pause, but Mrs Yarwood added nothing to her statement.

"Did my sister visit Clyde too?" Charlie prompted.

When Mrs Yarwood spoke again, Grace recognised the hostile change in her tone and had a déjà vu moment involving a shotgun.

"Your sister promised she was coming here. Why didn't she come to see me?" Mrs Yarwood's agitation grew with each word until she was shouting. "Ezra ought to have brought her to see me before they got married!"

Grace hurried out of the bedroom. "My brother is getting mixed up, Mrs Yarwood. I've only been in Clyde for a few days. It was nice to see …"

"Who are you?" Mrs Yarwood struggled to her feet and reached for the cupboard that held the shotgun.

Grace yanked Charlie from his seat. "Lovely to see you, Mrs Yarwood." She hauled open the door. "Mustn't keep you any longer."

The shotgun went off as they were halfway across the garden. Fortunately, Ezra's mother had dreadful eyesight. A flurry of peaches and leaves bumped and fluttered to the ground fifty yards to the left, as Grace vaulted over the gate with Charlie close behind her.

Grace pushed herself out of the dirt behind the hawthorn hedge – again – and groaned. "Next time we throw ourselves over a gate to escape a shotgun blast, can you try to land beside me, rather than on top of me?"

"Next time?" Charlie brushed off her clothes. "If we're threatened with another shotgun this side of Christmas, I'm going to take up a quieter line of work. My apologies for squashing you, Grace. In my defence, I was trying to stay between you and death."

"Apology accepted."

"Please tell me it was worth it." Charlie stuck his head out from behind the hedge far enough to ascertain that Mrs Yarwood had retreated to her sanctuary.

Grace held up a tiny hard teardrop of wood attached to a thinner protrusion, broken off close to the end.

Charlie raised a dubious eyebrow. "If you're about to tell me that little thing – whatever it is – is the solution to this exasperating case, I'm calling in the lunatic asylum. What is it anyway?"

"I found it in the seam of the knapsack. I know it isn't the evidence we were after, but it was all I could find. Ezra must have been clever enough to clean out his knapsack before the police arrived." Grace showed him under the magnifying lens. "I think it's a seed from a pinecone with the wing bit broken off."

"Oh well, it was worth a try. Learning that Ezra's girl was Zachary Dawson's sister might prove useful, if she's not a figment of Mrs Yarwood's befuddled brain."

"Dawson's sister will be long gone if she was ever here. How would we find her after all this time, Charlie?"

"I have it in hand already. When my father mentioned that Zachary Dawson had a sister in Cromwell, I sent off a telegram to the Cromwell police for more information. Let's go back to town. I want to check on my parents and visit the post office to see if I have had replies to my telegrams."

Grace took Charlie's arm as they set off towards town. "Why did you have the extraordinary foresight to think Dawson's sister might be involved?"

"I didn't expect anything to come of it when I sent the telegram. We had so little to go on when we started this investigation that I followed up every possible line of inquiry I could think of. I was glad I did, though, once I heard your account of your first meeting with Mrs Yarwood. She assumed you were

Ezra's girl, coming to marry her son, and I knew Dawson's sister left her position in Cromwell to get married. Now we have reason to believe they are the same woman."

"How do you think finding her will help us?"

"It probably won't, unless she knew what Ezra and her brother were planning. If she did come to Clyde to marry Ezra, she might have heard about his other women and decided she would rather have the gold than the man. Can't say I blame her. We can't afford to ignore any potential lead, no matter how unlikely."

Grace walked in silence for a few minutes before speaking. "Connie worked in Cromwell before she came here, and Matilda said she came from her family farm 'up the valley', which could mean the Cromwell area, I suppose. They both arrived in the months before the robbery. Could either of them be the mysterious sister of the robber?"

"Not Matilda. Her young age and skill at dairy farming when she arrived in Clyde doesn't fit at all, because Dawson's sister was a parlourmaid in a wealthy household. I cannot imagine Connie as a parlourmaid, although Vern did say his wife was more of a lady than people gave her credit for."

"I keep coming back to Connie's comment that Vern would be nothing without her."

"That might mean anything, Grace. I could say the same about you. In my case, it could mean that without you I would be lying battered and dead in a gully right now, or that I wouldn't have fulfilled my dream of becoming a detective, or something as simple as not being able to look at a Victoria sponge without my pulse rate racing."

Grace stopped under an overhanging tree and slipped her hands around his waist. "Despite being thrown into an unexpected mystery, it's been a wonderful honeymoon, hasn't it, Charlie? Apart from when you were kidnapped, of course."

"Despite the unexpected mystery?" Charlie leaned down to her ear. "Are you sure having a mystery to solve hasn't enhanced the enjoyment? Don't think I didn't see the surgical textbook in your trunk. You were worried about being bored in a little country town."

Darn the man – he knew her too well. "Idiot man. Of course I didn't expect to be bored. I simply expected to have a little more time on my hands to sit under a tree with a good book. I should have known better." Grace's breathing quickened at the touch of his lips. "Are we going to dilly dally all day or are we going to see about these telegrams?"

"Can I vote for dilly-dallying?" Charlie removed his lips from her ear and took her arm again. "But you're right, we ought to check on the telegrams. We can't forget that Dawson's parlourmaid sister could be anyone and anywhere. If she is in Clyde, I'd have to say that Miss Dewer, the Summerfield's maid, is the best fit. Dewer seems far too skilled to be stuck in a small town and there was something in the way she gave her title as 'Miss' that held a touch of sadness, as if her chance at marriage had passed her by. If so, it seems ironic she ended up working for the Summerfields."

They walked in silence, each deep in thought, until they reached the outskirts of Clyde.

Charlie stopped at the crossroads. "Do you want to visit my mother while I am at the post office? I'll be as quick as I can."

"I'd like to come with you, in case the telegram replies are in," Grace said, "but I also want to ask your parents about potential hiding places for the gold. We know the gold was not buried or stashed on the Yarwood's property, because the police searched thoroughly, but Ezra only had the early hours of the morning to hide it elsewhere. Assuming it hasn't been retrieved by Connie, Vern, Jake, Sylvester, or persons unknown."

"Good point, Grace. If we found the gold, we would at least know that it wasn't the source of the Summerfield's wealth. And that £500 reward is very tempting. Ezra would have decided on a hiding place in advance. Somewhere he wouldn't be seen, and where nobody would dig up the gold by chance. A place where the digging wasn't obvious, which wouldn't be easy in mid-winter when the ground was frozen."

"Unless he put it under a pile of rocks or in an attic or under the floorboards or any of dozens of other places."

"The spade my grandfather saw in his hand suggests Ezra buried it. Besides, if the gold was in a building, it probably would have been found by now."

Charlie's face took on the vacant expression that made strangers think he was slow-witted, but Grace knew it meant he was deep in thought, sifting the evidence in his brain into new patterns. She turned away to avoid distracting him, which made his sudden embrace all the more unexpected. Grace yelped, while Charlie burst into laughter and swung her around.

"You clever devil, Charlie Pyke. You know where the gold is, don't you?"

"I believe I might have an inkling."

His sparkling eyes said it was more than an inkling. Grace waited for him to tell her.

Instead, he took her arm again. "I fancy a visit to the church after we've been to the post office."

Grace didn't push him. She merely hoped his idea was more substantial than praying for divine inspiration.

They didn't get back to Rose Cottage until dusk, having stayed at the Pyke's house for dinner. Blaze ran in excited circles around them when they arrived. Grace preferred to think of it as the thrill of seeing her human companions, rather than the special meatloaf Jasmine Pyke had made in Blaze's honour. Blaze made it clear both were welcome. Blaze's starring role in Charlie's rescue had assured her heroine status forever in the Pyke household. Grace had been treated like royalty too, for her part in rescuing the Pyke's only child.

Charlie's parents had been stunned by the news that they would attempt to recover the missing gold tomorrow. After a busy afternoon involving a little research and a great deal of cajoling, all the necessary arrangements were in place.

Charlie's theory about the location of the gold – based on a single pine tree seed, a few finely crushed stones in Ezra's boots, and a perusal of the parish records – had definitely cheered the mood. In fact, Sergeant Pyke had pulled Grace into a joyous embrace and danced her around the sitting room, before disappearing to arrange for his constable to guard the site overnight. A wise plan, Grace acknowledged, given the likely frenzy that would erupt if word of the possible gold recovery spread from the supposedly sealed lips of the few people who had to be told.

They decided to have an early night to be fresh for the busy day ahead. Grace curled up against her husband's chest and sighed at the softness of the bedding. An overhead canopy of stars might be the loveliest sight on heaven or earth, but it took a lot to beat a comfortable bed when it came to a night's sleep.

"Our honeymoon is half over," Charlie said. "We have not had the peaceful break from crime that we intended so far. After tomorrow, I promise to have eyes only for you, my love."

"We should be pleased we have unmasked the second robber and found his body, even if we don't find the missing gold. However, finding the gold would be wonderful too. We could be £500 richer this time tomorrow, thanks to your detective skills."

Charlie gathered her hair to the side so he could reach her neck. "We did it together, as always. What would we do with such an enormous reward?"

"Perhaps we could honour your grandfather by donating part of it to a relief fund for Chinese miners?" Grace felt his smile against her skin.

"I'd like that. And I love that I don't need to hide my origins from you, Grace."

"You don't need to hide your Chinese ancestry from anyone, Charlie. It's people like the Fanshawes who ought to be ashamed of their attitudes."

"Who?"

"Nobody important. Merely a couple on the train who kindly allowed us a compartment to ourselves."

"Even after the donation, we'd have plenty left of the reward to build our own future."

"Enough for a lifetime supply of dog food," Grace suggested. "And husband food. Or food for a family, perhaps."

"All excellent suggestions." The third suggestion took a moment to register. "Grace, are you … could you be with child?"

The delight in Charlie's voice warmed Grace to the bone marrow. She turned over to look into his face, which was radiant with hope. "It's far too early to know, but we have not been as careful as I had planned. You are simply too irresistible, Charlie Pyke, and the stars were too bright and beautiful."

"I feel as if I should apologise, knowing we had agreed to wait until you graduate, but I cannot. A child would be a blessing, no matter when it happens."

"I agree, Charlie. Common sense tells me to wait until our financial position is sound, but I long for a family too."

"We would cope, with or without the £500 reward. I could take only the more profitable investigations. With a family in mind, I would not want to take the risks I have taken in the past. Alistair has made a name for himself with fraud cases. I could learn from him."

"Only if you would enjoy it, Charlie."

"I think I would. Being shot at, stabbed, beaten, and kidnapped are starting to lose their appeal."

"Whatever the future holds, right now we should sleep. It'll be a big day tomorrow, when my brilliant detective husband dazzles his hometown with a missing £7000 fortune."

"If they don't run me out of town for being born with a murderous grandfather," Charlie muttered.

228

A Grave Matter

The following morning, Grace and Charlie walked out of Clyde beside the county magistrate and the Anglican minister.

Grace's stomach churned at the thought of everything that could go awry. If they were wrong about the location of the gold, they would commit a deeply disrespectful act for nothing. If they were right, somebody else could have beaten them to it by twenty-four years, in which case Grace's desire to elevate Charlie in the eyes of the townsfolk might turn him into a laughingstock.

Even if the gold was there, it might be seen as proof of the rumour that the Pyke family knew more than they were telling all these years. Their goal had been to exonerate Charlie's grandfather, Lee Hope, and in that they had failed miserably.

Charlie was explaining how he had come to his conclusion. "We were thinking about where a robber could hide the gold when the ground was frozen over winter. Bearing in mind that Ezra Yarwood was seen with a spade in his hand."

"I see how you concluded that Ezra Yarwood was coming home from burying the gold, Mr Pyke," the minister said, "but why the graveyard? You will understand my concern, naturally. To disturb a grave is not a matter one takes lightly."

"I share your concern," Charlie said, "but don't you think it would be worth it to free the town from decades of uncertainty and suspicion? The evidence of the pine tree seed in Ezra's knapsack and the stones in his boots point to this location, as that combination is found nowhere but the graveyard."

The flimsy evidence rang hollow in Grace's ears, and she saw the doubt on the minister's face, but Charlie forged on with the final tentative link. "The cemetery register recorded a burial two days before the robbery. Thus, the ground would still have been easy to dig. Can you think of any other place that is close to town and yet out of sight of any neighbours, and where nobody would think to question newly disturbed soil?"

The minister exchanged a worried glance with the magistrate, who had heard the evidence yesterday. The magistrate had reluctantly agreed it was worth following up, given the stakes, but only after gaining the consent of the deceased's family. As luck would have it, the grave belonged to one of the many men who had no known family in the area.

Grace's stomach moved beyond simple churning into a state of acute distress. Vomiting or fainting were not options at this late stage. Should they call it off? Fortunately, Charlie had sworn the magistrate, minister, and gravedigger to silence. If their quest failed, the townsfolk need never know.

Their small party rounded the bend to find a chattering crowd gathered in the graveyard. Fear clutched her heart as Grace realised the entire town of Clyde had turned out.

Charlie nudged her arm. "You can see why Pa posted a constable here overnight. I did warn you that you cannot keep a secret in a small town."

Grace wanted to remind him that some people obviously had kept a secret, considering the mystery of the missing gold hadn't been solved in the quarter century since the robbery, but she felt too queasy to talk.

The crowd went eerily quiet at their arrival. Grace's boots crunched over the chips of stone on the path, which matched those in Ezra's boots. A large pine tree blocked the early morning sun.

Grace stood by her husband on the far side of the grave as the gravedigger began his work in the Anglican section of the graveyard. With each thump of the spade into the hard ground, the crowd crept a little further forward, their eyes alight with both curiosity and the insatiable desire for gold. Was one of these now-familiar faces a murderer who had failed to get the vital information on the gold's location before he killed Ezra? If so, how would the killer react now? Her eyes skimmed over the onlookers.

The prominent citizens took pride of place at the foot of the grave, their backs as erect as the lofty stone crosses that marked the passing of their ancestors. Mr and Mrs MacEwen stood front and centre, next to the mayor, the magistrate, the minister, and other local dignitaries and landowners.

Hovering at the edge of them were the worthy citizenry, including Matilda and Bob Trent. Matilda's arms wrapped around the swell of her belly, and her usual rosy cheeks looked flushed and blotchy. Her husband clutched her arm to support her. After a few minutes of standing, he ushered her over to a raised tomb. Matilda shook her head at first, presumably at the disrespect of sitting on a grave, but gave in at Bob's insistence and sat with a visible look of relief. Grace returned to her scanning of the crowd, hoping that she would not be called upon to act as an emergency midwife to a premature baby in the middle of a graveyard.

Further away, amongst the Presbyterian gravestones to the rear and side of the crowd, Vern and Connie Summerfield stood, looking both tense and exhausted. Several members of their household stood behind them, including Miss Dewer, the Summerfield's helpful and efficient maid. Despite the kidnapping, Grace sympathised with the anguish Vern and Connie must be suffering with their son in gaol. Nathaniel Summerfield hadn't been born when the robbery took place, but the repercussions had helped push him along the path to self-destruction.

Connie saw her watching and shot Grace a venomous glare. Jasmine Pyke, who was beside Grace, must have seen it too, because she flinched and dropped her head in prayer. Grace tucked her arm around her mother-in-law. Jasmine understood the deep hurt that came from being an outcast. Grace hoped she and Charlie wouldn't have to leave Clyde without freeing the Pyke family from the stigma of suspicion.

As the spade dug into the hard ground with a monotonous thunk, Grace looked beyond the crowd. On the margins, away from the rest of the townsfolk, a group of old miners, ground down by time and ill fortune, slouched against the stone wall surrounding the graveyard. If men of their ilk had gravestones at all, it would be a simple stone saying, "Here Lies X". No scripture about a life well lived, no "rest in peace" and no "forever missed by his wife and children". Perhaps not even a date of birth.

She searched the shadows but could see no sign of Sylvester Healey.

At the far side of the graveyard, near the Mixed Section, a cluster of people of Chinese ancestry had their heads bowed. Grace imagined them praying that their mortal remains would be returned to long-abandoned families in the home of their birth.

A grunt from the gravedigger drew Grace's attention back to the grave. The crowd surged forwards, despite the best efforts of the constable and Sergeant Pyke.

Charlie lowered himself down beside the gravedigger to help him lift heavy sacks, which sagged and threatened to tear. Grace felt weak at the knees, and thankful to have Jasmine Pyke beside her, holding her up.

The magistrate shouldered his way forward. "Everyone back, please. If you would do the honours, Mr Pyke."

Charlie sliced open the topmost sack and lifted out a nugget of gold, prompting the townsfolk to let out a collective gasp, before bursting into spontaneous applause.

All Grace could think was thank heavens they hadn't made fools of themselves in front of her husband's hometown. And then the reality hit her like a train appearing from nowhere.

"Breathe slowly, Grace," Jasmine whispered. "By all that's holy, I never would have believed you and Charlie could perform a miracle after all these years. Two miracles, in fact. Finding both the second robber and the missing gold."

Charlie gathered Grace and his parents around him to share in the moment. Through her daze, Grace slowly became aware that the Mayor of Clyde was making a speech along similar lines, praising the town's newly favourite son and most famous detective, Mr Charles Pyke, for achieving a miracle. Grace shook her head at the sudden elevation of a man who had left the town with a mixed reputation, based on little more than the coincidence of his birthday and the ancestry of his mother's family. Despite the irony, her heart filled with pride for her husband and joy that Charlie was finally getting his due.

The crowd demanded a speech from Charlie, and he obliged with a few words, acknowledging that it was a team effort from his family and his extraordinary wife. He did not mention the fact that Ezra's killer had not yet been unmasked, and fortunately, nobody in the crowd thought to ask. Yet.

Grace knew it was only a matter of time before fresh doubts would be raised about Charlie's grandfather, who was now known to be the last person to see Ezra Yarwood alive – apart from the murderer. At least they could now prove that it was Ezra who took and hid the gold, thanks to a few little stones and a pine seed.

The magistrate held up his hand for silence. "I can confirm that the reward of £500 for the return of the gold is still valid. As two young people, newly married, I imagine Mr and Mrs Pyke will be delighted to hear it. I look forward to hearing of their future exploits, which I have no doubt will reflect well upon our fair town."

Under the cover of another round of applause, Jasmine whispered in Grace's ear. "What on earth do you plan for an encore, Grace?"

"We're going back to our secluded cottage for a few days of peace and quiet." Blaze poked her nose into Grace's hand, as if she has something to say about that idea. "I'm looking forward to spending time with you and Sergeant Pyke as well, before we have to return to Dunedin."

"Just as well," Jasmine said. "I'm not sure Clyde could stand much more excitement."

Vern Summerfield had rushed over for the unveiling of the gold and was now clasping Charlie in a bearhug. Grace wondered how many people had secretly thought Vern's wealth had come from the stolen gold. A great many, if Vern's delighted response

233

was anything to go by. His eyes shone with tears of relief, as befitted a man finally absolved from blame for an age-old robbery he did not commit. The moment of joy would be fleeting. Vern and Connie would be reminded of the damage that suspicion had done to their family every hour of every day their son spent behind bars.

Connie stood in the background, seething at her husband. Their son was incarcerated, her glare reminded him, and every person in Clyde would wonder why Vern was embracing his captor. She turned and walked towards the exit with her head held stubbornly high. The crowd separated before her with the haste of the Red Sea parting.

Sergeant Pyke was watching Vern's reaction too. Any man with a son in strife would understand the heartache Vern was suffering – Thomas Pyke more than most. He stepped in front of Vern, shielding him from the gawking crowd.

Duncan MacEwen came up beside Thomas. "Back to the Molyneux Hotel, folks," Duncan shouted. "The drinks are on me."

A cheer went up, and the graveyard emptied in a tidal wave of jubilation. Duncan, Thomas, Vern, and Charlie followed them at a slower pace.

Grace wanted to retreat to the sanctuary of Rose Cottage. Was she the only one who understood that this was not the end of the saga? Yes, the missing gold had been found at long last, where logic and a shred of evidence had told them that Ezra had hidden it after he committed the fateful robbery. But Ezra's killer was still at large, assuming Sylvester and Jake were telling the truth. Inevitably, the shotgun of suspicion would become a sniper's rifle aimed squarely at Lee Hope, and the Pyke family would never be free of the taint.

Julia MacEwen took one of Grace's arms. Jasmine Pyke took the other. The love of these two exceptional women gave Grace the strength to put one foot in front of the other, towards the Molyneaux.

A Bridge Too Far

Charlie entered the Molyneux Hotel surrounded by a tide of well-wishers.

Connie Summerfield, ever a woman with an eye to opportunity, even in a crisis, had hurried ahead to take her place behind the bar. She was already dispensing ale and banter with the look of a woman back in her element. There was a new barman, who looked familiar. Charlie mentally stripped away the newly barbered whiskers, clean clothes, and dirt-free skin, until he recognised Sylvester Healey, who looked surprisingly at home on the opposite side of the bar.

When the telegram arrived – hand-delivered by the postmaster – Charlie was squeezed up against the counter with a line-up of drinks in front of him and a crush of men behind him. Grace had disappeared within a crowd of ladies to a separate private lounge, so he went outside to read the telegram alone.

He had been hoping for a telegram from the police in Cromwell. Since he was asking about events that had happened twenty-four years ago, his expectations were low. The most important piece of information was the name of Zachary Dawson's sister, who had worked as a parlourmaid in a wealthy household near Cromwell before the gold robbery. Good maids were hard to find, and Charlie's suspicions had been roused by the Summerfield's maid, Miss Dewer. Some unfortunate twist of fate must have been responsible for her seeking work in the small town of Clyde, and it was a coincidence he could not ignore.

However, the telegram was from Dunedin. The results of Alistair Stewart's inquiries added unwelcome complications to the case. Charlie shut out the noise of celebrations within the

Molyneux and tried to think logically. Not easy when his body was trembling as if it had been drenched in freezing cold water.

Charlie was so distracted he didn't hear the footsteps behind him. He crumpled the telegram to stop the person from seeing its contents before realising it was only his father and another policeman.

"Charlie," his father said, "this is Sergeant Donnelly from the Cromwell Police."

"Pleased to meet you, Mr Pyke," Donnelly said. "I had to come to Clyde to see the magistrate on another matter, so I thought I would answer your telegram in person. Well done on finding the gold, by the way. If I had known what all this was about, I wouldn't have pinched my pennies all those years ago."

"You've lost me, Sergeant Donnelly," Charlie said. "Perhaps you could give us the full story."

Donnelly handed Charlie a thin file. Charlie looked through the case notes while the story unfolded.

"You'll see the original telegram from Arrowtown only asked the Cromwell police to ascertain the whereabouts of Zachary Dawson's sister, without specifying the reason for the inquiry." Donnelly turned to Thomas Pyke. "You know what it was like back then. It was more like the army than a police force. Follow orders to the letter and don't waste pennies sending unnecessary words in a telegram."

Thomas Pyke nodded. "How well I remember those days, when polished boots were more important than initiative."

"I'd only been on the job for a week," Donnelly said. "The address given was a respectable household. The lady of the house told me that Miss Dawson had been an exceptional parlourmaid until she left without giving notice. She left her mistress a letter, apologising for her sudden departure and forfeiting her wages as compensation for the lack of notice, explaining that her fiancé wanted to get married. Dawson's mistress was cross but understanding. Love comes first, she told me, and Miss Dawson

236

had been an exemplary worker. Never any male callers, cleaned the silver to a shine, never any trouble. It's all in the file."

Charlie finished reading the brief notes as Donnelly spoke. Donnelly had done as ordered and sent off a telegram saying, "parlourmaid sister gone, married," without giving a full name or date of departure. But he had recorded those details in the case file. Dawson's sister had left the day after the robbery. Charlie experienced one of those heart-pounding moments when you look in a mirror and see someone unexpected standing right behind you. It wasn't a good feeling.

He pushed aside his reaction and shook Donnelly's hand. "Thank you for taking the trouble to see me. Father, perhaps you could take Sergeant Donnelly into the Molyneux Hotel for a drink. I need a few minutes alone to think."

A few minutes dragged out until he had lost track of time. Charlie knew what he had to do, but the consequences frightened him. Twenty-four years was a long time. Could he not let sleeping dogs lie?

It was Mrs MacEwen who finally sought him out. "There you are, Charlie. We thought you must have gone home. Why does the hero of the hour look so grim when you should be celebrating?"

Charlie couldn't find the words to explain his dilemma.

Mrs MacEwen took his arm. "Come for a walk and tell me about it, Charlie. You often brought your problems to me in the past, when you and Hamish got into a scrape. I like to think it helped you to talk to someone outside the family."

"It did, Mrs MacEwen. Your family meant the world to me. I will be forever grateful to you for the advice you gave me when I came back to Clyde last year after leaving both Grace and the police force."

Mrs MacEwen guided him down the road towards the river. "As I recall, I told you to stop being such a blithering idiot and get back to Dunedin right away to tell Grace you couldn't live without her. She's a wonderful woman, Charlie. I'm glad you took my words to heart."

"So am I, Mrs MacEwen. I thought I didn't deserve Grace, but you convinced me that love is more important than foolish ideas of one's status in life."

"Quite right."

They walked between the stone pillars supporting the end of the Clyde bridge and into the centre of the bridge, where the sound of the river would muffle their voices.

"Flowing water is so soothing, don't you think?" Mrs MacEwen said. "Tell me what is worrying you, Charlie, when you should be cock-a-hoop at receiving a well-deserved reward. You and Grace will be set up for life."

Charlie had to fight back the tears. "All I wanted to do was prove my grandfather was not involved in the robbery, to clear my family of suspicion once and for all. I was a fool to have dredged up the past. I wish I had never come back."

"Why, Charlie? What have you found out that is causing you such distress?"

He was reluctant to start, but it came pouring out anyway. "Mrs Yarwood said that her son Ezra was going to marry Zachary Dawson's sister. I got the police to check what happened to the sister, but there has been no trace of her since before her brother's arrest for the gold robbery. The police accepted she had left her position in Cromwell for an unrelated reason, to get married. The sister had an excellent reputation, and there was no evidence she had anything to do with her brother. However, fresh evidence has come to light."

"I see. And you believe you know who Zachary Dawson's sister is?"

"Yes, I do. Her mistress was forgiving when Miss Dawson left, because she had been an exemplary worker. The constable's interview notes record the mistress saying Miss Dawson was always as poised as a lady, polished the silver to a shine, and made

238

the best scones she had ever tasted." Charlie looked Julia MacEwen square in the eyes, so she wouldn't turn and see that Grace and his father had followed them. He gestured for them to stay out of sight by the end of the bridge. This was a discussion he wanted to have with Mrs MacEwen alone.

Julia MacEwen's eyes brimmed with tears. "After all these years, I felt safe. I never intended –"

Charlie cut her off. "Don't say anything to me or anyone else, Mrs MacEwen, I beg you. Not until you have engaged the best lawyer in the land. I know an excellent barrister in Dunedin by the name of Kenneth Drummond. He is retired, but he would help you as a personal favour to me."

Julia MacEwen swiped the tears away and looked him straight in the eye. "No, Charlie. I have no intention of putting you or your father in a difficult position, or your grandfather, for that matter. The truth has been eating away at me for years. I have to stop hiding. I can only throw myself at the mercy of the court and hope that my decades of honest living and charitable work will balance the scales of justice. You've always been a clever one, Charlie Pyke. Far too clever. I knew I was in trouble when you started sniffing around. Tell me, what made you think of inquiring into my origins?"

Charlie leaned on the bridge railing. "I asked my business partner to search for information on all the people in town who had prospered after the robbery. To be thorough, I included your family. I received a telegram a short while ago. The Matheson family is well known, yet there is no birth record for anyone named Julia Matheson, the name you put on your marriage certificate when you wed Duncan MacEwen. The policeman from Cromwell supplied the details of Dawson's sister they hadn't sent at the time. Her name was Julia Dawson."

Julia MacEwen leaned on the rail beside him, staring into the depths of green-blue water below. "After the robbery, I stayed with a cousin far away from here. His surname was Matheson, but a stonemason rather than one of the wealthy Matheson family. I deceived Duncan abominably, but I fell in love with him at a country dance and I couldn't bear to risk losing him. He would never have married me if he knew I was a lowly maid and the sister of a notorious criminal, let alone if he knew I had a hand in a man's death. The shame of having my past revealed now will devastate him."

"Your husband loves you, Mrs MacEwen."

"Now perhaps, but I doubt he would have even asked me to dance back then if he had known the truth. It's rather ironic that he deceived me too, telling me he owned a large sheep station, but failing to mention he was up to his ears in debt. He said the station was in the Manuherikia Valley, which meant nothing to me. I didn't know that it was a stone's throw from the scene of my brother's crime. What a shock that was. Over time, the worry died away. My dowry saved the station, we prospered, and the years passed in bliss."

"That wasn't your only deception, was it?" Charlie said. "Your role wasn't spotted at the time simply because the various policemen involved tried to save the expense of too many words on a telegram. The Cromwell police sent only what they saw as the essential information at the time: 'sister gone, married'. No name, but also no date of departure. Julia Dawson left Cromwell hours after the robbery, two weeks before Zachary Dawson was arrested. Your brother must have passed through Cromwell and stopped to see you. I suspect he gave you part of the gold he stole to hold on to for him, in case he got caught. That was what you used as your dowry to seal the deal on your marriage to Duncan, wasn't it?"

Mrs MacEwen's eyes were pleading now. "Charlie, please believe me when I say that Zachary didn't tell me about the robbery. He turned up that morning before my mistress had risen, telling me he had struck gold on his claim and giving me a share to allow me to marry well and choose my own life. Zachary tried to convince me to go far away and marry someone other than Ezra, because he said Ezra wasn't to be trusted. Fool that I was, my first thought was to pack my bag and take the coach to Clyde to speak to Ezra myself. I believed in my so-called fiancé, young innocent that I was. Ezra could charm the tail off a peacock."

"What happened, Mrs MacEwen?" Charlie had begged her not to talk to him, but now she had begun her tale, he couldn't stop himself from asking.

"I arrived late in the afternoon and found Ezra out mending a damaged wall on his mother's property." Her voice cracked, but she forged on. "He was already in a foul mood and furious at my brother. He assumed I knew about the robbery and told me the original plan had been to bury the gold and come back to Clyde once the fuss had died down. But Zachary must have realised Ezra was planning to double-cross him and escape with all the gold. My brother insisted on taking his half of the gold with him. A tragic move, as it turned out, because my brother's horse foundered under the weight, which led to his eventual capture. Ezra's duplicity killed him."

The tears were back now, streaming down her face. "Zachary had always been a good boy and a hard worker. Ezra could see I was shocked at hearing of the robbery and furious at him for turning Zachary into a criminal. He turned on me in a fury and yelled at me, saying I was a stupid little tart if I thought he would still marry me now he was rich. You can imagine how angry that made me. Angry and stupid. I threatened to go to the police."

Charlie could see in his mind the terrible scene plunging into a spiral of violence. He wanted to stop his best friend's mother from talking, but she brushed him away.

"Ezra grabbed me around the throat, strangling me. I suddenly realised how badly I had underestimated the man I thought I loved. He intended to kill me, without a doubt. I couldn't shout for help. I couldn't breathe." She turned away from him, her body racked with sobs as she relived the awful moment.

Charlie wrapped an arm around her shaking shoulders. "I'm so very sorry, Mrs MacEwen."

She slumped under the weight of his arm. "I know these facts will be revealed in court. The shame will be unbearable for Duncan

241

and the children, but I know what I must do. Please, let me be the one to hand myself in to your father."

"Of course. Never forget that you mean the world to Duncan and your children. They will see that you were not to blame, especially as you knew nothing of the robbery. Ezra attacked you and whatever you did was pure self-defence. There is no shame for you in this dreadful situation."

"Thank you, Charlie. You always were kind. May I have a moment alone to compose myself, please?"

Charlie withdrew his arm. "Of course, Mrs MacEwen. I will never forget that you were always kind to me and my mother, when others weren't."

Charlie walked back to the end of the bridge. He was sure that Julia MacEwen had had no option but to kill her attacker by any means possible. If it wasn't for the fact that the townsfolk would demand that Jake Blackthorn be tried for Ezra's murder, or forever believe that Lee Hope was guilty of it, he would be sorely tempted to tear the telegrams into shreds. But he wouldn't. He couldn't forsake his principles and take the wrong path for the right reason.

Grace and his father saw him approaching. Grace ran towards him, her face tight with distress. Sergeant Pyke held back, sensing his son's need for time alone with his wife.

Before he reached Grace's open arms, her expression transformed into one of horror. Charlie jerked his head around, fearing what he would see.

Julia Dawson MacEwen had one foot on the crossbars of the bridge railing with a look of grim determination etched across her face.

Charlie sprinted towards her, knowing he couldn't make it in time. "Don't jump," he yelled. "I'll be forced to jump after you."

She hesitated.

"Mrs MacEwen, please. You don't want Grace to be a widow, do you? She might be with child."

Julia's eyes widened. Nobody moved.

Then – slowly, deliberately – Julia put her foot back on the railing. "I'm sorry, Charlie. If I hand myself in to face justice, the entire town will find out. Far better to die than bring disgrace to my family. I beg you not to risk your life trying to save me."

"Duncan loves you, Mrs MacEwen. That won't stop because of what happened half a lifetime ago."

Julia hitched her skirt and swung one leg over the top rail.

There was no way Charlie could reach her in time, but a scrabbling sound on the deck of the bridge behind him opened a new hope. Charlie went to the rails and began to climb too, making her hesitate and ensuring her eyes remained on him. He tried a final plea. "You stopped me from running away from the person I loved last year. I can't let you make the same mistake, even if I have to follow you over that rail and into the river."

"I'm sorry. Tell Duncan and the children I love them more than life itself –"

A cannonball of black and white shot down the bridge at astonishing speed. Blaze grabbed onto his former mistress's skirt before she could finish her sentence. The sudden unexpected tug of the collie flipped Julia MacEwen back over the railing onto the deck of the bridge. She scrambled up, but Charlie was already upon her, pulling her into his arms. Grace arrived a second later, but stood back, waiting for his signal.

Charlie held Julia until the fight went out of her. "My father will sort this out, Mrs MacEwen. You killed Ezra in self-defence. We can say Ezra was killed by Zachary Dawson's sister when Ezra attacked her. In fact, all we need to say is that the sister left town and your identity need never be revealed. Whatever happens, you were not to blame. Duncan will understand, just as Grace stood by me through my foolishness."

Mrs MacEwen was shaking now – a shaking that went as deep as her bones. But her eyes refused to meet his. With sudden clarity, he saw what should have been obvious. Ezra had been killed by a blow to the rear of his skull. If he had been strangling Julia Dawson, she couldn't have picked up one of the heavy slabs of rock from the wall, let alone struck the lethal blow at such an awkward angle. Somebody else must have seen them struggling and come to Julia's rescue. Ezra's death had never been about the gold after all.

"It wasn't you who killed him, was it? It couldn't have been." Charlie took his coat off and put it around her shoulders. "Was it Bob Trent or his brother, Mrs MacEwen? Did one of them see Ezra attacking you and think he was attacking Matilda? They had the brute strength and motive, and they knew the old well shaft was nearby, which you did not."

"No! That's not what happened." Mrs MacEwen struggled to get free of his grip, giving herself precious seconds to think. "Terror gave me strength I didn't know I had. I … I got free and hit him from behind. I could see he was dead, so I went for help at the house across the fields. My mind was reeling – my body too. Suddenly, it hit me that if I told the police, Zachary might be caught. Fate made me stumble upon the old well. I know I shouldn't have done it, but I dumped Ezra down the shaft and fled, all alone, terrified of the consequences if I was caught."

Charlie wanted to shake her until she came to her senses and saved herself. He pulled the sobbing woman to his chest and murmured soothing words. Was her version of events plausible? Yes, but only just. Charlie couldn't see why she would protect Bob's brother, or even Bob Trent, whom she didn't know then and probably didn't much like now. Unless he had it wrong. Was Julia Dawson MacEwen protecting somebody else?

Over her shoulder, Charlie saw his father hurrying towards them. Duncan MacEwen was sprinting along the bridge behind him, calling out to his wife. Charlie was too far away to see the expression on Duncan's face, but his voice was frantic. Had Duncan come to town that day to collect Jethro Quinney, his injured shepherd? Had he seen Julia being attacked and gone to her aid? How easy it would have been for Duncan to whisk away the damsel in distress to his farm and hide her.

Duncan dashed past Sergeant Pyke, his face tormented with worry and confusion. Julia wrenched loose of Charlie's arms. But it was not Duncan she was looking at. It was Matilda Trent, who stood at the end of the bridge clutching her rounded belly with both hands as if her life depended on it.

Julia MacEwen threw a fierce glare at Charlie and strode past her husband to Sergeant Pyke. She held her wrists out to be handcuffed. "I killed Ezra Yarwood. I acted alone, in self-defence."

Duncan MacEwen had the look of a man who'd been shot in the chest – a man unsure in that split-second if the wound was fatal or even how it had happened. His mouth formed a question, but he bit it back and rushed to his wife's side. "Julia, I don't know what is happening, but I am beside you all the way. I love you."

Matilda stumbled towards them with tears running down her rosy cheeks.

The sight of her forced Charlie to see the evidence from a fresh perspective. Matilda Trent, who had seemed so helpful, had led their investigation astray several times. Telling them she thought Ezra had left town and that Ezra's girl was a figment of Mrs Yarwood's addled brain. Saying it was Bob's deceased brother who had been out that evening and that he had overheard male voices arguing, not a man and a woman. Matilda Trent, who was one of the few people who might know about the abandoned well shaft.

Had Matilda really spurned Ezra early in their acquaintance, or had she believed Ezra was her man right up until the moment she had heard him arguing with Ezra's fiancée, Julia Dawson? Which begged the question – had Matilda killed Ezra out of jealous rage, or had she resorted to uncharacteristic violence to save a woman who was being throttled to death? Julia MacEwen was taking the blame for the blow to Ezra's head, which suggested she believed Matilda had acted heroically to rescue her from a violent brute. Charlie was inclined to believe that version of events, because it was a far better fit for Matilda's character.

Julia looked directly at Sergeant Pyke again and repeated her statement at a raised volume, loud enough for all those present to hear. "I am confessing to killing Ezra Yarwood in self-defence. No other person, including my husband, had any knowledge of my crime, either at the time or subsequently."

Matilda halted, uncertain.

"This is no time for your neighbourly kindness, Matilda," Julia said. "Duncan, take Matilda back to Bob immediately." When her husband hesitated, Julia snapped, "now, Duncan, before the poor woman gives birth on the bridge."

Duncan did as he was ordered, while Charlie closed his eyes and prayed for guidance.

Grace's arms wrapped around him, providing both comfort and physical restraint. "This is the only way, Charlie. No jury will convict Mrs MacEwen once they hear the evidence. I doubt the magistrate will even send the case to trial when she was so clearly defending herself while being strangled."

Charlie drew strength from his wife's embrace. His tears blurred the sight of Julia MacEwen being led away, her head held high.

He let her go.

Farewell

The day before they were due to return to Dunedin, Grace had her feet up on the bench seat with two cushions behind her and a cool drink by her side. The textbook on surgical procedures slipped from her lap as her eyelids sagged from the warmth of the day. Pleasant as it was, Grace was beginning to feel that if she stayed here much longer, vines would grow up around her and she would slowly turn to compost.

Sometime later – it might have been a minute or an hour – Grace was jolted awake by a slobbery tongue and dusty paws. "Hello, Blaze. What have you done with your master?"

Charlie had disappeared on another of his long rides on Nyx. He had lapsed into ever-deeper silences since the day on the bridge, rousing himself only to answer direct questions. Grace let him be. She was on edge too, as the days passed without a decision on whether charges would be laid over Ezra's death. She joined her husband on the rides most days, partly for the peace and beauty of the countryside, but mainly to avoid the steady trickle of townsfolk who stopped by to hear the tale of the recovered gold.

When she heard hoofbeats approaching, Grace went inside to put the kettle on. By the time she had fetched a pail of water for Nyx, Charlie had the saddle off. They washed the horse together and released her into the paddock. Still damp, Nyx gleamed a silvery black, until she reached her favourite spot for an energetic roll in the dust.

Grace leaned on the fence next to her husband. "You're going to miss Nyx."

Charlie watched the mare rolling for a moment longer, before taking her hand and heading back to the cottage. "I will, but I'm looking forward to getting home too."

"Had enough honeymooning?"

That won her a smile. "Never enough. I'm looking forward to a lifelong honeymoon." Charlie's smile vanished again at the sound of approaching visitors. "I'm going inside to wash. Whoever it is, tell them I'm not here."

To their relief, it was Thomas and Jasmine Pyke.

"We received a message this morning inviting us to luncheon at the MacEwen's house," Jasmine said. "How soon can you be ready?"

"Five minutes," Grace replied. "Is there news of the decision?"

"I presume so, but the message did not say what it was."

It took ten minutes to get ready, because Charlie's hand was shaking so badly Grace had to help him shave the three-day growth of whiskers from his face.

They shared the buggy ride in silence. Duncan MacEwen was waiting alone at the bottom of his driveway – an ominous sign. Charlie and Grace jumped out of the buggy to hear what he had to say.

Duncan saw the look on Charlie's face and hastened to reassure him. "Don't look so grim, lad. Julia doesn't blame you in the least for doing what was right. In fact, she is grateful to you for finally bringing resolution to the matter."

Thomas Pyke asked the question on everyone's lips. "What's been decided, Duncan?"

"Matilda Trent insisted on giving evidence, which cleared Julia of any wrongdoing. It's Matilda we've been worried about, but in the end the magistrate decided Ezra was killed in self-defence."

Grace clutched Charlie's arm to prop him up as he sagged with relief. "Did Matilda say what happened that day, Duncan?"

"Ezra strangled Julia close to the point of passing out, which is why Julia's recall of events was hazy. There's no doubt whatsoever that Matilda saved Julia's life, for which she has our eternal gratitude. Julia assumed Matilda hit Ezra with a rock, which was why she was reluctant to come forward, worried she might implicate the girl who was trying to save her life. Matilda was too hysterical to give a coherent account at the time."

"Are you saying Matilda didn't hit him?"

Duncan nodded. "Matilda yelled at Ezra and he turned on her. He attacked her with a stonemasonry chisel. She's still got the scar. By the sound of it, it was only a matter of luck that Ezra stumbled, allowing Matilda to shove him away. Unfortunately, or fortunately, Ezra went down backwards and hit his head on the wall. If you ask me, the magistrate ought to have made his decision straight away, but you know how they are, always cross-examining and considering every last detail of evidence. Of course, he admonished them for not coming forward at the time, but he did concede that the word of two terrified young women wouldn't have carried much weight. Neither Matilda nor Julia will be named in the judgement, which describes only Ezra's attack on an unknown woman who was passing through town."

"So it's over?" Grace said.

"Yes, thank the Lord. Our children don't know and we'd prefer to keep it that way. I only wish I'd known. When I think of all Julia went through without my support ..."

Charlie threw his arms around Duncan and squeezed the air out of him. When he pulled away, both men had tears in their eyes. They turned away quickly and headed up the drive together. Grace and Jasmine followed, arm in arm, while Thomas Pyke took the horse and buggy to the waiting stableman.

The sound of laughter grew steadily louder as they went around to the back of the house, where a long table had been set for luncheon under a pergola shaded by grapevines. Matilda Trent must have been telling an amusing anecdote, because Julia MacEwen and the two men with her were laughing. It took Grace a second to recognise one of the men as Bob Trent, because he looked so different when he was cheerful. She assumed the second man was Charlie's old friend, Hamish MacEwen, or one of the other MacEwen brothers, because he was a younger version of Duncan.

Charlie broke into a run and flung himself at Julia MacEwen.

"What's got into everyone today?" the second man said. "My mother's acting like an excited debutante at her first dance and now my best friend is ignoring me."

Charlie released Julia and flung an arm around the man's shoulder. "Not used to playing second string, eh, Hamish? Why don't you take me over to that keg of ale and tell me what you've been up to since I saw you last?" The two men sauntered off, trading jibes as they went.

Julia watched them fondly. "I'm sorry my son didn't wait for me to introduce you, Grace. I can only apologise for his manners and say he's been eager to catch up with Charlie, especially as he's been busy with farm business until today."

"I'm just delighted to see Charlie happy again," Grace replied. "The last few days have been a strain. We're so glad that the future is brighter for all concerned."

Julia answered with a face-splitting smile that spoke louder than words. "Is it true that you and Charlie have set up a charitable fund with part of the reward for finding the gold?"

"The Lee and Elsie Hope Fund for the welfare of Chinese miners," Grace said, "with Mrs Jasmine Pyke at the helm." It had been one of the best moments of Grace's life when they had made their offer and seen her mother-in-law's eyes light up.

"You'd be surprised how many local families and businesses have already pledged contributions," Jasmine said, her entire body radiating excitement and pride. "We will soon have enough in the fund to extend the hospital to the benefit of the whole community."

"Guilty consciences after all those years of persecuting Lee Hope," Thomas muttered, but his grin took the sting out of the barb. "Jasmine and I feel as if the weight of the world has been lifted from our shoulders."

Julia leaned in to avoid being overheard by the approaching maid. "I'm glad. We feel the same." She whisked crystal glasses from the proffered tray and distributed them to her guests.

Jasmine waited until the maid had passed on. "Surprisingly, the biggest donation was from Vern Summerfield. He wanted to make it anonymously, so please don't tell anyone I mentioned it. I suspect he hasn't told Connie."

"If Vern is making a donation, you'd better put us down for a contribution too," Duncan said. "Can't let the old gold digger think he owns the town. Besides, with my beloved wife and family at my side, and that darned rustler behind bars for the foreseeable future, I'm feeling in a generous mood."

"How is Connie taking Nathaniel's incarceration?" Matilda asked.

"About as well as you would expect," Thomas replied. "After browbeating me and Jasmine over it, Connie has turned her talents to rallying a legal team to defend Nathaniel. Vern is supporting her, of course, but privately he is not optimistic. I feel sorry for Vern and Connie. The shame of their son's crimes has hit them hard."

"I suppose I will have to encourage Connie to continue her good work," Julia said. "The sins of her son ought not to ruin the family, after all. Besides, the Vincent County Horticultural Show cannot continue without its chairwoman."

"Enough of this serious talk," Duncan declared. "Today is a day for celebration."

Grace left the older generation to their merriment and went over to a woman of about her own age, who was standing alone. Her rosy cheeks and engaging smile identified her as the oldest Trent daughter. "You must be Etta. I'm Grace."

"Nice to meet you, Grace. I presume this celebration is in honour of your recent marriage. We're honoured Mr and Mrs MacEwen invited us, although I must admit I was a little surprised as our families have never socialised before." Etta gestured at Hamish and Charlie, who were now doubled over with laughter and trying not to spill pints of ale. "Is that your husband? He's quite famous, I hear, and handsome too, if you don't mind me saying so."

"Charlie and Hamish make a handsome pair. Do you remember them from school? Were they always this excitable when together?"

Etta stole another glance at Hamish. "I was three years younger, but I remember they were good fun at school. Charlie was the quieter one back then. Hamish was the prankster, but never mean, like some of the other boys. All the girls were sweet on him. I doubt either of them would remember me."

Charlie saw them watching and beckoned them over. "Hamish, it's about time you met my wife, Grace."

Hamish took her hand and kissed it with the elegance of a lord of the manor, although his eyes flicked to Etta, whose cheeks went a deeper shade of rose. "Grace, lovely to meet you. I suspect Charlie has kept you from me on purpose, fearing I would sweep you off your feet before he could get you to the altar."

252

"Then his fears would be unfounded," Grace replied. "Once I'd met Charlie, it would have taken an army of cutthroat soldiers to keep me from his side."

Hamish bowed. "And now I can only envy my old friend's good fortune."

Grace mimicked him with a mock curtsey. "Charlie, do you know Miss Etta Trent?"

"Miss Trent. I don't believe we've met since you were in pigtails."

"And still as beautiful as ever," Hamish said. "The belle of the Clyde school choir, as I recall, with the voice of an angel. I hope you like to dance, Miss Trent, because my father has threatened to bring out his old fiddle after the meal, in honour of Charlie and Grace's nuptials."

"I love to dance, Mr MacEwen," Etta replied.

Etta and Hamish were soon so caught up in conversation, they didn't notice Charlie and Grace slipping away for a stroll around the gardens. They found Blaze under a tree by the edge of the party, watching on.

"You were supposed to be tied up at the cottage, Blaze." Charlie bent down to ruffle the collie's fur. "But it is nice to have every member of my family with me today."

Grace could only hope that her great-aunt was as welcoming to the new member of their Dunedin household, although she was confident Blaze's charms would win her over in the end. "We have a lot to celebrate today. Not least the wonderful end to the perfect honeymoon."

"Perfect? Only you could say that, Grace, after all we have been through."

"Charlie, my love, we have solved a quarter century old mystery, proved your grandfather's innocence, gained a faithful canine companion, and been blessed with a large reward, all without any deaths or major injuries. Not to mention many unforgettable romantic moments. Honeymoons don't come any more perfect than that."

"You're right, as always." Charlie wrapped Grace in his arms. "I want to apologise for behaving like a bear with a toothache these last few days. Without your love, I hate to think how I would have got through it." He paused and smiled. "I'll have to find a way to make it up to you."

Grace didn't fail to notice the sparkle in his eyes. "I like the sound of that, but we should get back to the party now, because it'll be our last chance to enjoy the company of our friends before we go home. However, I could be tempted to indulge in a little personal celebration tonight, because this honeymoon isn't over until we step on that rattletrap stagecoach again and head back to mundane married life."

Charlie took her hand. "Grace, my love, I cannot imagine our lives together will ever sink to mundane, and I wouldn't have it any other way."

Read on

In Book 8, *Empty Cradle*, Grace and Charlie Penrose Pyke must put their own troubles aside to rescue a kidnapped infant.

Thank You

Thank you for reading this story. If you enjoyed it, I would be very grateful if you would leave a rating or review to help other readers discover it.

Find out about other books and sign up for notifications of new releases at https://RosePascoe.com

Map of Locations

Map of Otago, annotated to show locations mentioned in this story. Source: Department of Lands and Survey, 1963 (from LINZ, via the National Library of New Zealand. Crown Copyright reserved.)

A: Arrowtown. **B**: Cromwell. **C**: Clyde.
D: Conroys Gully/wilderness. **E**: Lawrence. **F**: Dunedin.

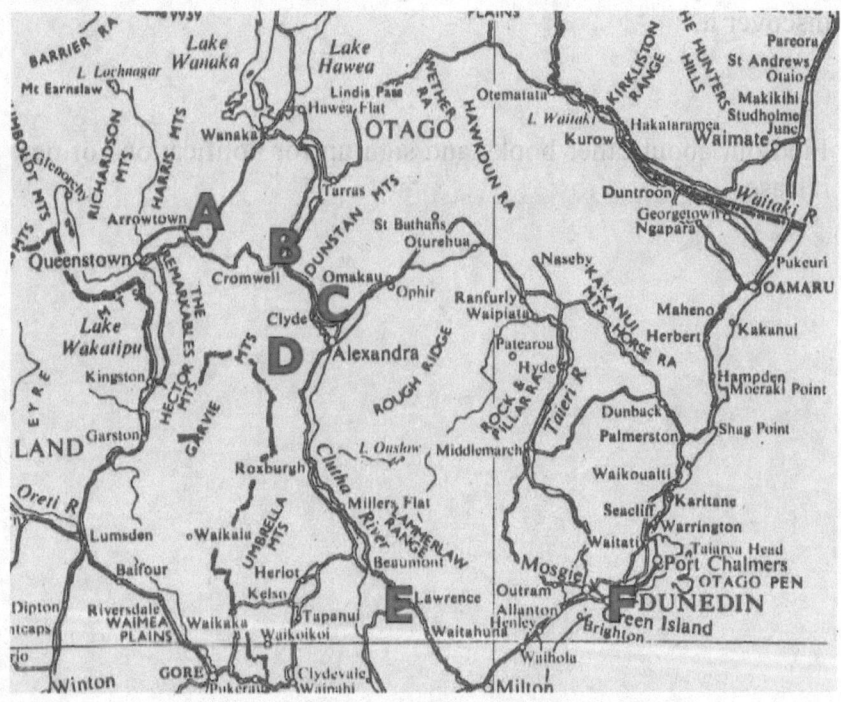

Historical Notes

Today, Clyde is a pretty town, full of relics of the gold mining era, including many historic buildings built of the local schist rock. Clyde sits above the mighty Clutha River, which is now lined with trees and perfect for a walk on a hot summer's day. When I was retracing my family links to the town, I discovered the first female doctor in New Zealand was born in Clyde. From this small nugget of gold, the *Penrose & Pyke Mysteries* were born, although it is Charlie Pyke who was born there in my stories.

The early town of Clyde was a far cry from its modern self. Within a year of the first discovery of a rich source of alluvial gold in 1862, around fifteen to twenty thousand miners were digging along the banks of the river and the surrounding gullies, which yielded seventy thousand ounces of gold in the first year.

The era of easy gold passed quickly, but sluicing, and then wholesale dredging of the bottom of the river, extended the gold era into the twentieth century. At one stage, about thirty dredges operated on the Clutha River between Clyde and Alexandra. This section of the Clutha River was often called the Molyneux River at the time, although both names were in use. I have kept to the modern name because "Clutha River" was used on the official 1897 map of Clyde I used for era-specific locations. As a nod to the past, I have named the fictitious hotel in the story the Molyneux Hotel.

Conroys Gully was one of the gold mining areas near Clyde, and every bit as dramatic of landscape as in the story. A clip from a film about Chinese miners of the era can be viewed at: www.nzonscreen.com/title/illustrious-energy-1988. Most of the Chinese men who flocked to the area during the gold rush were miners earning money to send home, but other members of the

Chinese community became notable citizens. For example, Charles Wong Gye worked as a Special Constable and raised a large family with his English wife.

Another prominent Clyde citizen was called Vincent Pyke – an unfortunate coincidence, since I had already used the Pyke name for my main character in earlier books. To be clear, my story is fictional and none of the characters are based on real people.

I had always planned to set one of the stories in Clyde, based on a gold robbery. When I started research for this book, I was delighted to discover that there had been a real gold robbery of epic proportions. In the depths of the winter of 1870, the gold lock-up was broken into the night before the Gold Escort was due to take almost £14,000 of gold and cash to Dunedin. In an era when wages might be £50 a year, one can imagine the shock of such a massive theft.

I have used the details of the gold theft from newspapers of the time, as sourced on *Papers Past* (National Library of New Zealand), but I have changed a few key details to suit my fictional tale: my story is set two years earlier that the actual robbery, names have been changed, nobody was killed – indeed, the lock-up was inexplicably unguarded at the time – and almost all the gold and cash was recovered soon after the actual offender was apprehended. The thief said he had an accomplice, but the trooper he implicated was found not guilty and no other person was ever arrested.

The first vineyard in the South Island was established in Clyde in 1864 by Jean Feraud and was producing medal winning wines by the 1880s. This property, named Monte Christo, also included a dairy farm, a large orchard, a market garden, pigs and poultry, and fields of oats. It was sold to the Bodkin family in 1889 (as related by A. W. Bodkin in: *An Account of Monte Christo: The Historic Farm, the Place and Its People, 1864-1960*). I have reimagined this property to include the fictional Rose Cottage, vineyard, orchard, and a separate dairy farm. The real vineyard has been resurrected in recent years (www.montechristowinery.co.nz).

I am grateful, as always, to the National Library's *Papers Past* digital collection for other real snippets of life from late January 1893, when the story was set, including local excitement around the inaugural Vincent County Horticultural Show and other social events.

Many books and pamphlets provided historical details for the story, especially:

Isobel Betty Veitch's fascinating *Clyde on the Dunstan,* Square One Press, Dunedin, 2003.

Grahame Sydney's *Promised Land: From Dunedin to the Dunstan Goldfields*, Penguin, 2009, which inspired by its gorgeous photographs and epic tales of early miners and runholders.

Stevan Eldred-Grigg's *A Southern Gentry: New Zealanders Who Inherited the Earth,* Heinemann Reed, Auckland, 1989, which provided insight on New Zealand's version of landed gentry – the families who grew rich from wool on the vast acres of cheap land of the early sheep stations – and their reaction to the radical plans of the Liberal government to break up some stations into small farms in 1893.

Other sources included: *A Fruitful Land: the Story of Fruitgrowing and Irrigation in the Alexandra-Clyde District,* John McCraw, Square One Press, Dunedin, 2005, and *Dunstan Hospital 125th Anniversary,* Alexandra, 1988.

Acknowledgements

A huge thank you to my fabulous beta readers: Mary, Jenny, Kathy and Ross. Their continued enthusiasm is very much appreciated.

Two new writing friends have joined the beta reading group: Bronnie Thomas and Tracy Chollet. Check out their books on: www.tracychollet.com and www.bronniethomas.com.

About the Author

Rose Pascoe writes historical mysteries with a dash of romance, when she isn't plotting real-life adventures. She lives in beautiful New Zealand, land of beaches and mountains, where long walks provide the perfect conditions for dreaming up plots and fickle weather provides the incentive to sit down and write. After a career in health, justice and social research, her passion is for stories set against a backdrop of social justice. Her heroines are ordinary women, who meet the challenges thrown at them with determination, ingenuity, courage, and humour.

Visit her at: https://RosePascoe.com

www.ingramcontent.com/pod-product-compliance
Lightning Source LLC
Chambersburg PA
CBHW021443210626
46816CB00020B/2510